BLAZE ORANGE

BLAZE ORANGE

A MIDCOAST MAINE MYSTERY

ALLISON KEETON

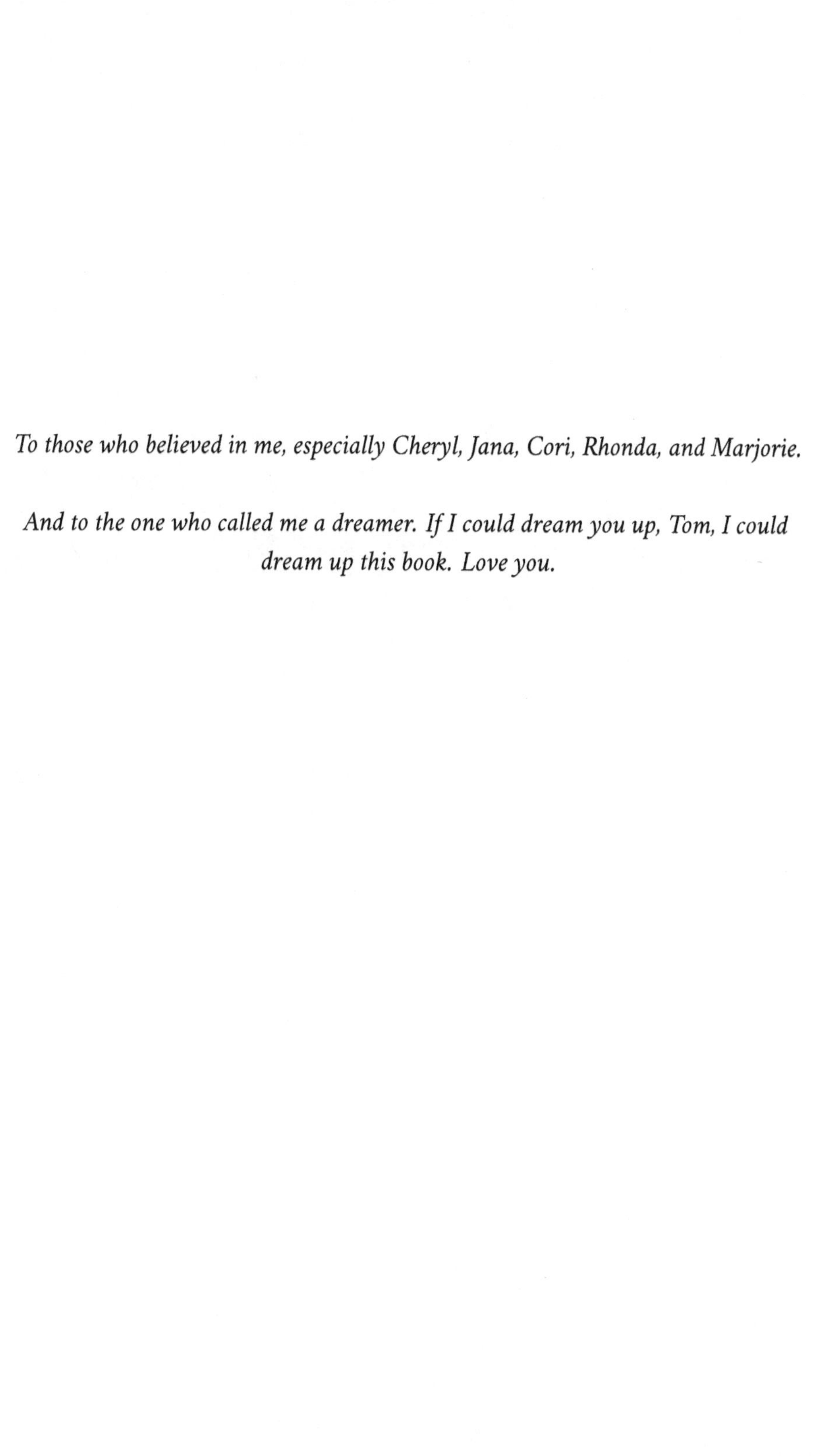

To those who believed in me, especially Cheryl, Jana, Cori, Rhonda, and Marjorie.

And to the one who called me a dreamer. If I could dream you up, Tom, I could dream up this book. Love you.

Chapter One

The yellow Labrador sniffed the air and dashed up the path into the woods.

"Lily! Come!" Raven Ouellette called out to the lab, her problem child. This was supposed to be a short walk. Raven hadn't finished cleaning the cabins, and the Thanksgiving guests were coming in two hours.

Lily's thick yellow rudder tail waved back and forth like a windshield wiper as she disappeared up the snow-packed trail and out of sight. She didn't care what Raven said.

The black, wavy-coated dog next to Raven pranced back and forth, going a little ahead in the direction of Lily, and then rushing back to Raven. He knew better than to disobey.

"Don't you dare leave me too, Dukie," she said to the Portuguese Water Dog, a gift from a longtime client when Raven's mother passed away. "I only agreed to this afternoon walk if it was brief, remember?"

At the tone of her voice, he sat on the trail and faced her, waiting for her next instruction. She shook her head at herself. Speaking to the dogs as if they were children was a trait she learned from her mother. Raven was confident, though, that they fully understood her.

"It's okay," she said, tussling the soft hair on top of Dukie's head. "Go have fun with Lil. Run. Run."

He spun around and sprinted like a greyhound in Lily's direction. Raven zipped up her down jacket to keep out the cool breeze and followed.

At the edge of the woods, she saw the tip of Lily's tail poke out from under a winterberry bush, its branches bright with red dots and its leaves long dead from earlier frosts. Winter weather came early this year to Secretly. She made a mental note to come back in December for cuttings of the red berried branches for her Christmas wreaths and vases.

Then she remembered it was still hunting season.

"And again, I forgot to wear my orange hat and to put on your orange vest, Dukie," she said to the pooch who had returned to her side.

It was November, and hunting season in Maine was in full swing, even in the preserves. The conservancy trails posted large warning signs to hikers and dog owners about the need to wear blaze orange, but Raven always entered on a side path closer to Pine Acres, the cabins she owned and managed, and never saw those reminder signs. But she should know better. She had lived here her entire life.

Before Raven and Dukie reached Lily, who was now sniffing the ground like a bloodhound, she took off at full speed further into the woods, off the path, and on the hunt of something she couldn't resist. A hiker must have dropped a peanut butter sandwich or something.

"Lily, no! No!" Raven knew she was wasting her breath. Even if she yelled "cookie" or "snack," nothing she could provide could match Lily's tastebuds for that sandwich or a dead squirrel.

"Dukie, go get Lily."

He raced off again into the woods in Lily's direction, purposely leaping over every log he could find, demonstrating both what an athlete and a clown he was, but he quickly returned alone and did laps around Raven.

"Dukie, you have many talents, but being a search-and-rescue dog isn't one of them."

She again ruffled the hair on his head and bent down to kiss his black nose. He gave hers a quick lick in return. Stepping off the path to find Lily, Raven's boots sank in the fluffy snow. Following Lily's prints was the obvious task, but other animals had earlier walked through much of the same brush, making it impossible to differentiate Lily's tracks from theirs. Raven muttered under her breath and yelled Lily's name again as she weaved between the branches. Dukie followed close on her heels. As they walked further into the woods and farther from the path, Raven paused occasionally to call out again, and then listen. No rustling. No jingle of a collar. No Lily.

Raven gritted her teeth. "We should be heading back home now, not walking aimlessly in the woods. I have so much to do."

She only had herself to blame for falling behind. Thanksgiving week was always a busy time. Those cabins should have been cleaned days ago. If she hadn't volunteered to help sew the pilgrims' costumes for the library pageant, she'd be ahead. If she hadn't been chatting at Lane's Market, she wouldn't have seen Betty Hart, who wouldn't have asked her to sew in the first place. Marcel was always saying she made more work for herself. She needed to learn to say 'no.'

The sun's light shifted, lowering itself toward the horizon. Desperately, she called out again as loudly as she could.

"Lily!! Lily!! Now!!" She listened again. Silence.

Shaking with anger, Raven decided to chance leaving Lily in the woods, with the hope she'd find her way home on her own. It made her sick to leave her, but what other choice did Raven have? Otherwise, she'd never have the cabins ready in time.

"Come on, Dukie." Raven turned abruptly towards the trail, glancing down before taking a step.

Within an instant of looking down, Raven couldn't control the scream that forced itself out of her lungs. It echoed through the empty woods. Its guttural force shook her insides, and vibrated throughout her body, from her toes to her mouth.

Lying in the snow in front of her was a person.

Part of a person.

A former person.

The remains of a person.

At least Raven thought it had been a person once.

She screamed uncontrollably again.

Shredded red jacket fibers covered the ground, mimicking blood on the snow.

A twisted pant leg with a boot at the end of it almost touched her boot.

She scooted backwards. It wasn't the type of Bean boot she and most

Mainers wore. This one was fancy. Black and leather. Like something worn by someone from away.

The leg—there only seemed to be one—was still attached to a coat-covered torso that was wrapped around the base of a small tree—as if a coyote had tried to drag the body away, but the trunk had grabbed it.

Laying at an angle at the top of the torso was a blue knit hat. Raven assumed it covered a head, and a face.

On the snow next to the hat was another bone—a partially detached arm, picked clean through the red fabric. This body had been here for a while.

Glued to the spot, she talked herself into moving and finding the path to home. She had to get Marcel. She had to get help.

Amazingly, Dukie hadn't been the least curious to sniff or smell the carcass.

The carcass. No. It was a person. The person, she meant.

Probably a man based on the size of the boot.

As she quickly trudged back towards the path, branches slapped her in the face. She grabbed onto small tree trunks to steady her shaking legs as she willed herself forward toward home.

She felt her pockets for her phone but then remembered plugging it into the charger before the walk. She picked up her pace, running, stumbling over fallen limbs, trying not to spend time on crying. She reached the path only to find Lily standing on it, large blockhead cocked, like she had been there the whole time, and wondered where Raven went.

No time to scold her. Raven ran down the path with the dogs following behind her, her heart pounding, squeezing the air out of her. The dogs thought it was a game. Dukie raced beside her and leapt up, nudging her elbow in hopes of a cookie. Lily grinned and ran faster, ahead of Raven, glancing over her shoulder to get Dukie to chase her.

As Raven ran, she blinked to forget what she saw. As soon as she could, she'd call Marcel to bring him and his men back there, though she struggled to remember where in the woods it was. He would tell her, again, that she complicated her life.

She stopped to gasp for breath.

That blue hat.

The blue hat on the body haunted her. She recognized it. Her mind raced with her feet as she started down the path again.

The emblem had read "Mathematical Society," an insignia only worn by one person she knew.

Charles Kearns. A recent transplant from Boston.

He had bought the Lane Mansion in the summer and instantly went to work renovating it. Of course, coming from away, he'd have lots of money to dump into it.

She only officially met Charles less than a month ago at a Halloween church social, standing around a bonfire made from the fall clean-up debris. He had said he was an expert witness for hire, that he testified in lawsuits against construction companies for faulty design work and code violations. All by using math, she had guessed by the hat he had been wearing. Math didn't interest her as much as the renovations of his Federalist home. She always admired and envied that property. He told her the work involved redoing both center chimneys and promised to show her inside when it was finished.

Raven stopped running again and bent over her knees. Lily licked her cheek. Charles' voice filtered in.

"Literally, my first floor is full of bricks," he had said. "I'm having them take apart the chimneys brick-by-brick to ensure their structural soundness and to straighten them. When I'm up from Boston, I'm ensconced up on the second floor in a bedroom to sleep, eat, and work. That is, when I'm not out photographing birds, my real passion. Maine's a treasure trove for birds."

Those in earshot around the bonfire had chuckled. Howard, another neighbor, who had come from away with his own dole of cash, rolled his eyes at the chimneys' expense.

Raven hadn't seen Charles since that night. Hadn't thought about him at all. Maybe he had returned to Boston, or maybe the bonfire was the last night anyone had seen him alive. Maybe that wasn't him after all.

She straightened and walked towards home, quickening her pace the best she could.

The remains didn't have on an orange vest, or hat. Raven couldn't say "what a dummy" because she was guilty of the same thing, and she knew better. She wondered if the hunter had even known he had shot a person.

If the person was shot. He also could have tripped and struck his head while hiking. Or broke his ankle on a day that had its night temperature dip into the teens.

What a terrible way to die. Alone in the woods. What a tragic accident.

If it was an accident.

Chapter Two

Raven reached the edge of Pine Acres' compound as Marcel's county-paid-for Jeep pulled in front of their greying cedar-shingled house. She waved her hands wildly to get his attention before he went into the house to take his pre-dinner nap.

"Marcel!" She called out to him.

Upon spying their dad, the dogs took off in his direction. Dukie reached him first, racing forward in a tucked form with Lily trotting behind in her wiggly, chunky lab way. Marcel looked up in their direction and waved back at Raven before kneeling down to receive the dogs' kisses and scratch their ears in return.

"Marcel." Raven puffed out his name and slowed her pace. Her lungs and legs burned. She never was athletic but was blessed with a trim body naturally. "From your father's side," said her slightly plump mother when she was alive. She had to take her mother's word for it since she didn't know anyone on her father's side of the family except for her father, and she barely knew him.

"You look like you've seen a ghost," said Marcel, grabbing her around the waist and leaning down to kiss her hello when she finally reached him. She was tall for a woman at five foot eight, but he was also tall for a man, standing easily at six foot five, the perfect height for law enforcement.

Raven nodded. "I did. I have." The reminder of what the human remains actually looked like in the woods flashed in her mind. She pulled away and doubled over on the gravel driveway. On her knees, she wretched, her long black hair falling against her face. The burning sensation of the bile scratched the back of her mouth. She had been too busy to eat all day, and now nothing came up to soothe her throat.

Marcel knelt down beside her, placing a hand on her back. The two dogs licked her face in support.

"Seriously, Raven. What happened?" His eyes widened, not used to seeing Raven fall apart for anything.

She wiped her mouth and took a deep breath. "I'll show you." She coughed and cleared her throat. "But call the station first. Get reinforcements or the medical examiner or whatever happens."

He remained rooted and calm next to her, stroking her hair. "Or whatever happens when?" he said, pulling her fallen hair back to study her face.

She gulped for more air. "When a dead body is found."

"A dead body?" Barrett County's lead sheriff leaned back on his heels. She sat up too and noticed grey hairs coming in on his five o'clock shadow and the slight bent of his nose from a break years ago, an altercation with a drunk who wouldn't come quietly. She was five years younger than Marcel and hadn't noticed one grey strand yet on her own black-haired head.

She nodded, and Marcel took her thin hands in his large, rough ones and pulled her up.

"Where did you see the body?" he said, still holding her hands.

Raven glanced over her shoulder to look towards the path, suddenly feeling that a zombie could walk out of the woods.

"In there. Off path. I was looking for Lily."

Marcel remained silent. Waiting for more. This must be how it felt to be interviewed by him if you committed a crime or witnessed one. Like she did.

She swallowed and plunged forward. "I think it might be Charles Kearns."

Marcel's brow knitted together, trying to place the name. "Charles Kearns? The geeky guy from Boston?"

She nodded. "I'm guessing."

He squinted. He only liked facts. "You're guessing because?"

Her memory flashed back again to being in the woods, standing in front of the partial body. She felt cold and shivered. "Because there's nothing left to him but a few bones. And his blue knit hat."

Marcel whistled low as he released her hands and walked over to the Jeep. Opening his driver's door, he picked up a receiver and radioed his office. He then called the county coroner on his cell, and then sent a text. Raven assumed he was contacting Tom Pinkham, one of his deputies. The dogs stood, sensing the tension. Raven leaned against his vehicle and steadied her breath by focusing on the faces of Lily and Dukie. They waited eagerly for their next move or hers.

Marcel spoke to her over the open Jeep door. "There's no rush in getting back to the body. We'll wait for Tom and the others. You okay with going back in to show us where you found him?"

She nodded, although she'd rather not go. "I think I can find him. It's all Lily's fault, going off path again."

The lab thumped her tail on the dirt driveway at the mention of her name. Dukie, not to be left out, did a circle dance around and barked.

"Mr. Jealous Pants," Raven said as Dukie crashed into her legs for attention.

"Maybe Lily could find it again, and you wouldn't have to go," Marcel said.

Raven checked her watch. Besides not wanting to stumble upon Charles Kearns, guests were coming in less than two hours.

"She never saw him, I don't think. Just Dukie and me. I'll be all right." She swayed.

He reached out and grabbed her again. Her eyes filled with tears, and she exhaled into his arms. She'd love to stay right where she was until she couldn't any longer. But those guests arriving gnawed at her. Although she had no ambition to finish making beds and fluffing pillows, it would kill the time while waiting for the others to arrive.

"Let me finish up those two cabins while we wait." She whispered into his neck.

She had just tucked the last flannel top sheet under the base of the mattress and straightened the down comforter when the sound of Tom Pinkham's SUV roared up their driveway. Tom was Marcel's right arm and the best deputy on the force, Marcel always said.

"Local as they come," Marcel said about Tom. "He knows every mole and wrinkle on every soul in this county."

At least all the moles and wrinkles on the ladies.

Tom had no ambition to be lead sheriff, wanting nothing to stand in the way of his side business of lobstering. Or his crowded dating schedule. His stature was the opposite of Marcel's, standing even shorter than Raven, but he made up for his size in his skill of putting people at ease with his joking demeanor. Both locals and tourists spilled their guts to him, often not realizing they were confessing to a sheriff's deputy.

"What's this I hear about free deer meat?" Tom climbed out of the white sheriff's SUV and slammed the driver's door behind him, grinning from ear to ear. The emblem for Barrett County painted on the SUV's door also showed the branches of the other two Midcoast Maine counties and the State Police, a symbolic gesture of law enforcement cooperation suggested by the current governor. The last thing any of the county sheriffs wanted was assistance from the State. Or to waste money on a new logo. But they complied. At least with the logo.

Marcel put up his index finger to slow down Tom's often off-putting humor and then pointed towards Raven walking up the path. She had already heard him, and her eyes swelled again at the thought of Charles being shot instead of a deer. His death wasn't a sport.

Tom, seeing Raven, instantly apologized. "Sorry, sorry, Raven. Where're my manners?"

He tipped his official trooper-style brim hat, cleared his throat, and addressed Marcel. "Sir, what do we have here?" A tone and phrase he used in front of strangers when trying to sound official.

Marcel nodded toward Raven. "I'll let her tell you."

Tom's face showed its surprise, but he said nothing. He took his small notepad out of his breast pocket and clicked his pen.

Her head felt heavy and her tongue thick. If she said the words again, she was afraid they'd leap out of her mouth and strangle her.

"I'd rather not talk about it," she said. "Better to show you."

Tom cocked his head but nodded without asking her any questions.

The dogs again ran ahead, with Marcel and Tom trailing behind Raven.

At the edge of the woods, Lily, this time, veered off the path to the right.

Raven mumbled. "Please, not another body."

But Lily soon returned to the regular path that the dogs and Raven had made over the years, during all the times they walked from Pine Acres to the official trail and down to the riverbed on the other side of the preserve. Raven's breath steadied as much as it could with the notion of seeing Charles again.

The three of them and the dogs walked deeper into the woods in silence and finally reached the main trail. Raven veered left, but that was all she remembered from earlier. With the packed snow and limited light left to the day, it was difficult to remember where she had gone off this trail in search of Lily. The snow tracks weren't any help either—too many from her, the dogs, wild animals, and possibly other hikers. She finally stopped by a decaying pine.

"I don't remember where I went in," she said, tears brimming over her eyelids and trickling down her face. "I was too mad at Lily and too distracted with the cabins."

She hadn't wanted to see Charles again, but she did want to find him, to get him out of the woods, to have him be as safe as he now could be.

Marcel came up next to her and put his arm around her shoulders, kissing her temple. "That's okay. We'll go back to the edge of the forest and wait for the others to come. We'll find him. I promise. Why don't you go back to the house and wait for the renters."

Raven nodded and whistled for the dogs. As she walked back, not waiting for Marcel and Tom to follow, she remembered more of her last conversation with Charles.

"I love the secrets that old homes keep," he had said at the bonfire. What secrets did he mean? What did his house know? Could his house now spill what it knew about him?

Chapter Three

Back at her house, Raven scrubbed her face to hide the red marks from her tears. The first guests arrived minutes later.

They were a friendly Rhode Island couple in their sixties who confessed to having never come to Maine before. Raven forced herself to shrug off the ridiculing thought of them choosing November to visit for the first time. Her mother's voice, reminding her that everyone was different, and a paying customer was the most different of all, kept her judgment in check. After bringing them to their cabin and thanking them for their compliments on the decorating, the "Maine coziness," as the wife said—whatever that meant—Raven went back to the house to wait for Marcel and the next guests to arrive. She had told the RI couple not to be alarmed about the sheriff's vehicles—that her husband was the head sheriff and others were coming over to walk in the woods with him. They had nodded and smiled, probably thinking that it made the place more safe for them. Little did they know.

Raven looked out her living room window at the little lights of the cabin she just left. It was one of ten on the property, all built by her grandfather; all painted white with small, inviting front porches. Each had its own bathroom with a small shower. A few had fireplaces, now converted to gas—she didn't trust a renter not to burn the whole complex to the ground. The ones without had baseboard electric heat. She didn't often try to rent any after mid-October, especially with the rise of private homes for short-term rentals, but this year she surprisingly had more people from away interested in the old-fashioned style.

She heard two more sheriff county SUVs pull in and park in the driveway, and despite the fading light, she saw a group waiting at the wood's edge. Someone turned on a large, bright light on a pole.

Her phone beeped. The next couple sat in traffic on I-95 by the New Hampshire-Maine border, inching their way towards the Piscataqua River Bridge. They were two hours away at the very least and probably more like four on a holiday week. All it took was one fender bender or a breakdown, and the lanes backed up even further. Even in Maine, after crossing the river, getting off the highway wouldn't help as Route One traffic along the coast crawled, especially in Southern Maine, due to the volume of visitors and traffic lights. She told the guests not to worry about the check-in time and to drive safely. She was actually grateful for the extra time to catch her breath.

She fidgeted with her phone for a few more minutes and then glanced at a large pot on the stove, ready for peeled potatoes for tomorrow's Thanksgiving meal. She was in no mood, however, to prep food.

A brisk walk would do her good and clear her head. She threw on her old down jacket, the one with the duct tape on her right arm holding in the down where Dukie had punctured a hole with his nail on a nervous car ride. Her favorite blue wool knit hat covered her ears and matched the scarf she wrapped around her neck, both long-ago handmade gifts from her mother. She felt in the pockets of her coat to ensure she had gloves and a flashlight and took off down the long dirt driveway.

At the bottom of the driveway, instead of turning left up the road towards her neighbors, Betty and Howard Hart, who always welcomed a visit, she turned right, towards town. It was about a mile walk into the small downtown area, all on the side of the road. She was grateful the residents had shot down a proposal to add sidewalks, a measure wanted by those from away who moved to Secretly for its charm but then tried to suburbanize it to match what they had left. Their logic was far from logical.

Raven wielded her flashlight to avoid any potholes or roadkill as dusk settled into the early evening. She walked with purpose, although she had none. There was something about being speedy that felt more deliberate and liberating than slow-poking about like she did daily with the dogs on their walks. The cardio effort pushed out more of her nervousness and a few tears. When she saw the white fences of the nearby horse farm, she relaxed. The horses would be in for the night, she suspected, but she paused briefly to inhale, hoping to get a whiff of one of her favorite smells on earth. As a child, she always hoped she could own her own horse, but now she couldn't imagine adding that extra work to her day.

Next to the fenced-in field was one of the town's twenty cemeteries. Maine was like that, with small family plots sprouting up on the sides of roads or in the back of pastures, all official. This one was more organized and formal than most. She shined her light in at the wrought iron gate and saw the word "Johnson" but was too far to see the smaller print that said her mother's name. "Julia, beloved mother." Earlier that week, she had weeded the area around the stone and prepped it for a holiday spray she'd put there after Thanksgiving.

She saw a few headstones with plastic mums shoved in front, locals who wanted to remember their loved ones on Thanksgiving. Small American flags dotted the deceased veterans, placed by aging VFW members on Veteran's Day earlier in November. Veterans of Foreign Wars. What did Civil War veterans think of the VFW when it was founded after World War I? Or was it earlier than that? Spanish American? Her grandfathers were both World War II veterans. She couldn't imagine going off to war or even knowing anyone who did, yet thousands of soldiers still went.

Across from the cemetery sat the Secretly post office, a favorite stop for many of her guests, always marveling at the lack of patrons in line. Summer regulars brought up packages to send and joked they were going to leave Christmas gifts with Raven to ship for them. These dilemmas always made Raven wonder why people continued to live in such crowded, inconvenient places. She understood some had to for work reasons, but what about the others? No wonder so many were taken with Maine and its lower population and easier life. She just hoped Secretly wouldn't become the new Boothbay or Kennebunkport with its fancy restaurants and shops. And crowds. Simpler was, by far, better.

Around a corner, just past the cemetery, stood Lane's Market, a town fixture for a couple of centuries or more. There was a larger corporate grocery store in the next town, about fifteen miles away, but that store didn't have the local fishermen's catch or the town chatter. She had gone to school with Christopher Lane's younger sister, and her own mother always advocated for supporting local businesses. She agreed. Plus, who wouldn't want to shop where everyone knew your name?

The store was still open, and she stood in front of the windows, hidden from the cashier and customers by the indoor light reflecting back inside. A new cashier, whom Raven didn't recognize, manned one register with Evelyn Poole, Lane's senior cashier, leaning over her. Evelyn was probably training her. She had been the sole cashier for months since the last one, Sarah Wolf, ran off with Evelyn's husband, Rusty.

Raven wondered how Evelyn was doing, living totally on her own without his second income and coming back to the store day in and day out. Maybe it was good she had to pick up Sarah's shifts, although it had to be hard to stare at the empty register and know that it was empty because the woman ran off with her husband.

Everyone was surprised Rusty had just up and left with young Sarah last summer. He even left his lobster boat behind with his traps still in the water. Love made you do stupid things. Another quote from her mother. But this seemed dumber than normal.

Evelyn soldiered on. One day, to a customer in front of Raven, Evelyn joked that she was going to get a lobstering license to use Rusty's boat and pull his traps. Raven had heard that other lobstermen had been checking Rusty's traps and giving Evelyn the profit. That's what the lobstering community was all about.

Tonight, Evelyn, her brown hair pulled back into a ponytail, smiled at an approaching customer, Karl Wolf, the owner of the Wolf Marine Store, and Sarah's husband. He and Evelyn had the same dilemma, left by their spouses, although the rumor was that he'd had his own candy on the side for quite a while anyway. Maybe that's why Sarah was looking herself for a different lollipop.

The new young cashier picked up an item to scan while Evelyn and Karl chatted. Raven didn't feel like talking with Karl or anyone. She rushed away from the door before the transaction could be finished and Karl could exit the store.

She now stood in front of Charles' house, the Lane Mansion, separated from the store by a small parking lot and a patch of grass. The house stood on the highest peak in the very center of town, originally built by Isaiah Lane, a wealthy merchant, who built it the same year as the store. The Lane Family still owned the store and the parking lot but had sold off the family homestead with ten acres during the Great Depression. Despite the decades that had passed, it was still called the Lane Mansion, and the current Lanes, having never been able to buy it back with the price of coastal real estate soaring, could not hide their disdain for the revolving door of owners. Actually, all locals were getting outbid for homes by those from away. The Us vs. Them mentality was growing. Marcel had said it was a dangerous mindset. Charles was the seventh or eighth owner of the large white Federal-style home.

The original slate sidewalk went from the house to the store and still remained out in front of both, forever connecting the two. A stone pillar with a wrought iron ring for securing horses stood to the right of the sidewalk that led up to the house's large wooden front door. Despite the recent snowstorms and impending winter weather, scaffolding ensconced one side of the house as well as both chimneys that Charles had mentioned at the bonfire.

Raven walked up the slate sidewalk and stopped. Her heart beat fast. If it was Charles in the woods, he'd never be here again.

She stepped up onto the stone slab and turned the knob on the wide front door. She and Marcel kept their house unlocked, as did most of her neighbors, but she didn't expect someone from away to do the same.

The brass knob turned. It was unlocked.

Raven caught her breath, her hand still on the handle. She should walk back down the sidewalk and go home. The Massachusetts guests might be earlier than she thought. It had happened before.

Instead, she pushed the wooden door open and stepped inside.

Her flashlight's glow revealed she had entered the large center hall. Charles wasn't fooling about bricks being everywhere. Piles of them spilled out from a doorway, probably from the dining room or kitchen. Before venturing further inside, Raven paused and listened.

No sounds of workers were heard. Not that she had seen any pickup trucks out front or in the side yard or any lights on inside. With the sun nearly set, the hall was quite dim, almost dark. Her flashlight's beam bounced off the walls, casting spooky shadows. The stillness added to the eerie feeling creeping up from her toes. She reached for a light switch but didn't see one. She swallowed and stepped deeper into the hall.

The house was a mess.

Raven's mind flashed back to the night of the bonfire. Charles had continued talking about his house plans without noticing or showing he heard the murmurs around the circle from the locals.

"I'm paying extra for more workers so I can be in the house for Christmas," he had said, beaming as he looked into the flames. "Which means by mid-December in my book. I have to have time to put up a tree."

He turned and grinned at Raven with the assumption that many people had—that she loved Christmas trees. Which she didn't. Not when her earliest memories of Christmas were the tree flying out the front door, ornaments included, with the lights still on until the cord couldn't reach the outlet any further, and it finally went dark. The sound of tingling glass as the ornaments broke and the wails of her mother had floated into her brain at the bonfire that night as it did again as she stood in Charles' hallway, remembering his comment.

But she had played along that night with Charles and just nodded as she played along with everyone who made Christmas comments. More groans had come from the bonfire crowd, and a whispered "he should learn to shut up" hit her ears.

She glanced in that direction and saw Christopher Lane, the current owner of the family grocery store, scowling towards Charles.

"And Evelyn is struggling to keep her house, and this guy waltzes in and flaunts his money," Chris said under his breath.

Raven was glad Evelyn was on the other side of the bonfire, hopefully out of earshot to hear any of the comments, including Chris'.

Raven focused back on her current surroundings in the Lane Mansion hallway. Besides the bricks, the few pieces of furniture in what Raven assumed was the living room were turned upside down, haphazardly, and strewn about. They weren't covered to be protected from the brick dust that was all over the wooden floor. She saw various footprints in it from Charles and the many workers she figured were needed to complete this project. White loose paper, copy machine-like, splayed, disorganized on the floor. A glint of a silver laptop in the corner, also on the floor, peaked out from under a chair.

"A strange place to leave that," she said, remembering Charles saying he worked upstairs in a bedroom.

She pivoted to cross the hall and heard a noise at the front door. Shutting off her flashlight, she knelt behind a brick pile, flattening herself against the wall.

The noise increased, and the front door swung open. A man, about six-foot tall, stood in the outline of the frame. All she could make out was his stature—thin. He paused in the doorway and seemed to survey the dark hallway, looking for something.

Raven's heart pounded heavily. She held her breath, to both calm her nerves and to stop a sneeze.

The man stepped into the hall and shut the door behind him.

Chapter Four

"Raven." The man's voice called out. "Raven?"

Raven let out her breath.

"Dad!" She switched on her flashlight and stood up.

Ethan "Johnny" Johnson squinted and threw up his arm to shield his eyes from Raven's beam.

"Hey, lower that, will you? Trying to blind me?"

"Trying to scare me?" She said back, annoyed, her voice rising. He had a knack of showing up at the wrong time. Over and over again.

"Actually, I'm trying to save you. B and E is illegal." His voice was extra authoritative in the dark.

"I didn't break in. The door was unlocked," she said back.

"All right. 'Unlawful entry.' Kinda the same thing."

She shook her head to herself. Once a cop, always a cop. Even though he had retired over five years ago, he still acted like he was on the city of Boston police force.

"Charles Kearns isn't going to care." Her mind flashed to the image of him lying on the snow, crumbled and literally disjointed.

Johnny came further into the hall. "You sound confident. Why's that?"

She swallowed. "Because I found him dead this afternoon. In the preserve behind our house."

"What? Dead? Did you tell Marcel? Why didn't you call me?" His voice elevated.

"Marcel was just getting home when I ran out of the woods. He and his guys are in there now." She took a deep breath. "I needed to go for a walk. To get out of there." She ignored responding to his question about her calling him, and Johnny didn't push it. She didn't grow up relying him, and she wasn't going to start now.

"What happened to him?" Johnny entered the circle of light made by the flashlight and stood close to Raven. She saw his white five o'clock shadow on his unshaven face. His white eyebrows seemed bushier than usual, perhaps from the bounce of the light off the floor. His blue eyes danced at the prospect of a good story.

"I don't know. Tripped and fell? Mistaken for a deer? I'm not sure there is enough of him left to know what happened, I'm telling you."

"Jeezum Crow! Raven, you're fooling with me."

"I wish I was." Her voice caught in her throat.

"So, naturally, you thought entering the dead man's house immediately after finding him was the right thing to do."

"Yeah, wicked creepy. Though I didn't plan it."

"Yep, wicked creepy indeed." He paused. "But you're right. You had to do something to keep busy. Seeing your first dead body always stays with you, too." He looked down at the floor. "Why are there bricks everywhere?"

"He was redoing the chimneys. Brick by brick, he said."

"I didn't realize you knew him."

"Just met him. At the church bonfire last month."

"Hmmm." Johnny looked further around the hall and meandered into the front rooms. He called out, "What are you and Marcel doing tomorrow?"

Her shoulders sagged. She had toyed with the idea of inviting Johnny for Thanksgiving dinner, but the whole concept of the holiday was about giving gratitude. She wasn't sure yet if she was grateful to have Johnny back in her life.

"I'm working. More or less. We have two cabins rented for the long weekend."

She remembered the couple stuck in traffic. They'd still be inching their way up the coast.

"Hope you're soaking them for the rental." His voice sounded like he was speaking from one of the chimneys. She made her way around the brick pile and followed his muffled words. The beam picked up more piles of brick and dust balls, the kind that she had at home. Hers were mostly made out of Lily's white fur. If Charles had a dog, where was it?

Johnny knelt on the hearth, looking like a beheaded man. His head, up to his shoulders, was shoved up the center flue.

"Let me see that flashlight." He reached his hand out. Once he held the torch, he shined the light up. "Nice work happening here. It looks like they had finished the interior and could start on the cosmetic reconstruction of this one."

Sitting back on his heels, he trained the light on the front of the fireplace and stood. He followed the beam with his hand and paused in one section. He wiggled the brick, and it easily came out into his palm. The light showed a perfectly rectangular hole in the wall. Empty.

"Bingo. A secret hiding place. Woo hoo. I was hoping to find one. Maybe because of the Revolutionary War. What year is the house again?"

She had walked by the house a million times and looked at the white sign with the house's year painted on it but didn't remember it now.

"I don't know. 1795? 1805?"

"Well, if not the Revolutionary War, then the War of 1812. Maine saw action, you know."

If he was such a Maine history buff, why hadn't he stayed living in Maine? Why did he move to Boston and away from her and her mother? Her continued annoyance with him was why she couldn't yet have him over for a holiday meal despite him being back in Maine, and her life, for two years. Marcel's nudge for her to let bygones be bygones was easy for him to say. His family had always been intact. "But he's still your father," Marcel insisted. Well, he hadn't acted like one. At least not until recently.

Raven kept her thoughts to herself and said, "Yes, I remember learning about it in school. 'Maine's second fight for independence' or something like that."

"Yep, all of America's second fight, really. Those redcoats weren't going to give us up that easily. This hiding place could have been for war documents. Or the Underground Railroad. All sorts of uses. I've read about them but have never seen one. This is so cool."

The beam flashed around the room in his excitement. His other hand contained the brick that closed up the hole.

"Makes you wonder if Charles or the workers found anything interesting still in the hole. The brick came off easily. I'll bet it did for them, too," he said.

Raven stepped forward to touch the brick. A lawn sign out front bore the name of the bricklayers. Maybe they knew if anything interesting was found.

She followed Johnny's movement to stay with the light. He crossed the hall to the living room after placing back the brick.

"Jeezum Crow, what happened here?" He said.

"I'm guessing he didn't get to cleaning this room yet with the brick mess and all." Raven stood next to Johnny.

He shook his head in disagreement, "I'm not so sure." He slowly shined the light around the room, training it mainly on the floor.

"What's this?" He said when the light picked up a dark stain near an overturned chair. Raven had seen it earlier but thought it was a flaw in the floor stain or a burnt mark from an old ember.

Johnny walked over to it and knelt. "That doesn't look too good."

"Oil?"

He shook his head and looked at her with a blank face.

"No, I'd say blood."

Raven inhaled quickly.

Johnny stood up. "We need to get out of here and have Marcel's team come in. Don't touch anything else."

Chapter Five

Johnny drove Raven back to Pine Acres in his old white pickup truck. It rattled and squeaked, but they rode in silence.

The county coroner's van was now in the driveway, which meant that he hadn't taken the body away yet. She hoped her Rhode Island couple were either in their cabin or hadn't seen the van. She'd have a harder time explaining that.

She also hoped that the coroner was able to confirm that it actually was Charles, though she suspected that, unless he had a wallet in his pocket, the identification would have to wait. Maybe it was someone else and not someone she knew. The odds, however, of two people in Secretly having the same nerdy math hat were nil.

Tom Pinkham stood outside his vehicle when they pulled up in the truck. His driver's side door was open. He looked ready to leave.

"Hey, Johnny," he said as they got out of the truck.

"Any identification of the body?" Johnny asked, strolling over to Tom, coffee cup from the truck's holder in his hand.

"Well, there's no jawbone left to the body, and the skull's badly damaged by the uppers. It'll make dental identification tough. Doc thinks it's—he's—been there for almost a month."

Raven swallowed. So, seeing Charles at the bonfire might have been one of his last nights alive.

"The animals must have come across his body and tore him apart," Johnny said, taking another sip. Raven eyed her father out of the corner of her eye and hoped there was just coffee in the cup.

"Maybe the limbs, but not his head. Someone else took care of that." Tom ran his fingers through his thick, auburn hair.

"What do you mean? Like that mountain lion we keep hearing about?" Raven said.

Tom glanced at Johnny and then back at Raven. "Sorry to be the one to say, but his face was gone before the animals got there."

Raven shrugged and shook her head, showing she still didn't understand.

"Close-range gunshot is my guess," said Tom.

Raven's eyes widened.

She took a deep breath.

Close range.

Gunshot.

That made it murder.

She covered her mouth with her hands.

Who would want to murder Charles?

"The blood at the house," Raven said, her words pushing out in billows.

"Blood?" Tom said, moving closer to Raven to catch her words. "Blood in your house?"

She shook her head. Her voice was gone.

"No," Johnny answered her for her. "Charles' house. In town. The Lane Mansion. We came back to get Marcel."

Marcel had come up behind the group and overheard Johnny.

"You were in Charles Kearns' house?" He addressed Johnny. "When?"

Raven went over to Marcel, but he was waiting for Johnny's response and didn't reach out to her.

"Just now. That's why Raven and I came back quickly. To alert you. I'm not sure if it is blood, but it sure as hell looked like it."

"You touched potential evidence by going in that house." Marcel didn't ask. He stated it as a fact.

"I thought it was an accident." Raven's thin voice piped in. "I thought he died by mistake. I didn't know he was..." She couldn't say the word murdered or shot.

Close. Range. Gunshot.

The words made her weak, and she reached out to grab Marcel, who steadied her but only as he would steady a stranger. He kept her at arm's length.

Headlights turned into the driveway, and Marcel moved towards the incoming car. Raven saw the Massachusetts license plate. The second renters. Ugh.

She steadied, took a deep breath, and then moved between the men to meet the renters at their vehicle. Their arrival was a welcomed distraction and allowed her to avoid further criticism from Marcel.

"What's going on here," said the woman, exiting the Mercedes SUV in one of those black over-the-top puffy coats with an arctic symbol on the shoulder.

A county coroner's van and sheriff's vehicles would spook anyone, Raven thought.

"My husband's the sheriff in the county," she offered, hoping they thought there was a social event despite the serious vehicles.

The woman nodded and turned towards her husband, who wore a matching expensive puffy coat in silver.

"Don't tip my luggage on its side," she said to him, standing at the back of the SUV to supervise.

The man smiled at Raven. "We're glad to be out of traffic, that's for sure."

"And in the middle of the woods," the woman said without expression. Obviously, she was the type who should have stayed ninety miles south, in Portland.

Raven steadied herself for their disappointment in the small cabin, but surprisingly, both the man and woman murmured compliments. The accommodations were cozy, warm, and what she jokingly called "cabin chic" on the website. And it was. A black and red buffalo plaid fleece throw laid askew on an overside chair. The gas-lit fireplace, already on, and the battery-operated candles in the windows added to its charm.

"Complimentary local sparkling blueberry wine." Raven pointed to a bottle in a chilled holder. Local foil-wrapped chocolates lay displayed on a plate.

"It'll be hard to leave for Thanksgiving dinner tomorrow," said the woman, removing her coat and smiling for the first time. "We should have just roughed it out here for an authentic Thanksgiving." As if Maine was Plymouth Rock.

Raven managed a smile back, but she could barely concentrate or act cheerful when they asked her about local Thanksgiving traditions.

Murder wasn't one of those traditions, but that was all she could think about.

Chapter Six

By the time Raven got back to the house, Marcel, Tom, and Johnny were gone from the driveway. Marcel's Jeep, however, stood next to her Mini Cooper. He must've driven down with one of the guys to Charles' house to check out the stain and whatever else they could learn. With the coroner's van also gone, Raven knew that Charles' remains were safely tucked inside it and would be identified eventually, somehow.

Inside their house, Lily and Dukie pranced around her. Raven glanced at the clock. Way past their dinner time. Before feeding them, she knelt down to accept their kisses and nudges. She needed it. Lily pushed her block head into Raven's chest. She tightened her arms around Lily's thick neck and buried her face into her fur. Always her snuggle bunny, thinking back to the last days of her mother's life. Returning exhausted from the hospital day after day, Raven always had support from Lily.

Dukie danced nearby and then sat perfectly still. Her perfect child, always trying to be the good boy to counter Lily's carefree attitude. When he was a clown, it was a calculated leap. Measured. More like Marcel than Raven.

Raven rose to fill their bowls with their food and watched as they inhaled their dinner in a nook of the kitchen. Life went on for them as if a man's body was never found in the woods.

She turned at the sound of the front door opening. Marcel was home. He didn't come right into the kitchen. She heard him fumbling with his coat in the foyer. Their house wasn't as old as the Lane Mansion, but it had its own quirks for being well over one hundred years old and added on many times before they bought it as newlyweds from her mother, who moved into one of the larger cabins on the property, now used as a year-round rental. The cabins were how her mother supported herself and Raven, all inherited from her grandfather, who had built them when he moved down from Newfoundland over a century ago.

Marcel's silence meant he was mad at her. She knew better than to go into Charles' house, but she really hadn't planned it, and she hadn't known it would be part of a crime scene. She wanted to call out hello to him but was afraid he wouldn't answer, and then she'd know for sure he was mad. She also wanted to ask if the stain was really blood but waited for him to round the corner to the kitchen.

But he didn't come into the kitchen. His heavy footsteps chose the other path to the bedroom. Keys dropped into a dish with a jingle. She knew then he was unbuckling his holster and hanging it on the closet door. At least he was home for the night.

She busied herself in the kitchen, sticking her head deep into the fridge, waiting for him to come in. Her hands shook as she pushed the bagged turkey in the brine further to the back. Lately, it had been difficult to talk with Marcel. She wasn't sure if it was her or him or something else entirely. Her behavior this afternoon only added to the awkwardness.

She didn't hear him come up behind her but saw his stocking feet walk by with his left big toe poking out. He didn't touch her or say hello. She straightened up.

"Hello," she said.

"Hi," he said with a clip without turning around and looking at her. No hello kiss. No warmth in his voice.

She swallowed. "The dogs ate, but I've been waiting for you. What do you feel like having?"

He checked the wood stove without answering her and sat down in his chair, flicking on the table lamp. Picking up the newspaper, the local one that came out weekly, he opened it wide and buried his face in the pages. Raven advertised the cabins in the rag although she suspected no one from away ever read it.

Minutes ticked by. She stood rooted to the kitchen floor and realized she was holding her breath. She eventually moved back to the fridge, its door still open. Removing bagged lettuce and a cucumber from a drawer, she started to make a salad. She might as well eat something even if he didn't want anything. Lily and Dukie, always her sous chefs, sat semi-patiently waiting for a sample of the cuke.

"You and your father are unbelievable," he said, finally breaking the silence.

"What do you mean?" She paused from slicing the seedless cuke into rounds.

"You both think you know everything. I understand his motivation somewhat. Former Boston cop. Thinks he knows more than us up here. Thinks we need his help. Plus, it's in his blood. But you. I don't get you."

She bit her lip. Whenever he felt undermined, he reverted to the old "you're a know-it-all" line. Lily moaned and motioned to the counter with her head. Raven resumed cutting up the cuke.

"Did you hear what I said?" He turned in the chair and looked over his shoulder.

"I heard you."

"Then how about acknowledging me? How about saying, 'Okay, Marcel, I hear you.'?" He turned back around and shook out the paper.

"I didn't say anything because it's a rerun. I'm sick of defending myself." Her eyes burned. She felt Marcel going down the rabbit hole. Not tonight, please. Not on a day she found a dead body. Not the night before Thanksgiving.

"You have to admit it's pretty strange you two went to the Lane house, and then we discover it's a murder."

"Are you saying we're responsible for Charles Kearns' death?" Raven swiveled, the knife in her hand. She couldn't believe Marcel was accusing them of murder.

"I didn't say that! I just can't believe you both stuck your noses into a crime scene. Possibly ruined evidence."

"First off," said Raven, her face flushing as her volume went up, "I didn't know it was a crime scene, nor did I plan on going there. I just needed to walk, and my feet led me there."

Now, it was Marcel's turn to be silent.

"And another thing, my father didn't go to the house. He saw me go in and followed me. He didn't even know that Charles was dead until I told him. Leave him out of it, okay?" She suddenly felt protective of Johnny and wasn't sure that was a good thing. Marcel's anger got her all turned around.

"Ow!" She dropped the knife, and drew up her finger into her mouth. Just a tiny nick by her fingernail, but like a paper cut, little nicks hurt as much as large ones.

"Death by a thousand cuts," her mother used to say. Is this what she meant? A thousand jabs?

"Just stay out of it. Stay. Out." Marcel's voice had a finality to it.

The room returned to its awkward silence. The air thickened. Raven picked up the knife but didn't resume cutting. She tossed a couple of cuke slices on the floor for the dogs and put the lettuce back in the fridge. She wasn't hungry.

Marcel rose and tended the wood stove, opening the flue and adding two more pieces of wood. More to have something to do, she thought, not because the room needed it. She was sweating, but probably not from the heat of the stove. She wished to hide and at the same time, she wanted to ask Marcel what was happening to them and why they've been bickering so much lately.

He walked toward her and drew her close in his arms. He put his hand on the back of her head.

"Please stay out of it. Okay? For your sake. It might get dangerous," he said softly into her hair.

She wrapped her arms around his thick, taut waist and nodded as she buried her face into his flannel shirt. She understood what he meant. That is what her nod meant. She didn't realize at that moment it was all her nod meant. It did not mean, she'd later discover, that she would comply.

His cell phone in his pocket rang. He pulled back from Raven and tugged to extract it.

"Ouellette." He walked away from her towards the hall as he spoke. His voice lowered, and as he rounded the corner, Raven thought he was whispering. To keep her from hearing details of the case, she assumed. But this wasn't the first time she caught him whispering this month.

Chapter Seven

Thanksgiving morning, Raven rose to get started on her day. After taking care of Lily and Dukie with their food and brief morning walk around the yard, she turned to her list of 'To-Do's" for Thanksgiving meal prep. The warmth of lying next to Marcel the night before and being held in his arms stayed with her, comforted her. Maybe she had been imagining their disconnection.

The holiday routine of peeling potatoes, sautéing onions and celery for the stuffing, and even putting the cold, wrinkled bird in the oven distanced her from the horrors of Charles' death. For a moment.

Then, other thoughts flooded in. Charles' body was lying there for weeks. She and the dogs must have walked that path dozens of times in the past month. Was it already picked clean when they had walked through the first time? Was he killed in his house and moved to the woods much later? Was he missed by anyone? Had anyone been looking for him? Family? Work?

Work. What did his hat say again? "Mathematical Society."

Raven quickly finished up the stuffing prep and covered the dish before washing her hands and going over to her laptop on the kitchen table. A search quickly found the information about that group.

Founded in 1938, The Mathematical Society was an international organization promoting education and research within the seven branches of mathematics.

"Archimedes. Founder of Math. That sounds familiar." Raven spoke out loud again to herself.

"What's that?" Marcel had entered the kitchen and was filling his travel mug with coffee.

"Just double checking a Christmas reservation," said Raven, grateful to have the laptop facing away from the counter. She hated to lie, but she had only promised the night before to stay out of the investigation, although simply learning more about Charles' interests wasn't really investigating.

"Where are you off to?" she said to Marcel as he rounded the corner to where they hung their coats.

His voice traveled around into the kitchen. "Just back into the woods. Tom and a state forensic expert are meeting me to walk the area again in better light." He peered around the corner and eyed her. She expected him to repeat "Stay put" again, but he didn't. She nodded an acknowledgment and gave a short wave. A moment later, she heard the front door close.

Focusing back on the screen, she read more about math.

"Mathematics is the queen of the sciences, and number theory is the queen of mathematics."

"And it's all mud to me," she said. Not that she didn't do well in school, but she was more of what Marcel would call a dreamer. She definitely never dreamed about math.

The Mathematical Society membership list on the website was private and password-protected. She wondered if Charles had passwords on his own laptop or in that upstairs bedroom at the Lane Mansion. She could bop in there and just look. It would take only a couple of minutes.

"Stay out of it," she said to herself.

But she obviously wasn't.

She next threw Charles' name into a search engine. Many 'Charles Kearns' came up, even when she focused the search just to Massachusetts. She fine-tuned the keywords to include his witness testimony role using phrases like "expert" and "SME," and, of course, "Math." Up came numerous newspaper articles about courtroom arguments, including a restraining order against a North Shore contractor who threatened bodily harm and death to a "Charles E. Kearns" for costing him a two billion dollar contract. Two billion dollars. Now, that was a motive to kill.

Was Marcel aware of any of this yet? Should she tell him despite being told to stay out? Internet searches were harmless, right? Public Knowledge. While she debated sharing the information, she popped up to see if he was still in the driveway waiting for Tom. Through a window, she saw him, Tom, and two others, including a tall, long-haired blonde woman, walking into the woods on the path near their property. Just as well. She shouldn't be the one to tell him anyway. How could she explain how she knew?

As she looked out the window, she saw the Massachusetts SUV leave for their Thanksgiving activities. She had forgotten she had two occupied cabins and people spending money on their vacation.

She checked on the turkey in the oven—it was browning nicely—and headed over to Betty and Howard's house. They were coming for dinner at two o'clock, but she wanted to speak to them privately first about what had happened without Marcel listening in and cutting her off.

Betty, a stylish woman in her late sixties, opened the door with a grimace and whispered, "Don't bring up Sally." Sally was their oldest daughter, a want-to-be-actress in Los Angeles. She usually called asking for money for rent, plastic surgery, or the latest fashion trends. Howard always said no, and then Betty covertly wired it to Sally via a private cash app.

Howard sat in his leather chair in the den, mumbling about learning to support oneself as an adult, when Betty loudly announced Raven's arrival.

"Oh, I thought we were going to your house today, not the other way around," said Howard, rising and showing his good manners. He grinned, always glad to see Raven. "Who's that hottie blonde with Marcel and Tom today? And I don't mean the guy in the baggie pants." Howard laughed at his own joke. He could see the trail entrance from their sitting room.

Raven shrugged. She had seen the woman but didn't recognize her, at least not from the back. Must be someone from the state.

"Have a seat." Howard motioned to one of the floral-patterned chairs.

Raven sat on the edge of the cushion.

"I wanted to tell you guys what has happened." She knitted her fingers and squeezed them together. "I'd rather have you hear it from me now than later wonder why Marcel and I didn't tell you today at dinner."

"You're getting divorced," said Betty with another grimace and a loud sigh.

"Oh, Raven, I'm so sorry, but it's probably for the best." She plunked into the chair next to Raven and touched her arm.

Howard shot Betty a look. "Will you listen!"

Raven shook her head. "No. No. It's not that." She paused to wonder what would make Betty think that. "Do you know something I don't know?"

"Oh, no. No," said Betty. "I just assumed since you mentioned last week that things have been strained between the two of you lately."

"You must think we're getting divorced every ten minutes, then," said Howard. He shook his head in bewilderment at the woman he'd been married to for forty-five years.

"Sometimes I do," Betty said with a frown. "You could be nicer to me." She rose abruptly and went to the stove. Raven heard the gas flame ignite under a metal kettle.

Betty returned composed. "A cup of tea, Raven?"

"I can't stay. I have the turkey in the oven. I just wanted you to know that a body was found in the woods yesterday. That's why Marcel and Tom are in there now."

"A body? Really?" Howard crossed his arms and leaned forward.

"A dead body?" Betty pulled a cup and saucer down from a shelf.

Howard gave her another look and turned to Raven. "Sometimes I have a hard time believing she was a school teacher. Do you think it's the onset of dementia?"

"I can hear you." Betty poured the hot water into the porcelain cup.

"Do they know who it was? How long it was there?" Howard leaned forward.

"I didn't hear about anyone being missing." Betty settled down into her squishy chair by the window and stirred her tea. "Maybe it's a cold case."

Raven again shook her head. "Not a cold case." She didn't know if she should reveal Charles' name. She shouldn't have come. This was a mistake. These two now would want to talk to Marcel about it over turkey, and he'd be mad again at her for giving out information. She gazed out the window past Betty and saw Johnny drive slowly by Betty and Howard's house. His head was angled towards Pine Acres' driveway when he came to a stop at its end. Howard followed her line of sight.

"Did you invite your dad for Thanksgiving?" he said.

"No." She felt a pang of regret. Just a small pang. Johnny, driving around alone on Thanksgiving, driving by hoping to catch her outside, still hoping for an invitation. The pang wasn't large enough, however, for Raven to want to reverse her decision.

"Oh, here they come," said Howard and directed Raven's attention towards the woods in the Harts' back yard, which also butted up next to the preserve. Tom and the baggie pants man were ahead, talking. The stranger carried a black bag similar to a medical kit. Marcel and the blonde were walking together, their heads close as they talked, the woman flicking her long blond hair around with a toss of her head. It seemed more personal than business.

Raven rose to get a closer look. The blonde flipped her hair again. Raven saw her face and inhaled quickly. It was Shannon McGrath, Marcel's high school sweetheart and the region's newly elected district attorney.

Chapter Eight

J ohnny slowed his old F-150 to a stop in front of the main driveway to Pine Acres. Tommy's deputy sheriff SUV was parked further up in the driveway, as was a newer Jeep Cherokee, the really expensive kind. Probably some state official in his private vehicle.

Johnny missed conducting investigations but didn't miss the danger of being on duty in the Boston area. Whichever mayor at the time was claiming that crime was down obviously wasn't out on the streets at two o'clock in the morning or going undercover. After two years of being back in Maine, he was finally able to sleep at night instead of jumping at every coyote howl or ATV revving by.

Yet, here was a murder in Secretly. Put a bunch of imperfect humans together, and it was bound to happen. He'd like to offer his services to help if Marcel needed an extra hand, but he didn't want to be perceived as thinking that the Maine sheriffs were less qualified than a Boston flatfoot.

He did need something to keep him busy, though. There were many opportunities to volunteer. That was the beauty of living in a small town. He was already on the decorating committee, scheduled to string Christmas lights tomorrow on all the town buildings and park entrances, but he needed more in his life, especially while he waited for Raven to let him back into hers.

The town had been more lenient than Raven about accepting his return to Maine, despite leaving almost thirty years ago. Raven was five when Julia, Raven's mother, asked him to move out.

"Don't come back until you're sober," she had said, standing in the middle of the road with broken Christmas ornaments at her bare feet next to the decorated tree he had just heaved out of the house.

They were living in Rockland at the time, a much larger town than Secretly, twenty-five miles up the coast. The rental home was old and drafty, but it was all they could afford on Johnny's rookie cop salary. He was a newly minted uniform and scared to death of failing—as a police officer and as a husband and father.

He became a self-fulling prophecy. He would have failed at it all, except Boston was desperate for police officers, and a drunk cop wasn't unusual in that city. He had a clean record otherwise—never used excessive force, kept his nose clean from bribes, and never missed a shift. He was also an excellent partner and an even better joke-teller.

Initially, he told himself he would only be going to Boston for a year. To make more money and prove to Julia he could be a good provider. He sent money every month for Raven. Cash. He didn't have to. No court ordered it because Julia and he had never divorced.

While part of his paycheck crossed the Maine border, he himself never came to Maine until after he retired. He never saw Julia again.

He had planned to return when he was sober for real. That effort took time, with many false starts, but now he proudly jingled the ten-year coin in his pocket. If he had come back then, Julia and he might have reconciled, and maybe Raven wouldn't be resistant to him, but he never trusted himself. Would sobriety stick this time? Even now, he wondered. His weekly meeting friends believed in him more than he believed in himself.

He didn't blame Raven for being distant. Thirty years of her witnessing her mother go it alone. Thirty years of her not having a father. He had hoped that Julia had shared with Raven that he had continued his financial support for her. Maybe Julia had, and Raven, rightly so, didn't believe that money was enough to erase the past or heal the present.

After he left Maine, Julia and Raven moved down to Pine Acres and helped Julia's father run the business. Johnny was proud the cabin business continued to thrive under Raven, with her fully taking it over from Julia about ten years ago. About the time of his sobriety. If only he had chanced it, if he had reached out then.

That was around the time of Raven and Marcel's wedding. He wasn't invited of course. In fact, he only learned of her marriage when he read Julia's obituary and saw Marcel listed as her beloved "son-in-law." All those years, he subscribed to the weekly area paper to keep track of Raven's track and field accomplishments in high school, to see the ads for Pine Acres, and then he had to learn of her marriage from an obituary. Reading of Julia's death jolted him. He should have been there for her and for Raven. They should have been a family. He reread the obituary notice three times before he realized what was missing—his name.

"Julia Fossett Johnson died peacefully in her sleep with her family by her side after battling a long illness. She managed Pine Acres Cabins in Secretly, first with her father, and then with her daughter, Elizabeth. Besides her daughter, she leaves her beloved son-in-law, Marcel Ouellette. Services and burial are private."

He knew the obituary by heart.

He was invisible. He was. He had earned that. Even with his financial support, he wasn't there to provide security or comfort, to share a life—not just when Julia was sick but in the happy times too.

Was it Julia's wish to use Raven's birth name? Was that a signal to him since he had nicknamed her Raven when she was an infant for her jet-black shiny hair?

Johnny's thoughts returned to the present when he saw Tommy and another gentleman emerge from the woods. He recognized the chemistry kit, as he called it, as the tools for a forensic expert. Today wouldn't be the first or the last day for exploring the area, especially with skeletal pieces of Charles Kearns scattered anywhere. In fact, if it was his investigation, he'd have closed down the entire preserve, until law enforcement was satisfied they found all that they needed to find.

"But it's not your investigation, dummy," he said to himself in a low mumble, "and Marcel is fully capable of knowing how to handle one."

Just as he said Marcel's name, out popped Marcel and a woman from the woods. She had long blonde hair and a coat that Johnny hadn't seen up in

Maine, just in Boston. She could have been Mrs. Charles Kearns, though it would have been in poor taste to have the widow at the crime scene. She was also too chipper to be a new widow, leaning towards Marcel as they walked, touching his arm, laughing. Laughing as she left a murder scene.

"Something's rotten in Denmark," Johnny said, "and I'm going to figure out what stinks." With his phone, he grabbed a photo of the Jeep Cherokee license plate before driving off. He still had plenty of friends who would run a plate for him.

Chapter Nine

After watching Johnny drive off, Raven returned home to finish prepping the Thanksgiving meal. The dogs ran over to the cellar door, giving away Marcel down below. She paused and heard the clack of his barbells.

"It's okay if I'm not ready to include Johnny," she told Dukie and Lily, who sat as her sous chefs in the kitchen. She tossed them diagonal slices of carrots, and they scrambled to get their fair share.

"How would you feel if your father was MIA your whole life—your whole life!—and shows up now?"

She cubed the potatoes with a force.

"Never once did he try to contact us. Never once did he check in."

She slammed the chef's knife into a peeled potato.

"For years! Decades!"

Lily wagged and hoped for a potato cube to bounce to the floor. Dukie, however, cowered under the dining room table, peering out from under a chair.

"He never knew Mama was sick."

Boom.

"He never saw her again."

Bang.

A piece of potato finally flew from the cutting board and across the kitchen, ricocheting off of a framed, faded photo of Pine Acres on the first day it opened. Her grandfather stood grinning as he cut a red ribbon across the small office door.

Marcel came up from the cellar, his face and shirt sweaty from his weightlifting exercises.

"I'm guessing you just talked to Johnny," he said, grabbing a sports drink from the refrigerator.

Raven was now on to celery sticks for the onion dip. She sliced the sticks with the precision of a table-side stir fry chef, surprising even herself.

"Wow. Being pissed has its value." Marcel passed behind her and over to the TV area. Raven had cleaned that room, and the thought of his smelly, wet sweatshirt rubbing up against the furniture boiled her further, which led her down a path she had wanted to avoid.

She should have kept her mouth shut, but she asked anyway.

"How did it go today in the woods?" She was giving him a chance to mention Shannon McGrath's visit.

"The coroner hasn't reported yet how many bones are missing. We'll do a more thorough search when we know what we need to look for."

"Did he confirm it was Charles?" She swallowed. How rude and insensitive. "That he's Charles, I mean."

"Not yet. If the Massachusetts courts are open tomorrow, our office will be able to confirm if he has been working this month or if he missed every court assignment."

Marcel popped the TV on. He usually had no use for the New York City Thanksgiving Day parade, also having no use for New Yorkers in general after pulling many of them over for speeding or OUIs. But the parade must have been a better option than talking to her, Raven assumed.

She wasn't deterred.

"Which forensic specialist came?" As if she knew anyone from the state labs, but if he talked about one of the visitors today, he better mention the other one, too. Raven felt sick to her stomach to be fishing for information and even more sick that Marcel hadn't offered it up yet.

"Frank Poland's boy. The one who just graduated from Cornell. Tom chewed his ear off on the co-ed life—how many girlfriends he had on campus, what his current love life was like—the poor guy's ears were red."

Girlfriends. That word hung in the air. Raven waited.

"We also looked for the casings, although I'm not convinced he was killed there."

"Because of the blood at his house?" Raven realized she was more interested in learning about Charles than hearing about Shannon.

"The blood stain was small. And there was no splatter. He definitely wasn't shot in the house, though he might have been injured there, abducted there."

Santa Claus in his sleigh flashed on the television screen, waving to the crowds battling New York's November chill and to the television cameras. Christmas was a month away.

Marcel punched the off button on the remote.

"If he was shot in the woods, someone was smart to do it there. Evidence lost to the elements and the animals. Footprints washed away or trampled by hikers. Actually, if you hadn't wandered off the path after Lily, we may never have found him."

Lily's tail thumped again at the mention of her name. She stretched from her spot in front of the wood stove and rolled on her back to her "rub my belly" position. Marcel knelt next to her to give her a scratch. Dukie barreled in from nowhere and pushed his head under Marcel's arm.

"Hello to you too, Mr. Jealous Pants."

"Who else…" Raven's question about Shannon was interrupted by Betty and Howard bursting through the front door.

"Happy Thanksgiving!" said Betty, coming around the corner and carrying a pie plate covered with foil. "Are we too early?"

Marcel rose to take their coats, still in his damp sweatshirt. "No, not at all."

Lily and Dukie hustled over to receive head rubs and hugs. Next to Raven and Marcel, Betty and Howard were their favorite people.

Raven tossed the celery sticks on a plate with the dip, crackers, and wedges of cheese. Extracting the information about Shannon would have to wait.

"Here's the apple pie, except I made it as a galette," said Betty. She never brought what she agreed to bring. Ever. At least this time, it was made with apples. One time, she offered to bring a chocolate cheesecake and showed up with oatmeal raisin cookies. Julia had taught Raven to be gracious about whatever a guest brings and to also never plan or expect for them to bring what they promised. Of course, Julia had learned the hard way not to rely on promises.

"You've been busy, I see," said Howard, settling into a cushioned chair near the wood stove with a tall glass of ginger ale in hand that Marcel had fixed for him.

"No more than usual," said Marcel.

Raven swallowed. That was Marcel's signal to her to keep her mouth shut about the Charles Kearns murder. Too late.

"Saw you and a lovely woman leave the woods this morning. I'd say that is unusual." Howard was similar to Tom with his comments about any breathing female.

Raven held her breath to hear Marcel's response.

Marcel cleared his throat, thinking.

"You'll hear this soon enough. I was just trying to keep the conversation light for Thanksgiving, but we found a body in the preserve. Actually, Raven found it."

"Oh…" Betty started to say, "Oh, we know."

"Betty, let him finish." Howard shot Betty a glare. Raven tossed a gratitude smile in Howard's direction, grateful for his astute business brain, even though he was long retired from a southern New England-based insurance company.

"Someone we know?" Howard leaned forward in his chair. Raven had purposely withheld that information earlier. Their reactions would now be genuine.

"I think you do," Marcel turned his back to the room, paying the wood stove extra attention.

"We know who was killed. It was Chris Lane." Betty spent a lifetime guessing instead of listening.

Again, Howard threw dagger looks at her.

Marcel cocked his head at her at the mention of Chris' name. For Raven, Chris was on a list—that of suspects—since he resented anyone living in his family home despite having never lived there himself.

Marcel shook his head. "No, not Chris, although I can think of a few employees of his who would like to see him six feet under."

"Add a few summer residents who want to be babied by everyone up here," Howard chuckled. Not only did Chris baby no one, he was barely civil to friend and foe alike.

Marcel smiled. Howard considered himself a native for having lived in Maine about eight years. To Mainers, no one born outside of the state's borders, no matter how long they lived in state, would ever be anything but from away.

Betty grew impatient. "It wasn't Chris? Who was it then? I'm dying to know. Oh sorry! I shouldn't have worded it that way." Her face heated up to a light pink.

"One of our new residents," Marcel started. "I'm just asking that you keep this to yourself. Let the news come out organically."

Betty nodded in understanding. "Like a mushroom on a warm, moist day."

Raven knew she'd be on the phone telling as many people as she locally knew as soon as dinner was finished.

"Charles Kearns," said Marcel.

Betty gasped, and her hands flew up to her mouth. "The bird photographer?"

Chapter Ten

"Bird Photographer?" said Marcel.

"Bird Photographer?" said Raven.

"Bird Photographer?" said Howard.

All three said it in an unplanned chorus.

"Yes, he is excellent. Oh," she said, frowning, "he was excellent. He gave a free lecture at the Owl Creek Preserve this past summer. He's an amazing speaker and bird expert, specializing in nighttime birding. In fact, he just won Barrett County's first prize for his Full Moon Owl in-flight photograph. Remember it was on the front page of the paper in September?"

Betty's puffed-up chest replaced her blush, obviously thrilled to know something that no one else in the room did.

Raven went over to the wood stove and the stacks of yellowing newspapers that sat in a bin to help start a fire on a stubborn day. It didn't take long to find the September issue with a large photograph of a snowy owl outlined against a huge full moon. The byline said, 'Secretly resident Charles Kearns wins county award for best in show.'

Raven's mind flew back to the bonfire night in October. She recalled Charles speaking about birds that night, too—some rare find. She remembered Betty being excited then, too. Charles' voice filtered back into her head.

"Everyone should go out to Blue Heron Pond when they get the chance," Charles had said. "Incredible to hear the owl chorus."

"Is there a best time to go?" Betty had called across the flames to him.

He had raised his voice, and anyone around the circle who hadn't heard what they were talking about now did. He had said, "I'd recommend going when the moon is full again. Not that you need the moonlight to hear, of course, but the ambiance of the pond lit by that light sets a mood to thoroughly enjoy it."

A groan had come from Raven's left.

"Aren't you afraid of tripping in the dark?" Christopher Lane had asked. Obviously, he wasn't an evening bird watcher or even an evening dog walker.

"It's so bright with the moon, you can easily see the path," said Charles. "You can see everything."

"Oh yes." Betty echoed. "Even the hand in front of your face. It's like daylight."

Betty broke Raven's train of thought and brought her back to the living room.

"Yes, that's the photograph. He took it in July at the Blue Heron Pond. I want to go there next month and see what I can capture," she said, looking over Raven's shoulder.

Howard turned to Marcel. "More importantly, how did Charles die? Anything we should be worried about?"

"You just have no respect for my birding interests." Betty snapped at Howard as her eyes filled with tears. "All you care about is your damn ham radios."

"Which you'll appreciate when the satellites are shot down by the Russians or North Korea," Howard said with confidence. He eyed Marcel. "So?"

Marcel gave it to him matter-of-factly. "Shot."

"In this preserve?" Betty pointed towards the back of the Ouellette property, where the side trail allowed access, and butted up against Howard and Betty's backyard. Her voice squeaked out in a reedy tone. "I'm in the preserves daily and also never remember to wear blaze orange. I'm so naive. I'll be next." She slumped into a chair and covered her head with her hands.

"I think you're probably okay for the most part," said Marcel. "Most hunters aren't wildly shooting at people, but you really should wear an orange hat or vest. I have extras if you'd like one."

Raven loved his gift for working with people, especially anxious ones.

Instead of chastising Betty for trouncing around in the woods without precautions, he comforted her and offered her a solution. Raven should listen to his advice about Johnny. She needed to. For her own sake. She just wasn't ready.

During dinner, Howard brought up Charles again.

"So a hunter thought Charles was a deer, huh?" said Howard from his usual spot at the head of the table because he loved a chair with armrests. Marcel always graciously allowed Howard this honor, respecting both Howard's age and size, although Marcel was taller. Howard was wider, however.

Before dinner, Marcel had briefly stepped away from the group and quickly showered, and now the foursome was gathered around a Thanksgiving feast, although what they were grateful for, Raven had to wrack her brain.

"I'm afraid not, Howard," said Marcel as he cut into a slice of turkey smothered in gravy. "Not an accident at all, we think."

"What?" Betty met Marcel's eyes, rising from the seat Raven preferred for its proximity to the kitchen. "We have a killer on the loose? A serial killer?"

"No, no, I hope not. No, I suspect this is a one-off. But start locking your doors at night just to be safe, but otherwise, go about your lives."

"Easy for you to say," said Betty. "You walk around with a gun."

Marcel smiled. Howard had a gun, too, if you counted his replica of a musket from the Revolutionary War.

Howard tucked the napkin under his chin to lighten the mood. "I'm starving. Can we change the subject? I love Raven's cooking and have been waiting all week—all month—to have it. I want to enjoy it. Seconds, please."

But it was too late to change the atmosphere in the house. Betty nervously dished the smallest of helpings of corn on her plate, her appetite ruined. Raven herself had lost her own pang for Thanksgiving dinner. Too many unanswered questions—was that really Charles? Why was he killed? What did he know or do? Who killed him? Where was he killed? And the biggest question of all, why was Shannon McGrath in the woods with the investigation team?

Raven hadn't even known Shannon existed until recently. Sure, Marcel had made references to a past girlfriend here and a past girlfriend there. Since she and Marcel hadn't grown up in the same town, she didn't know who these women were, nor had she cared.

That all changed in late summer. Soon, Shannon's face on political signs littered the county. Once, when Raven and Marcel were in the car together, he said, "Funny to see my ex's face everywhere."

The words ripped through her like a knife. They were each other's first marriage. No one in their past relationships seemed worthy of an "ex" title. Yet here he was, throwing that distinction around like it was commonplace.

"You dated her?" Raven tried to make her question sound casual.

"Yes, for six years."

Six? Six! Why hadn't she heard about this Shannon before?

Marcel continued with a huge grin—too huge. "All of high school and into college. Halfway through the University, she wanted to date other people." He shrugged. "I think she was pressured by her mother to expand her world. She was at Penn, you know. She's a wicked bright girl."

Raven hated her already. And definitely wouldn't vote for her.

It was one thing to have Shannon's face all over town and another to have her physically in her yard, walking next to her husband, looking up at him laughing, touching his arm.

"Raven?" Howard called out to her.

All three faces were staring her way.

"And what are you thankful for?" Howard smiled, a look that reminded her of someone who had an answer he wanted her to say. Probably about Johnny coming back into her life or having amazing neighbors. Raven had no words.

Marcel's work phone on the counter dinged. He excused himself and rose. He texted back and then cleared his throat.

"Please excuse me. There's something I need to check out."

Betty and Howard murmured their understanding. Raven joined him at the counter to kiss him goodbye as another text came on the screen, the phone still lying on the counter.

"Great," said the text from a contact named Shannie.

Chapter Eleven

Betty Norton Hart grew up privileged and wealthy along Connecticut's Gold Coast, one of the richest counties in the United States, near New York City.

The only daughter in a family of boys, her childhood of pink and puffy dresses and oversized stuffed animals was storybook—sailing in Long Island Sound, skiing the Vermont mountains, and attending plays on Broadway on a regular basis. She was given everything she asked for as Daddy's little girl. After graduating from a private day school, she studied at the all-girls Smith College in Northampton, Massachusetts—her mother recommended it to counter her upbringing in a male-dominated household.

Growing up cherished, she sought the same in a husband.

Somehow, however, she ended up with Howard.

Her mother had advised against it.

"Betty, he's not really an executive like your father, you know," she said, glancing up from her afternoon gin and tonic, swirling the ice around in a heavy crystal tumbler.

Betty's father traveled daily into Manhattan by train. Howard took the bus into downtown Hartford because he was too cheap to pay for parking.

Her father ran a division. His photograph was in Forbes Magazine when his team won an international award. He'd walk the quarter mile from the train station to their house on the hill at all hours of the night, doing whatever it took to keep the lifestyle her mother and siblings were accustomed. Yacht club. Country Club. European Ski Vacations. Betty thought all husbands were like that.

Howard had to catch the 5:30 bus, otherwise he'd be stuck in Hartford until 7 p.m.

Still, Howard was smart. To be an actuary, he had to be. She didn't even know what an actuary was until she met Howard. Hadn't even heard the word before, which surprised her since she majored in English, but no English or American Literature author ever spoke of an actuary. Why would they? Writing about one would be dull.

As much as she longed for a glamorous husband, Howard was a good provider. Their three girls went to good schools, paid for in cash. Their home was custom-built along the Connecticut River across from a bald eagle's nest. They took one large vacation every other year.

Having him home nightly for dinner surprised her. Her father made an appearance at the dinner table one or two nights a week. Howard was there every night, joking with the girls as they ate, helping with homework as they got older. He may not have been the storybook husband, but he was an ideal father.

The downside, however, was that he was home, keeping an eye on her and bossing her around. No one bossed her mother around. Betty wasn't prepared to have constant eyes on her as a wife and mother.

"Betty, why don't you put that bench over here," he said once when she was out digging the earth to plant tulip bulbs.

"Betty, what are all of these plants where I mow?" he said when she'd planted thirty hostas to replace the front lawn.

When she complained to her mother, now widowed, her mother asked if she would rather be questioned or cuckold.

"Cuckold?" Betty knew the meaning of the word but didn't know how it applied to her, especially since the definition was about the wife being the adulterer, not the husband.

"Your father was a cheater." Her mother's words fell flat without emotion or expression on her face.

"A cheater? With whom?" Betty had a hard time imagining her hard-working father having the time.

"It doesn't matter. Various women in the City. My point is you have a husband who is actually home. With you. Be grateful."

Gratitude wasn't Betty's strong point. Why would it be? She grew up having everything.

But she tried. Instead of being annoyed at Howard's questions, she included him. She meant it sincerely, but it accomplished what she actually preferred—to be left alone—gardening wasn't his bag. Neither was theater. Or art. Or dinner parties. The more she tried to include him, the more he stayed out of her business. It wasn't exactly what Betty's mother recommended, but it worked like a charm.

But then, just as she thought she had life figured out, she ended up in Maine.

How could her life get any worse?

When this thought pounded in her mind, she chastised herself.

"Betty, you're a boorish snob. There's nothing wrong with Maine…if you like pine trees and flannel."

Actually, all of Maine wasn't like that. If they had moved to Kennebunkport, where the Bushes lived, she'd have felt more at home, where LL Bean boots were worn as a fashion statement, not for utility. She was grateful for a college chum who lived in Ogunquit and invited her to art openings and theater fundraisers. To attend, Betty pulled out her heels and silk scarves, applied eyeshadow and mascara, and drove out of Secretly with her Mercedes' top down. Howard wanted her to sell the gorgeous convertible when they moved up. He said it wouldn't fit in, but she refused. Yes, she initially received stares at the grocery store or the nursery, but the locals got used to her. She drove in style when visiting friends back in Connecticut, and most importantly, it allowed her to feel like she still had command of part of her former life.

That really was the rub. Howard first ripped her out of her town, then out of her state, and now forced her to start over with a new life and new gardens. He'd deny it if asked, but that was how it was, and that was how she felt.

"Whoever has the money makes the decisions," he said when she balked at their move.

She hadn't worked in decades. Hadn't contributed a dime since the girls were born, and she felt too old to start over, both with a rebooted teaching career and a single life.

So, she left her beautiful, award-winning gardens and her book club. She was now four hundred miles from Manhattan and even farther from their two daughters in Philadelphia, who turned their noses up at Maine, even in the summer, preferring the bustle of the Jersey shore. The daughter in LA probably thought Maine was part of Canada.

Maybe if their Maine house was on the water, the girls would come up more because she raised them to be boorish snobs like she was. She hadn't meant to.

For months after she and Howard first moved up, Betty sat in a corner of the house and stared out the window.

"Build a garden. Create a club," Howard said. "Be a trendsetter."

At first, she scoffed at the idea of starting anything, but now there were five members of the Secretly Garden Club—three other disgruntled, transplanted women and a local girl who graduated in Plant Science from a vocational agriculture school. If Betty heard one more time about this young woman's prize lilies and lupines, she'd scream. Still, a member was a member, and it was a coup to snag a native Mainer.

She knew all too well what it was like to be unhappily married. Or unhappy in general. So when she saw Raven's face as Marcel left the Thanksgiving dinner table, she knew it wasn't an emergency that needed a sheriff on a holiday. It was personal. Her mother would agree.

Chapter Twelve

Raven blinked tears at the sound of the front door closing and Marcel's Jeep starting up. She was used to him being called away in the middle of a holiday, but this time, she wasn't sure it was legit.

"A pistol was found by a lobsterman in Whale Harbor when the tide went out," he said to Raven in a low voice and out of earshot of the Harts. "Tommy is meeting me there. We want to keep a tight hold on the case ourselves. Keep the staties out of it as much as we can."

He kissed her on the forehead and excused himself.

"Come back tomorrow for leftovers," he said to the Harts and was gone.

Raven busied herself at the sink, her blood pulsing. She had never been one to mistrust Marcel, never had any reason to, but if she could, she would have checked his phone to see if Tom Pinkham had actually been the one who reached out to Marcel. Or if Marcel had even asked Tom to go along.

Being a snoop was stressful. She snooped as a kid in her mother's drawers, looking for any sign of her father. As soon as her mother left for the store or was in a cabin changing its sheets, Raven was scouring through papers, looking under beds, leafing through books on the shelf, always coming up empty. All she wanted was an address or a phone number. All she wanted was an answer to why—why he had left them.

Now she had all the chances in the world to ask Johnny, and she didn't care anymore. She had bigger questions in front of her—like why was her husband's ex-girlfriend back in his life.

"You okay, Raven?" Betty stood next to her and rubbed her back.

Startled, Raven forced herself not to move away from Betty's patronizing tone or touch.

"Oh, yes, fine. Thanks," she said, swirling a sponge against the edges of the sweet potato casserole pan.

"We should get going," said Howard, rising.

Lily and Dukie, who took the emptiness of the dining table as a chance to get leftovers, sat and stared at Raven with pleading eyes.

Raven exhaled. She needed to be alone, but her upbringing, that guests came first, won out. A squash pie, a chocolate pudding pie, and that apple galette thing masquerading as an apple pie sat on the counter, untouched.

"We haven't had dessert yet." Raven waved towards the pies on the counter. "It's tradition."

"That's right," said Betty, reaching into the cabinets for plates. "Do you have vanilla ice cream or whipped cream?"

Before Raven could respond, Howard gripped Betty's elbow.

"We'll come back…"

"We're here already." Betty started to protest.

"We'll come back." Howard's style was to repeat whatever sentence he was firm about. Raven assumed it was a leadership technique taught at the insurance company in Hartford.

Raven joined in. "Great idea. Come back when Marcel returns so we can all have dessert together."

"Great idea." Howard beamed. Betty looked deflated.

Howard gave Raven a one-armed hug. "Thanks so much, kiddo. Come on, Betty."

"How about if I help you with the dishes?" Betty said, stalling.

"How about if you come home with me?" said Howard before Raven responded, and out the front door they went.

Raven resumed her pan scrubbing when she heard the front door open again. Dukie sat up, listening.

"Did you forget something?" She called out over her shoulder.

No response came.

"That latch must be wearing," she muttered as she turned from the sink to shut the front door.

"Oh!" She jumped. Johnny stood at the fringe of the kitchen, both dogs rubbing against his legs like cats.

"I didn't mean to scare you. I saw Betty and Howard leave and thought it would be okay to stop by." His tone was even and not accusatory for not including him.

She caught her breath and recovered.

"Did you eat? Do you want a plate? We have lots of leftovers." Raven wondered why she didn't feel guilty offering her father leftovers when she could have easily included him in the holiday meal. Was she an ice princess, as Marcel said? Maybe she was becoming colder toward Marcel, too, and that's why he was running off to an ex-girlfriend. Maybe…

She shook that feeling off. Don't invite trouble in, her mother always said when Raven was excessively worried.

Johnny shook his head at the invitation for food. "Thank you, though. Another time."

Did he mean another Thanksgiving? Another holiday? Another chance for Raven to thaw her heart?

"Marcel around, by any chance?" Johnny looked around the expansive room.

"He got a call about a gun. He left about fifteen minutes ago."

"Connected to Charles Kearns?"

"He thinks so."

Johnny nodded.

They stood in silence looking at each other like a kitchen game of chicken. Johnny blinked first and wandered into the family room portion of the room, picking up the newspaper and banging it against his hand as if thinking of the right words. The dogs followed at his heels, sniffing his pants pockets for treats.

Raven pondered if he was going to finally confront her about not letting him into her life. She steadied herself, wondering which approach he'd take—the pathetic sympathy vote or the hardened father method. She felt prepared to battle back either argument. How dare he think he could just reappear in her life after thirty years.

"Raven." His voice was soft, thoughtful. She was ready.

He continued. "I was thinking about Charles' house."

Anger seeped into her veins. This is why he was able to stay away for decades. He wasn't human. He wasn't even thinking about her. He still didn't care if he was with her or not.

She turned away, busying herself with a sponge on the counter, hiding the tears that streamed down her cheeks. She had been wanting to punish him, and he actually didn't care. She was only playing games with herself.

"...so I think we should go back and look."

"What? Look at what?" Raven had missed most of what he said. "Can you repeat that?" She pretended to scratch her nose before turning around, giving her a chance to wipe her face.

"Sorry. I'm mainly talking to myself." He rose and leaned against the counter's edge. "I was thinking, you said he told you he was an expert witness in Boston trials. Maybe there's something left in the house pointing to a case. Something we could look into deeper."

Raven nodded. Charles' voice floated back in.

"You wouldn't believe the guys I put away," Charles had said around the bonfire.

"Better hope they don't get out and come looking for you." Howard smirked.

"Wouldn't be a bad thing," Chris Lane said, again muttering under his breath.

Charles had just laughed it all off. "Why do you think I want to move to No-Man's-Land, Maine?"

Even Raven had felt her face flush at his insult to her hometown. Based on the glares around the fire, she knew she hadn't been the only one that day who felt that way.

Chapter Thirteen

Tom Pinkham looked twenty years younger than his real age. His youthfulness would come in handy, he knew, when he was in his fifties and older, but being a thirty-seven-year-old sheriff deputy but looking, in the wrong light, like a teenager, didn't help his credibility when he pulled someone over on the side of the road, especially someone much bigger than him.

Standing five foot five inches in wet feet and looking no more than fifteen years old caused many a drunk vacationer to take a swing, always missing as Tom dived low or jumped on a chair. Locals who grew up with him and played against him in football and, even basketball—believe it or not—understood that what he lacked in leg height, he made up for in speed, agility, and tenacity.

He also had the opposite personality than most expected. Instead of having the proverbial Napoleon complex, he was self-confident, charming, and easy-going, with nothing to prove to anyone. As Marcel once said in a performance review, Tom was the perfect cop mold.

When Marcel had reached out on Thanksgiving about joining him at the harbor, he jumped at the chance to escape the repeating stories of Uncle Frank and the wails of his sister's twin brats. He leaned against a post at the dock and watched a lobsterman come in, someone else who had decided to avoid a family dinner.

Tom had already pulled his own lobster boat, Peggy Sue, named after his mother, out of the water in October, along with his hundred lobster traps. He only dabbled in the business. His full-time responsibility was his deputy role, and he took that seriously. He didn't have the time for the deep water lobstering that many turned to in the winter. It could take an hour or more just to get out to the first trap.

His father had been a full-time lobsterman, pulling a hundred traps a day, six days a week all year round, and when he could pull no more, he gifted his thirty-six-foot Jarvis Newman hull, Peggy Sue, to Tom on his thirtieth birthday.

"Sail her proud, Tommy," he had said from his hospital bed.

Tom didn't know what really had killed his father—smoking cigarettes, inhaling too much diesel exhaust, or having his heart broken after being landlocked from a stroke.

Tom worked on Peggy Sue with pride, feeling with every day that he rode the waves, he still had his dad by his side. Each time he went out to sea, with each trap lifted up, with each lobster inspected and weighed, his Pop was right next to him.

Today, the harbor was quiet, deserted, actually, except for that lone lobsterman. Grey skies and a brisk northeast wind were enough to keep the weekend tourists in their inns. A white skiff motored toward the dock from the lobster boat that had just moored. Tom recognized the lobsterman, Clark Christianson, a classmate of his.

"Hey, Tommy, I'm glad it's you," said Clark, calling out from the skiff as it motored up. He tossed a line to Tom, who wound it around a metal dock cleat.

Clark climbed out and handed Tom a paper bag. "I have a present for you."

"I heard." Tom unfurled the oily bag with the standard "seafood" printed across it in blue and red. Peering in, he saw what he came for—laying flat on the bottom was a .32 caliper silver and black gun.

"Named after you, Tomcat," Clark said. The creases around his eyes reflected both his years in the sun and the years laughing at his own jokes.

This time, Clark was right. A Beretta Tomcat held the same name as Tom's high school nickname. Tom didn't dare tell him the nickname TomCat still stuck, at least with the female residents in Secretly.

"Where'd you find it?" Tom resealed the bag. He'd drive it over to Augusta today to the state crime lab. They hadn't found shell casings yet, but maybe there'd be a match with any nicks on the bone.

Clark pointed to a metal detector in the skiff. "On low tide mornings, if I have time, I entertain myself by walking Whale Beach. I can show you exactly where I dug it up. I didn't want to leave it there, obviously, and selfishly, I didn't want to wait for one of you to come to me, especially on Thanksgiving." He grinned, showing a missing front tooth, knocked out when his trawler hook swung back at his face in his first year out on the water on his own over two decades ago.

"I understand." Tom did. There was no reason to doubt anything that Clark said. He had known him his whole life. Then again, this was the town's first murder, and Tom wouldn't have expected that either.

Tom glanced toward the parking lot. Marcel should be driving at any moment.

"Can you hang out until the boss gets here? Then we can drive over to the beach together, and you only have to tell your tale once."

Before Clark could respond, Marcel's Jeep's tires sounded on the gravel parking lot. At first, Tom thought Raven had come too, but it was District Attorney McGrath who exited the passenger side.

What the heck was Marcel doing with Shannon again today?

Chapter Fourteen

Johnny's old white pickup truck rattled down the road toward the center of town. Raven braced herself for the holes and cracks in the road; all of the shocks were shot.

Maybe if she hadn't seen "Shannie" on Marcel's phone, she wouldn't have been easily talked into returning to the Lane Mansion to "harmlessly" peer in the windows of Charles Kearns' last home.

They bumped and jarred against the uneven pavement. A light shone in Wolf Marine Supplies.

"Odd they're open on Thanksgiving unless someone called in an emergency need." Johnny slowed down in front.

Standing in the doorway with a bag in her hand was Laurie Eldridge, a young woman who Raven went to high school with, widowed even younger when her husband died. She was talking to Karl Wolf, the owner, who saw Johnny's truck and gave a big wave.

There was once upon a time when Raven would have called Laurie her best friend. Funny how things changed, or was it only Raven who changed?

"Hmmm," said Johnny. "What could she use from there? She doesn't even own a rowboat. And on a holiday," he added.

At the Lane Mansion, Joe Morin's renovation company sign and the placard for Bryant Masonry stood at attention on the front lawn, close to the slate sidewalk, to attract potential new customers. Johnny had no fear of parking in the driveway behind Charles' Buick. American-made cars always signaled traditional values in a man to Raven. She was pleased Marcel's county vehicle was a Jeep.

"Might as well park here. Better to be upfront about things like that. If we park down the road and walk up to the house, we'd look sneaky." He exited the truck with his fresh cup of coffee, topped off at Raven's house.

"We are sneaky." Raven reminded her father.

This murder investigation was the first real together time she and Johnny had spent since his return two years ago. The family that sneaks together, stays together, she mused to herself.

Johnny stood on top of the bulkhead, peering into the living room window, the room that had had the blood on the floor. Across from the window, stuck in the ground, a metal hook held two empty bird feeders.

"You know, it's not enough blood to be where his face was blown off," Johnny said matter-of-factly. "If he was shot in there, the room would be a sea of red. The floors. The walls. Everything. We would have been covered in pieces of him, just walking into that room. Trust me. The human body splatters everywhere."

Raven's turkey lunch rose in her throat, grateful she hadn't eaten more.

"I believe you." She coughed out the words, choking back the food. She raised one hand as a plea for him to stop. Marcel, thankfully, always spared her the graphic details, and she never asked for more.

"Oh, sorry. Occupational Hazard." He cupped his eyes to block out the afternoon light. "The laptop may still be there, in the corner. I'm not sure. I can't see it. In any case, I'm sure Marcel grabbed it, but maybe something else will jump out."

Johnny nimbly hopped off the bulkhead and ran to the other side of the house before Raven had taken two steps. Hard to believe he was approaching seventy.

"Raven, come quick." His voice elevated with excitement from around the corner.

She doubled back around the house in a run but tripped over something hard. She lost her balance and landed in a small pile of brown oak, yellow birch, and red maple leaves, covered by a melting layer of mushy snow. Johnny rushed to help her to her feet and brushed errant twigs and leaves out of her hair and off her jacket.

"Here's your culprit," he said, picking up an iron rake lying on the lawn. He stepped back and surveyed the leaf pile.

"Hmm," he said, his hands on his hips, "when did you say you last saw Charles?"

"End of October." Raven eyed the rake and the pile of leaves as she rubbed her knees. Brown stains littered her jeans.

Johnny nodded. "The perfect time to start raking your lawn. Don't touch the rake." He pulled it back from Raven's outstretched hand. "I wasn't thinking when I picked it up. At least now we can tell Marcel my prints are on it when he checks for others."

Charles didn't seem like the kind of man who would leave a rake outside or even leave a raking job unfinished. Was he raking his leaves when his killer approached?

"That makes sense." Johnny agreed. He stroked his chin. "If that's the case, that would mean it was daylight, and maybe someone saw him talking to someone on the lawn while he raked. Unless he was a nut, who did things like mow his lawn in the dark. In Massachusetts, I lived next to a kook who did stuff like that. Even painted his house in the dark."

Massachusetts. Raven had no interest in hearing anything about that state. She didn't comment, avoiding the topic of Massachusetts and Johnny living there, footloose and fancy-free all those years.

Instead, she said, "If there was a witness, maybe they'll remember seeing him outside. Once the news of his death comes out." said Raven. Hard to believe that most people in town didn't know yet about the murder. It felt like she had been living in it for months already, even though it had barely been a day.

At hearing her idea of the witness coming forward, Johnny grinned and nodded. He grabbed her by the shoulders. "That's my girl! A natural detective!"

A chill ran up Raven's spine. She wasn't ready to be his girl yet. She wasn't sure she'd ever be ready. She kept her arms at her side, and he let go.

Johnny went quiet. "You know Marcel better than me. Will he be mad when we share these findings with him?"

At the moment, Raven didn't care if Marcel was mad at her or not, because she was madder at him. She just shrugged.

"Well, I just don't want him to think that I think he's incapable. I just have ants in my pants. I can't sit still. I need to be busy."

And Mama and I weren't enough to keep you busy? Raven wanted to ask but was too tired to get into it. Then she remembered him calling to her before she tripped on the rake.

"Why did you yell for me just now?"

Johnny snapped his fingers. "Oh, I almost forgot. Glad you brought it up. The front door is open."

"What?" Raven couldn't believe the door was open or that he had made it fully around the house that quickly. She was out of shape.

"Come, follow me."

He led the way around to the front of the house. Sure enough, the heavy wooden door was ajar. From the road, unless a wind gust came through to push it open further, a passerby wouldn't have noticed it. But up close, it was obvious.

"Either Marcel or Tommy left it this way yesterday..." Johnny paused and made a face, showing he didn't believe that.

"Highly unlikely." Raven agreed.

"Right." He scratched his head. "Or someone else has been here since last night. I doubt the masons worked today on Thanksgiving. Do you have your phone on you?"

Raven nodded. Of course, she did. He obviously didn't.

"Take a photo of it, the door. Please."

He stepped aside, and Raven obliged, shooting it from multiple angles.

Johnny leaned close and studied the lock without touching anything this time.

"Nothing jimmied. No splintered wood. I'd say someone just opened the door and walked in. I'm sure Marcel would have locked it if he could have. Bet there's no key to be found."

"I can't say I know where our house keys are," Raven admitted. "I just have the cabin ones since renters are so anal about protecting their bathing suits and flip-flops."

Raven understood that folks visiting were living in higher crime areas than she did. Her mother was always amused by their request for multiple keys.

"Locks are for honest people," she had been fond of saying to Raven after explaining to a guest that she was sorry she didn't have five sets of keys for one lock.

If the person who left Charles' door ajar had truly wanted to get into this house, he would have smashed a window if the front door had been locked. A determined person always found a way.

Raven said, "I hate to say it, but if we find anything of interest, I think we should take it with us."

Touching and moving evidence seemed like a horrible idea, but having the evidence go missing seemed worse, especially if people were now going into the house.

Johnny turned to face her. He shifted his weight. He stroked his chin. Finally, he nodded.

"Okay, I hear what you're saying. Let's film the whole thing, though. A video. From the moment we enter. Document our movement."

"Okay," said Raven, although proof of her meddling turned her stomach. "What are we looking for?"

Raven had agreed to go with Johnny because she expected a quick in and out. Showing Marcel a video of Johnny walking around Charles' home wasn't exactly in the cards for her.

"I'd like to see what Charles' paperwork says. If there are any client names on anything. Something I could call down to my contacts in Boston. Don't worry. I'll keep Marcel fully in the loop. I'm not trying to get any credit for this."

Taking credit wasn't what worried Raven.

Chapter Fifteen

Tom moved a stack of flyers with the words "Save Maine Lobstering" to the rear seat in Clark's truck. Clark was vice president of the local chapter of the state lobstering association.

"Seems like we just finish defending our livelihood from one pack of liars when someone else comes up with a story that gets the news hounds' attention again." Clark popped a couple of Chiclet gum squares into his mouth.

Tom nodded. He had attended last month's meeting. One of the most regulated industries in the United States and one of the most ocean-conscious and environment-loving groups of people on the seas. He had no hope that they would ever be fully understood or respected.

"Who's the hot babe with Marcel?" Clark grinned at Tom, revealing another gap where a right incisor should have been.

"Don't you recognize her from her posters?"

"Wanted at the Post Office?" Clark laughed at his own joke.

Tom shook his head. "That's your newly elected district attorney. You step out of line, and she'll be prosecuting your ass."

"Tempting. I'm sure for you, too."

Tom smirked. The last person he'd want to fool around with was an attorney, especially one who had dated his boss. "Did you vote for her?"

"Jeez, I haven't voted since I was eighteen." Clark lowered his window and spit out the gum. "Did you?"

"That's private."

"Hahaha. I'll take that as a no. So why is she here today? Is there someone to prosecute? And what's the big deal about this gun to cause so many of you to turn out?"

"We'll see." Tom knew better than to share too much with Clark. The information would spread faster than seaweed in a Nor'easter.

Marcel had followed Clark's truck, and both vehicles were now parked at the gate to the beach. The parking lot was locked up as it always was after Labor Day to protect it from mud ruts and the need to plow it come snow season.

Clark beelined to Shannon as she exited the Jeep. She really was beautiful. Blonde, slender, and tall like a model. Poised as if she went to finishing school, as his mother would say.

"Great to meet you in person," he said, extending his hand. "I voted for you."

Tom covered his mouth with the back of his hand to stifle his laugh.

Shannon grinned as she shook his hand. "Thank you. I hope to serve you well."

"Oh, I'm sure you will." He turned and winked at Tom.

Tom held his breath. He half expected Clark to pat her on the behind.

Marcel rolled his eyes and reeled in Clark and the situation.

"Clark, can you show us exactly where you found the gun?" he said.

The reminder of the gun made Tom pat his pocket. He felt the hard metal and heard the crunch of the paper bag.

"Sure. Let me grab my shovel in case we need it." Clark leaned into the back of his pickup.

"Shovel?" Shannon's eyes twinkled, and the corners of her painted lips turned up.

He bounced to the ground with a spade in hand. They walked around the locked gate and past the sign "Whale Beach."

"You know how many whales they see on this beach every year?" Clark asked, pointing his question at Shannon.

"None," said Shannon. "The whales don't come this close to shore."

"That's right, but that's the wrong answer," Clark said, his grin widening.

"Really?" said Shannon, her face showed surprise.

"I don't recall ever hearing about a whale on this beach," said Tom.

"I remember studying it in grammar school," said Marcel. "The native Indians laughed when the English named it "Whale Beach" because they also had never heard of a whale on it either."

"You guys are way off," said Clark, chuckling. "I came down once in the afternoon last summer with my metal detector. Low tide about three o'clock in the afternoon. There had to be fifty, maybe seventy whales on the beach. Yellow ones, black ones, red, striped, polka dots."

"Oh no." Shannon groaned and covered her face in mock protest.

"That's the oldest joke in the book," said Marcel.

"And you still fell for it!" Clark, almost carrying the same tall frame as Marcel, slapped him on the back as they left the path that led to the beach through the woods. They stopped at the small wooden gate that marked the path and protected people from randomly walking on the dunes and marveled at the ocean. Looking at the beauty of the waves crashing against the rocks never got old, thought Tom.

"So, we're going to have a bit of trouble," said Clark. "I found the gun over there."

He pointed to a large boulder, a reddish glacier erratic. Seafoam swirled at its base from the incoming tide.

"High tide. I hadn't thought of that," said Clark. "Sorry."

"That's Mother Nature for you," said Tom.

Marcel said, "You found the gun near the rock? By the rock?"

Clark pulled out his phone.

"I figured you'd want to know exact. Plus, I didn't want anyone to think I hid the gun myself or had anything to do with the gun." He flipped through screens, and stopped. "There."

He turned the phone around. The photo showed the gun laying in the sand at the base of the erratic at the bottom of a six-inch hole, dug by him when the detector went off. Next to the phone was an old metal nail, probably what set off the signal initially. He passed his phone to Marcel for a closer look.

"Shallow hole," Shannon said after viewing Clark's photo and passing the phone to Tom. "You'd think someone would dig deeper than that."

"The way I see it's one of two things," said Clark. "Either it was deeper, and the tide eroded the sand away."

"Or this past snowstorm brought the gun into the beach on a wave." Marcel finished Clark's thought.

"BINGO. Most of what I find isn't what folks have left at the beach, but what the tide has dragged ashore."

"So someone tossed this gun from a boat?" Shannon looked out into the vastness of the sea as she asked the question.

Tom wondered if Shannon had spent all of her Maine life in the western part of the state, away from an ocean. How do you grow up near the sea and not know its powers?

"Not necessarily," said Clark, turning to Shannon. It looked like he was going to hold her hand to reply. Thankfully, he kept his hands to himself. "It could have just as easily come off a dock, from anywhere, actually."

Shannon nodded. "I always hear 'the ocean doesn't give up her dead,' but what you're saying, Clark, is that eventually everything comes to the surface."

Clark laughed, revealing the two missing teeth. "Oh, I'm sure there's plenty still sitting at the bottom, waiting for the right storm to churn it loose. I can't wait for that day when I find that buried treasure strewed out piece by piece on the glistening sand. Pay Day!"

Marcel seemed to have enough of Clark's bravado, or was it watching someone flirt with Shannon? "Can I see the gun?" he said and looked at Tom, who pulled the bag out of his coat.

Marcel's eyebrows raised as he looked into the bag. "It's possible."

Tom nodded. He agreed. It was possible that this was the weapon used to murder Charles Kearns.

"What's possible?" Clark waited to be filled in.

"Clark, thank you for your help." Marcel rolled up the paper bag and then stuck out his hand.

Clark chuckled. "Oh, jeez, I know when I'm getting the brush off." He responded to Marcel's gesture with a shake. "But can't you give me a little nugget? Something to whet my appetite for more? As a thank you for finding the gun?"

"Let me just say I appreciate you being a concerned citizen and leave it at that," Marcel said with a smile as he turned to Tom. "Let's come back here at low tide. When is the next one in daylight?"

Clark answered first. "About nine tomorrow morning. I'll probably be here. I can help."

"One more thing," said Marcel to Clark. "Please don't tell anyone about finding the gun."

"Aye-aye, Captain." Clark saluted.

Chapter Sixteen

Raven turned on her phone's video-making option as soon as Johnny pushed the front door open with his foot. The brick piles in the hallway in daylight looked like crumbles of small chimneys tossed around. Johnny walked in front of her and pointed to the area of the floor of the living room where the laptop was. No laptop. Thankfully, it was retrieved by Marcel and Tom, she hoped. The room still had the dark stain on it, and papers still littered the floor despite the army of crime scene forensics that must have combed through the room last night. Johnny pulled a crumbled tissue out of his pants pocket.

"Raven," Johnny said at her phone. "Please note I am picking up this one piece of paper using a tissue." He maneuvered the slightly used tissue to have enough space for his fingers. Raven hoped the phone's microphone didn't pick up her "ew." Squatting, he turned over the paper.

"It's blank on both sides," he said to the phone, showing both sides. "Or at least appears to be." He dropped it near where it had been.

Raven wanted to say, "Oh, you think that there's invisible ink on it?" But didn't want that snarky comment to be recorded, too.

Johnny went over to the next piece of paper and did the same thing. Then the next one, and the next one. All blank.

"Is there a printer nearby?" Raven only had blank, single-sheet paper in her office near the printer. She used regular notepads elsewhere in the house for the very reason that loose paper sailed away from its ream on a regular basis if not in the paper holder or wrapped up.

Johnny stood and surveyed the room.

"I don't see one, do you?"

Raven looked around too, both with her eyes and by turning her body so the video also recorded the room.

"No, I don't." She spoke clearly to be picked up on purpose, this time in the audio.

"Let me just look to see if there's a printer anywhere under these chairs." He quickly bent and looked at all the upside-down pieces of furniture.

"Nope," he said. "Just some dust. Now, let's go back to the dining room chimney."

Again, using that disgusting used tissue, Johnny pulled out the loose brick of the soon-to-be rebuilt chimney.

"Get in tight here," he said, pointing to the gap in the bricks.

The room was darker than the living room. She glanced up at the overhead light.

"Maybe we should put that on." She pointed up.

"Maybe my truck in the driveway is as much attention as we want to draw to ourselves." He winked.

Raven swallowed. Maybe this was one video she should delete. Like right now.

But she kept on filming, doing the best she could in the dim light. There was nothing to see in the flat hole. The words "flat hole" stayed with her. Isn't a hole round by its very nature? Crevice might be a better word. Or hiding place. Whatever it was called, it was empty, for sure.

There was nothing else in the dining room but the fireplace with its partially unassembled chimney and more bricks on the floor. The kitchen also had nothing in it or its cabinets; all opened again by that dirty tissue. The only personal item was a tripod in the corner. Betty was right about Charles' level of seriousness as a bird photographer.

"I've always found the design of these old homes to be strange," said Johnny as they passed the brick pile that Raven had hidden behind when Johnny surprised her the night before. "They seem so large on the outside, but inside there are so few rooms. Would you ever think there were only three rooms on the first floor?"

Raven agreed. The Lane Mansion was more showy from the outside. Less rooms to heat, perhaps?

"And furnish," Johnny added. "People also didn't have to have so many things like nowadays."

The stairs creaked as Johnny climbed them.

"Coming?" He said over his shoulder when he realized she hadn't started up.

Raven paused. Herself, not the video. The deeper she went into the house, the deeper into trouble with Marcel. She shrugged and, with amazement at her stupidity, followed her father.

"I'm sure the Colonialists knew what they were doing. Practical Puritans," Johnny said when he reached the second-floor landing.

"This house was built in 1806," she said, remembering this time to read the small white sign by the front door. "That makes it a Federalist home, I think."

"Aren't we all colonialists, in a way?"

That isn't how Raven would describe an American. Or a Mainer. Leave it to Johnny to make new rules.

"I'm glad it isn't dark." Johnny's statement was exactly what Raven was feeling. That night in the dark in the house was only a day ago, but it felt like months had passed. She shivered at the thought of all she had experienced and learned in the past twenty-four hours, and that didn't just include Charles' death.

A short hallway revealed four doorways. Walking down the hall, they passed the first doorway to a small bathroom, probably the only one in the house and probably formerly just a closet. Standard bath supplies used by a man, like disposable razors and cheap shampoo, sat on top of the toilet tank. A crumbled towel lay on the floor where it had fallen after use, probably off a naked Charles, an image Raven wished she hadn't conjured up.

The next two rooms were also small, wallpapered, and completely empty. One had a bricked-up fireplace, closed in when central heating was installed. The third room at the end, the largest of the lot, was definitely lived in. Charles had said he was using the upstairs as his bedroom, dining area, and office, but Raven didn't realize he meant he was only using one room.

This time, Johnny flipped on the overhead light switch. A single bulb at the ceiling blazed on.

On one side of the room was an unmade twin bed, clothes in a pile, and a flattened, empty duffle bag. Against a windowsill sat a small table with a wooden chair pushed in. On the floor next to the table was a printer and stacks of unopened reams of paper. The printer was plugged in to an electrical strip. Both the strip and the printer's lights were lit, indicating powered on. Also plugged into the strip was another cord, probably belonging to the laptop. A third cord looked like a phone charger.

"Phone charger," Raven said unconsciously, forgetting she was still filming.

"But no phone. Did Marcel mention if they found Charles' phone?"

"No." Raven thought of Marcel's phone, though, with "Shannie" on it. She shook off the thought to concentrate on Charles.

"Maybe they did," said Johnny. "Hopefully, they did. Maybe they took it when they were here Wednesday night."

"Yesterday. When they were here yesterday," said Raven. It was hard to believe it was just yesterday.

"Ah, yes. Yesterday," Johnny echoed her comment.

"And hopefully, they're also the ones who took the laptop." Raven thought back to the front door being ajar. Was that a mistake by Marcel or the forensics team to leave it for someone to steal? She doubted it.

Remembering that her role was to capture their movement as well as the house itself, she turned three-hundred-and-sixty degrees to film the whole room. An empty cereal bowl with a spoon in it lay on the floor next to the bed. Wrappers of various food items were around it.

"Guess he liked potato chips," said Johnny.

"I don't know why I'm shocked to see how messy he was," Raven said, "but I am surprised. I thought the first floor was messy because of the construction, but this is— was—his own doing."

Johnny lay on his stomach and looked under the bed.

"Well, what do we have here?" His voice was muffled.

Please, not a mouse.

Johnny looked around the room. "I need a broom or an umbrella."

"For what?" Raven wondered if she should stand on a chair. She was good with snakes and spiders, but she drew the line at rodents.

"Screw it." He grabbed a shirt of Charles's from the pile and wrapped his hand in it. Reaching under the bed with his arm, he grunted, shoving almost his entire body under. Finally standing, with dust covering one arm and part of his chest, he showed Raven his prize.

"Taa-daa!" He held open his hands.

A thin book, curled as if rolled up and stuffed into a back pocket or backpack, laid inside the article of clothing in Johnny's hands. He flattened the front cover with both hands using the shirt and showed it to Raven. In bold red letters, it said "Maine's Guide to Coastal Birds."

"I thought it was something important," Raven stopped videoing just as her battery, long blinking an empty red symbol, stopped working, and her phone shut down.

Johnny tossed the shirt and flipped through the book, not caring about fingerprints. "He noted the birds he had seen and the date. Gee, I'm surprised he only saw the puffin this summer."

"Can we leave now?" Despite the overhead bulb, the light in the room was much dimmer than when they first started exploring the house. Raven also wondered if Marcel was back home. She hadn't left him a note, and now her phone was dead.

Even in the fading light, Raven saw the disappointment on Johnny's face. She refused to feel guilty about not cherishing her time with him. She also refused to fake it.

"Sure," he said, his smile disappeared, and he stopped meeting her eyes. "Let's go."

He pocketed the bird book and turned towards the door.

"You're keeping it?" Raven couldn't believe she was seeing her retired cop father taking something from a crime scene.

"Time for me to get a hobby," he said, not turning around as he left the room.

Chapter Seventeen

Johnny concentrated on his driving. The headlights of his old Ford followed the narrow road from the center of downtown back to the woods of Pine Acres.

He had pushed against the front door of the Lane Mansion after he shut it. The latch worked fine, so the wind couldn't have blown it open. He doubted it was Marcel or Tommy who accidentally left it ajar. They were professionals.

Someone else had been inside. Who? And just as important, why?

Raven sat in his passenger seat with her hands folded on her lap, but they hadn't spoken since leaving the second floor of the house. Not that she hadn't tried, bringing up the rake found on Charles's lawn and the mystery of the front door

Johnny just murmured back acknowledgment, but today his patience with her was thin. He had been trying for two years to gain her trust and love. It suddenly and overwhelmingly felt like a losing battle. She'd never turn around. Never love him. At least not, maybe, until it was too late. And he didn't want to win her with the sympathy vote. He wanted her to love him because she got to know him as an adult. He wanted her to love him for him.

He knew he needed her forgiveness, too. He struggled with forgiving himself for walking out on her and Julia. He allowed himself all those years to say it was okay because of the money he had sent Julia's way. He didn't actually know if she had received most of the money. He didn't have any canceled checks as proof except for the first one. She had cashed it but never communicated back to him. After that, he just mailed cash. That way, he couldn't be hurt for not receiving a thank you, an invitation to come up for Raven's birthday, or a copy of her latest school photo.

He sensed that Raven didn't know about the money he sent. Or maybe she did and didn't think financial support was enough. It wasn't. Throwing money at a situation wasn't the same as living day in and out with someone. He wasn't there to help raise Raven. He could persuade himself he vanished to save her, but that was only an excuse. He left so he didn't have to deal with himself.

But now all he had was himself, staring at him from every direction, making him face his life.

He glanced over at Raven. She now angled her body towards the window, seemingly content to not talk with him either. If it were daylight, she might be watching the scenery go by, but at this time of the evening, there was nothing to see but the edges of the road that his headlights illuminated. Lumps of dirty, crusty snow left from a plow.

Maybe a reunion for them was a lost cause. Maybe moving into town was a mistake. Maybe he should just slink away into the sunset like a worn-out cowboy in an old Western.

After driving up the long, dirt driveway and pulling into the expansive parking area of Pine Acres, Johnny saw that Marcel was home. Or at least his Jeep was. Johnny parked his pickup truck next to the Jeep and put it into park. He had planned on backing right out as soon as Raven disembarked.

"Why don't you come in for some leftovers? We have so much." Raven's voice was reedy as she slid off the seat. Johnny had forgotten all about Thanksgiving dinner and about how much he had wished Raven had invited him. It no longer seemed to matter.

When he didn't respond to her or kill his engine, she stood on the ground and faced him from the open door. "I'm sure Marcel would like to see you too, and we could tell him about our visit to Charles' house."

Our visit.

Johnny had been waiting to be an "our" with Raven. Here it was.

Or did she simply want company? Johnny's mind flashed to seeing Marcel and that woman. He shook it off. Marcel and Raven seemed too solid to have issues like he and Julia had. First off, neither Marcel nor Raven had an addiction problem. Julia always called his drinking "the third person" in their marriage. She was right, he now saw. He was too far in it, though, to see it then.

"Sounds good," Johnny said, shutting the engine off and getting out of the truck, even though he really just wanted to leave. Whatever the reason that Raven had to want him to stay, he should take it. He followed her into the house. Lily and Dukie greeted them in the foyer, with Lily's thick white tail banging against the bench. He sat for a moment to remove his boots.

"Oh, that's okay," said Raven. She had, however, kicked off her own shoes before continuing into the house.

He finished taking his boots off and received a gentle kiss on his hand from Dukie. Nothing like a dog's love. Lily had run off after her mom in hopes of a cookie.

A light shone in the family room, a carve out that was adjacent to the kitchen. The rooms themselves, however, were empty, and the house was quiet. Raven padded in her stocking feet down the hallway and returned with one finger to her lips. She hoarsely whispered.

"He's asleep. On top of the covers. I'm sure he'll be up soon. He's a light sleeper."

What cop isn't, thought Johnny. Sleep? What was that? Actually, close your eyes and trust that when you wake everything will be okay? He just nodded in understanding.

Raven took plastic containers out of the refrigerator and a large clear food bag with a partially cut-up turkey carcass.

"Please make yourself a plate," she said, motioning to the food.

Johnny realized that he and Raven had never actually shared a meal together since he moved back.

"Are you having any?" He longed for a normal relationship with her, whatever normal was supposed to be.

"No, but only because I'm not hungry." She pulled a plate down from a shelf in a cabinet.

Was it his imagination, or had the bitterness and guard in her voice disappeared?

Seeing the food, his stomach twitched. He had to admit he needed to eat something.

Filling a plate with sweet potato casserole, mashed potatoes, stuffing, green beans, turkey slices and dotting it all with chucks of solidified gravy that would soon melt in the microwave, he marveled at the array of home-cooked food. He hadn't really had any since leaving Julia. His own cooking skills capped out at scrambled eggs and grilled hamburgers.

Raven hovered over and placed a paper towel over the plate and lifted it into the microwave. A couple of minutes later, he was seated at her table, a glass of water within reach and a cloth napkin on his lap. She sat at the other end of the table and worked on a laptop.

"I'm not sure if you've looked up Charles Kearns yet," Raven said quietly, eyeing the computer screen, "but I did find an article about a North Shore construction company not being too happy with his testimony."

"You don't want to mess with any Boston area construction company, trust me," said Johnny, finishing off a mouthful of turkey. The melding of flavors was insane. Raven cooked as well, no, better, than her mother.

The flavors brought him right back to his early days with Julia. She'd send him off to his shift every morning with a foil-wrapped egg sandwich with melted cheese and a slice of bologna that had briefly touched the frying pan to take its chill off and slightly singe. He'd come home for lunch if he could get away and have more bologna, this time on a brioche roll smeared with mustard. Having someone make food especially for him always made him lightheaded. Not that he believed a way to a man's heart was through his stomach. It wasn't the food itself but the gesture of love and caring. Even though the dinner in front of him was a plate of leftovers, and he hadn't been invited to the main meal, Raven's insistence that he eat was comparable to being handed that egg sandwich many years ago.

"Do you still have contacts on the Boston police force?" Raven's voice remained low, and Johnny leaned in to hear it. He didn't think she was whispering because Marcel was sleeping but to keep their espionage a secret.

He answered back in the same quiet tone. "Oh, yeah, many guys, including my former chief. What do you need?"

She put her thumbnail into her mouth and then wrinkled her nose. "Just a thought. If we could find out any information about the cases Charles worked on and what and who he testified against."

Johnny nodded. Solid idea. In theory. If it was his case. But it wasn't his case. It was Marcel's. In fact, it might already belong to the state police.

The last thing he wanted to do was step on his son-in-law's toes, but it was an incredible opportunity to do something with Raven. For Raven.

"You two look like you're up to no good." Marcel stood by the sink, half his hair standing up from his intense nap.

He was right.

Chapter Eighteen

Raven was grateful Johnny took the lead.

"Full confession," he said, hopping up and extending his hand. "First, Happy Thanksgiving, by the way. How do you not weigh eight hundred pounds living with this expert cook and pastry chef?" He winked at Raven and displayed his empty plate to Marcel.

Marcel looked over at Raven and smiled. She knew he was pleased she made an effort with Johnny. Her heart leaped. Maybe they were actually okay.

"It ain't easy. I keep telling her to stop making sweets because I have no willpower." He patted his stomach area. Raven knew there was a six-pack under that shirt. Who was he fooling?

"How did it go with the gun?" Raven rose from the table and walked closer to him. He leaned down and kissed her hello. The dogs, who had already received their warm hello from him at the door an hour ago, butted between them for additional hugs and kisses. Marcel released Raven and hunched down to cater to them while he updated Raven and Johnny.

"It's possible that it's the right gun. Tom brought it to Augusta for processing. Once we know more, Shannon'll look to see if it's been used in other cases."

Raven stiffened at the mention of Shannon's name. She felt her blood drawn out of her legs and her face heat up.

Johnny glanced at her before he said, "Who's Shannon?"

Raven knew that Johnny knew but was grateful he just baited Marcel for an answer.

"Shannon McGrath.   Our new county DA." Marcel stated it like a newscaster.

"The pretty girl from the election signs?" Johnny smiled up at Marcel, not looking at Raven.

Marcel laughed. "Yes, the pretty one. That's what her father used to call her when we were in school."

"You knew her in school?" Johnny crossed his arms, in for a good, long story. "Grammar school?"

"Yep, all through high school. She was my senior prom date." Marcel's eyes twinkled. He strode over to the fridge. "Got any leftovers in here for me, babe?"

Raven cleared her throat. "Sure, let me help you."

She pulled out the containers again. "Have more, too," she said to Johnny, motioning to the leftover food.

"Don't mind if I do!" He grabbed his empty plate from the table.

"Let me give you a clean one." She turned to the cabinet.

"No way. This isn't a buffet restaurant." He winked at her. She was afraid he was going to kiss her on the cheek. Not tonight, please. He didn't.

"What did her sisters think of her father calling her 'the pretty one'?" Raven tried to keep her voice light, tried to feign polite interest and show she didn't care about Shannon McGrath, ex-girlfriend, one way or another, but that she was also listening. It was so much work.

Marcel laughed. "She only had brothers!"

Johnny laughed, too. Then stopped. "But she is pretty."

"Oh yes, that she is." Marcel heaped turkey and mashed potatoes on a plate. "Can you toss me a spoon, hon, for the gravy?"

Raven pivoted, grabbed a large spoon out of a drawer, and handed it to Marcel. He scooped a clump of tan gelatinous mass from the plastic container and tried to spread it across the meat, potatoes, and stuffing.

"I'm not seeing any vegetables on that plate," said Johnny, laughing, offering him the carrots, green beans, and creamed onions.

"I'm all set." He popped the plate uncovered into the microwave. Raven forced herself to not grab a paper towel to put on top. She'd be cleaning the gravy spray later.

While Marcel's plate rotated, Johnny again crossed his arms and eyed Raven. "I meant it when I said, 'Full Confession.'"

Marcel cocked his head, ready to listen. Raven's heart thumped, her mind still on Shannon.

"We want to come clean, Marcel. We were just walking around the Lane Mansion," Johnny started to explain.

"We?" Marcel asked, his voice now with an edge, but Raven knew already that he knew the answer.

"Raven and I. Or is it 'Raven and me'?" Johnny shrugged and laughed, holding his plate next for the microwave.

Marcel turned and glared at Raven without comment. She remained still and expressionless. He wasn't happy she was still involved.

"Any who," Johnny said, keeping his voice light and casual. "A couple of things, if you don't mind. I don't want you to think I'm butting in."

"Once a cop, always a cop. I get it. Go ahead. I appreciate your input." Marcel used a dishtowel to remove his hot plate and put his hand out to receive Johnny's. "Ninety seconds?"

"Sure," said Johnny, agreeing on the heating time. "Thank you for that, and thank you for indulging an old man."

Marcel smiled and grabbed a beer from the fridge. "What would you like to drink, Johnny?"

"Not that!" Johnny laughed as he pointed to the beer. "If you have a coke or a water or a ginger ale or whatever. Thanks." Johnny paused while Marcel settled at the table with his plate of food. "So we were walking around, and we both saw some things we'd like to bring to your attention."

Marcel chewed and shook his head, and then nodded. He pointed to the plate and his mouthful and gave Raven a thumbs up. She exhaled and smiled. His appreciation for the meal made her feel like they were still friends, which was a ridiculous yet rational thought.

"First off, there's a rake outside by a pile of leaves." Johnny made his way over to the table with his heated plate and a can of soda.

"So, you're thinking that he just finished raking before he died." Marcel took another mouthful and moaned in delight.

Raven interjected. "Rather, he was interrupted while doing it. By his killer. Maybe someone saw him talking to someone while he was raking. Someone who was at Lane's Market or walking by and took it as ordinary at the time."

Marcel nodded. "Great point. Go on," he said to Johnny and took another forkful.

"And number two, the front door was ajar." Johnny raised two fingers up, counting the clues.

"The wind must have blown it open. I shut it myself."

Johnny shook his head. "The latch works fine. I tested it."

Marcel put his fork down. "You're saying someone went into the house last night or today."

"Yep."

Marcel scrunched his eyebrows together. "Why now? We think he's been dead for almost a month."

Johnny, with a mouthful, muffled, "That's a good question."

"And we haven't released anything about his death yet. Only a small, tight circle know about it." He eyed both Raven and Johnny.

"That eliminates nosy people. I mean other nosy people." Johnny laughed. "So, you can probably guess I couldn't walk away without checking on the house. Since the door was ajar, of course."

Marcel shook his head with a smirk. "Go on."

Johnny continued. "Just so you know what went on, we filmed it. Videoed it. Whatever the right term is. To show we didn't disturb anything." He turned in his chair to see Raven, who was still standing by the counter, waiting for Marcel's neck to turn red and his cheeks puff out as they did when he was upset with her. "Raven, show your hubby what we did."

Raven lowered her eyes to avoid Marcel's and brought him her phone, attached to a portable charger. She opened up to the video and hit play. The muffled sound of her turning the phone in the right direction was followed by a visual of Johnny turning towards her.

"Is it on?" Johnny's voice asks on the video.

Raven knew she nodded to him in response.

Then Johnny's voice again. "Raven, please note I am picking up this one paper using the tissue."

At the table, Johnny let out a howl of laughter. "Yes, Marcel, it's a used tissue! Barely used! Hey! It's what I had on me."

The video continued through Johnny's investigation of the loose pieces of paper in the living room.

"Hit pause for a second before I lose my train of thought," Johnny said. "I'm not a spring chicken, you know."

Marcel did as Johnny asked.

"You guys took the laptop, right? The one Raven and I saw on Wednesday night?"

"Yes, Tom brought that to Augusta too to be cracked open—it's password protected."

"Oh, good. Just making sure whoever broke in, went in after you did, didn't get it. What about a printer on the first floor?"

"I don't recall seeing one." Marcel took a sip from his beer.

"Neither did I. On Wednesday." Raven clarified.

Johnny nodded. "Nope. The same. And not one in the living room today, although there is one upstairs. That doesn't explain the printer paper on the first floor, though," he said. He was thorough. He must have been a great cop. Even if he was a rotten father.

"One of my reasonings for videoing—because I'm sure you'd trust us that we weren't causing mischief—was to have you compare the house to any photos that you may have taken on Wednesday night. Last night. I keep forgetting it was just last night."

Marcel nodded in appreciation. "Yes, good idea. The photos are on Tom's phone. I'll have him come by tomorrow, and we can look.

"Did you take Charles's cell phone?" Johnny asked

Marcel shook his head. "No, we didn't see one."

"Hmm, neither did we, but we saw the phone charger. Upstairs."

"It could be in the woods. Fallen out of his pocket." Raven offered, although she wished she hadn't because it made her think of Charles lying in the woods. Alone.

"I'll put someone on that tomorrow to look in the woods," Marcel said. "We'll also check with his carrier."

"Oh," said Johnny, "if the killer took it, then maybe we can track right to him. Even if it's just from the day of the murder, right?"

"I think so." Marcel scraped the last of his mashed potatoes onto his fork.

Raven couldn't advance her mind past the scene in the woods. When did it happen? Did someone shoot Charles there, or was his body dragged in? What was she doing the day he was killed? She could have been in the woods with the dogs right after it happened. Did she see anyone that she didn't normally see walking the trails lately? Actually, she couldn't remember the last time she saw anyone in the woods now that the seasonal people had left.

Or was she doing something mundane when he was shot, like making beds in the cabins or doing laundry, or worse, doing nothing, just sitting and sipping coffee. Ordinary tasks on a day that were far from ordinary for Charles, on a day when he was executed five hundred yards from her house.

Executed. Someone who lost money or reputation or worse, freedom, might have a lot to say to Charles and his expert testimony. Enough to make the trek from Boston to Secretly. Wouldn't be the first time Maine was entangled with Massachusetts.

"We've lost you." Marcel's voice was soft. She looked up and met his gaze. His eyes reminded her of when they first met, and she shared her upbringing, being alone with her mother and grandfather, being abandoned by her father. She later learned of his intact nuclear family. His perfect mother and dutiful father. His loving siblings, all five of them. All friendly and happy to welcome her into the fold, overwhelming her with love. She didn't love them back. It was all too much.

"My family is tiny." She had said to Marcel when he asked why she didn't want to spend every Sunday at his parents' house for large family dinners. "I grew up being quiet, being private. Your family is very…nice, but I don't need to know every detail of their lives or have them know mine."

She knew she had hurt him by saying that, but it was the truth, and it needed to be said. Early in their marriage, he occasionally went over on a Sunday without her but didn't stay long. Her mother-in-law still tried to bring her in closer, mailing her coupons or favorite recipes, calling here and there to check in. Raven wasn't ready to be loved that much or to share Marcel.

But if she didn't change, would she one day end up dead and alone in the woods, waiting for someone to stumble upon her? She just might.

Chapter Nineteen

The day following a holiday always depressed Betty. The holiday itself was often anticlimactic, too, and that didn't help matters. All the prep work that went into the big day—the planning, the menu decisions, the money, the cleaning—egads, the cleaning—but then it was over in a few hours and swept away. Forgotten. Not even really appreciated. And to top it off, there was very little to look forward to until the next holiday and the whole cycle started over.

When the kids were young, they kept her busy with activities and needs, and then later, caring for her mother, she was almost overwhelmed and couldn't wait for the time when she had nothing to do. What she wouldn't do for more of that hustle now.

Howard was content with just being—reading, watching TV, fiddling with his ham radios, dreaming about owning this boat or that lake cabin, with Betty fully knowing that he'd never pull the trigger to spend that kind of money. But wouldn't that be grand? Give her something to do. She could make curtains for the cabin or cushions for the boat. And pack picnic lunches and invite friends from Connecticut. They'd finally have a reason to visit. She missed all of her old friends.

Until then, she was forced to look for other ways to keep busy and happy. Lately, as part of her strategy, she took to doing all of her shopping at Lane's Market, even though the inventory was smaller than the large commercial store in the next town. Sure, Lane's was known for its excellent meats and fresh-off-the-boat fish, but that wasn't the draw for Betty.

She went for the town gossip. It even beat the dump.

Today, despite taking her time, wheeling the small metal shopping cart up and down the few aisles, reading more ingredient labels than an FDA inspector, she remained the lone customer in the store except for an occasional town worker coming in for a made-on-the-spot egg sandwich or a mom needing more milk for bowls of cereal. Of course, she knew all about Evelyn losing her husband to her coworker. Such a pity, but that was old news from the summer. Betty was hungry for something meaty, something new. Eventually, she gave up and began her checkout.

"Slow today, huh, Evelyn?" Betty unloaded her groceries onto the belt. "I should have come in later."

"Ugh, no, Betty. You don't want to be here later today when the Massholes arrive for the weekend." Evelyn scanned and bagged in one swoop.

Actually, Betty did. She had finally been in Maine long enough to blend in as a local amongst those from away, and thus, she was invisible to anyone on vacation or in town to use their parents' house for the weekend. She learned about what these visitors thought of Chris Lane, the store owner, and their neighbors—full-time people Betty knew—and gas station owners and the beach personnel. The list went on and on. It's a wonder these people enjoyed anything.

Yet she saw herself in them. She criticized instead of enjoying. She worried instead of relaxing. She was susceptible to crowd pressure. To the rest of America, the Friday after Thanksgiving was Black Friday, and if she was still in Connecticut, she'd have been running around with the best of them, hunting for bargains, buying things neither she nor her family needed, but heck, it was on sale and at an incredible price that no one should pass up. Maybe that's why others from away who had houses in Secretly and Whale Harbor didn't arrive until after every deal had been grabbed.

"I would have thought those…" Betty searched for a better word than Evelyn had used, "people would have come up on Wednesday. Spent the whole holiday here." She stood at the end of the cashier area, helping Evelyn load the groceries into her recycle bags.

"Some did, but most will come in tonight." Evelyn wrapped a package of ground beef in a separate plastic bag. "You don't want this leaking all over your whoopie pies."

Betty barely heard her. Her attention was riveted by what she saw out the window. A pickup truck with the lettering Bryant's Chimney was parked on the road across from the Lane Mansion. Betty couldn't see the house from that angle but knew the workers must be back at repairing the chimney. Howard had said the work would need to be finished for Charles' estate to get full value for the house. Maybe a realtor or an attorney had already spoken to the chimney guys and asked them to speed it up.

"Thanks, Evelyn. Have a good day," Betty said, grabbing all four bags at once.

"Don't you want help getting those out to your car?" Evelyn called after her, but Betty was already out the door and halfway to her car.

Emil Bryant stood on the slate sidewalk leading up to the Lane Mansion, talking to a woman. Betty tossed all the bags into her backseat, causing them to tip and spill their contents. She shut the car door without fixing them and straightened her jacket. Nice day for a short stroll. As good a place to walk as any. She hoped to eavesdrop on the conversation.

In less than a minute, however, she saw that the woman with whom Emil was talking was Raven. Why was she there again?

Part of her wanted to walk up to the two and fully hear their conversation, or walk by, hoping to be noticed by Raven and invited over.

Instead, Betty decided to wait by her car to see what Raven did next. Why not? She had nothing else to do.

She didn't have to wait long. Raven hopped into her green Mini Cooper and spun it around. Betty, less speedy and sporty, jumped into her Subaru SUV, her other, less conspicuous vehicle that she used in colder weather, and whipped around the corner, narrowly missing a fieldstone wall that encased a yard.

The Mini was easy to follow, and even if Betty lost her, as long as Raven stayed within ten miles or so, Betty could find her by finding her car.

The Mini bopped along and passed the post office. It didn't turn up the road that led both to Betty and Howard's home and Pine Acres Cabins. It drove past the town offices and Rachel's Diner and passed the swimming hole. It finally made a right into the town library.

Betty had always wanted to be a librarian and dreamed that one day, she would be the head librarian of this particular one. She pictured herself as a customer, browsing amongst the stacks, and the current one-hundred-and-twenty-year old librarian saying to her, "Betty, you are such a bookworm. You should run this place when I retire. In fact, take it over right now. Today. I have finally found my perfect replacement."

But for all the times that Betty was in the library, Marie Claire had never said anything remotely close to that to Betty, and she also never seemed ready to retire either.

Betty pulled her practical Subaru up next to Raven's Mini. Raven looked up from the driver's seat and up from a folder she held in her hands. She had been reading some papers. Both women waved simultaneously.

"Looking for something new to read?" Raven asked Betty as they walked into the library together. Raven had the folder with her. Betty noticed the file folder tab didn't have a subject written on it.

She quickened her pace to keep up with Raven. "To be totally frank, I'm bored and followed you here. I saw you talking to the chimney guy outside the Lane Mansion."

"Really?" Raven stopped and studied Betty and then shrugged. "Well, I could use the company."

Betty smiled and felt the day would finally have purpose. She almost skipped.

Raven caught her up as they walked up the sidewalk from the parking lot.

"The chimney guy is the librarian's grandson, you know. Emil Bryant. Mrs. Bryant."

Betty did not know.

"You guys who grew up here know everyone," she said. She thought about the meat and milk in her car and wished she had parked in the shade, but at least it was forty degrees out or so.

Marie Claire Bryant, not really one hundred and twenty years old, but absolutely looking so, stood in her usual spot behind the front desk with her stamp in hand. She had refused to modernize the library by scanning the codes in books, which made inter-library lending difficult. Her short, thick hair-sprayed white hair was impeccably molded to her head. Her gold-rimmed glasses completed the look.

"Two for the price of one," she said as Betty and Raven approached the desk.

'Good morning, Mrs. Bryant," said Raven, giving her a large smile. "How was your Thanksgiving?"

"Marvelous. Simply marvelous. How about yours?"

Betty internalized this exchange. Cordial. Friendly. Measured. Timely. Not how she would have done it. Not how many in Connecticut would have, being so accustomed to rushing, storming in, getting the needed information, and then rushing off to the next thing. Connecticut's pace was definitely faster than Maine's.

"Mine…" Raven started and turned towards Betty, "Ours…was interesting. To say the least. I'm the one who found Charles Kearns, if you've heard about that."

Marie Claire nodded. Betty assumed there wasn't much that would surprise this ancient woman.

"I did get wind of that today. Emil called to tell me you'd be over. Such a shame. Charles hadn't even finished the Lane Mansion to enjoy it."

"Yes, it is horrible." Raven kept it short. Betty was grateful to not relive what Raven had described finding in the woods.

Marie Claire hung onto the counter for balance as she spoke. "I only met him that one time. When he came in with that paper he found."

Paper? Betty smiled, happy she was here. This was getting interesting.

Raven nodded. "Emil said he found it when he moved the brick in the dining room chimney?"

Brick?

"Yes, Emil said." Marie Claire went on. "And Charles was standing next to him. You would have thought that Emil found a million dollars, he said. Charles was just as excited when he came here with it. Caring for it so gingerly. Wrapped in a hankie."

Betty was lost.

"I'm sorry. I'm behind. What was found? Where was it found? What brick? A gold brick? An Indian relic?" These locals always spoke in code, and she was sick of it.

Marie Claire waited for Raven to explain.

"In the Lane Mansion, there's a place in the dining room chimney where messages could be left. Hidden messages behind a brick. Possibly used during the War of 1812. A loose brick comes out from the mantle area. I can show you the video I have of it later. It's an empty hole now."

Now Betty was impressed. "And it was full of notes the day that Emil moved the brick?"

Raven nodded again and turned back to Marie Claire. "Any chance you have the notes? They may be at the Lane Mansion, too. I just haven't found them."

"I don't have the original notes, but I made copies. I love to keep copies. One moment."

Marie Claire swirled around extremely slowly, faced the back of the receptionist desk, and paused. A large metal industrial filing cabinet, two feet taller than her, was the centerpiece of the area. She gingerly stepped over to the cabinet and pulled on the middle drawer—once, twice—and just as Betty was about to ask if she needed help before she hurt herself, the drawer squealed open, scraping the metal like nails on a chalkboard. Betty almost covered her ears.

Minutes ticked by as Marie Claire practically buried her head into the manila files. If Betty was the librarian, she'd automate everything, making it streamlined and paperless. Not that she was a certified librarian or even had a good grasp of technology on how to convert documents or book catalogs, but she'd be up for the challenge. It had to be easier than this, and she had to be a better librarian than this woman.

"Here it is," said Marie Claire, holding on to the cabinet to regain her balance as she turned. While her thin, papery hands clasped the metal, Betty held her breath and took out her phone in case they needed to dial for an EMT. Marie Claire slowly turned back and crossed the open space, placing the manila folder in front of Raven. She laid one veiny hand on it.

"Why did Charles Kearns come to the library with the notes?" Betty asked. It would be one thing if he knew what to research, but without proper technology here, any research would be hard. He would have had more success on his personal laptop.

"Because besides being the town librarian, I'm also the town historian," said Marie Claire. Not with a note of bragging or boast. Simply a fact. But how many roles did Marie Claire need?

"And President of the ladies' auxiliary of the VFW," Raven added with a smile.

Marie Claire beamed. "Founding member. Yes, my Ernest was in the army. Drafted. Trust me, he didn't want to go. But he went and thankfully came back."

Betty looked at the closed manila folder. How did Raven do it? She had the patience of a saint. Betty debated grabbing the folder out from Marie Claire's hand but was afraid the movement would cause Marie Claire to topple backwards.

Marie Claire looked down at the unopened folder. "Charles was very disappointed to find out the notes weren't old."

"Oh, they weren't?" said Betty. "How old were they?"

Marie Claire flipped open the file. Photocopies of handwritten notes took up three or four pages of photocopy paper. There were two types of handwriting—frilly girl and chicken scratch man.

Chapter Twenty

Raven picked up the pages from the folder and huddled close to Betty to allow her to see them, too.

One note in the woman's handwriting said, "Can't wait to kiss you." The handwriting was the large, loopy kind that a few of Raven's classmates had, the girls who wore fancy clothes and spent more time applying lipstick than applying themselves to their studies. Raven had a prejudice towards this type of penmanship: Dumb Girl.

Below that note was a copy of one in a man's thinner, slanted writing.

"Tick. Tock. Tick. Tock. How slow the hands on the clock move," it said.

"Is that a bad attempt to write a poem?" Betty asked.

Raven and Marie Claire smiled.

"Or a good attempt to write a bad poem?" Raven added.

Marie Claire giggled. "I'd say so. No Keats or Browning, for sure."

"I prefer Stanley Kunitz." Raven's love for the New England poet came from her mother, who spoke of the time Stanley and his wife stayed at Pine Acres to take a break from the crush of the summer tourists on Cape Cod.

"They were so nice," her mother had said. "What a treasure to meet him in person." Julia had always hoped they'd come back, hoped she could have a poetry reading session with the Pulitzer Prize-winning one-day-to-be National Poet Laureate, but they never did. It was a long drive from New York City to Secretly.

"I don't think of Kunitz as a love poet," Marie Claire said. "'My mother never forgave my father for killing himself.'"

Raven smiled. "So true." Kunitz' "The Portrait" was her favorite.

Betty, not a fan of poetry, and having no poet or poem to add to the mix brought them back to the hidden messages. "If it had only said, 'tick tock tick tock. How slow the hands move on the clock.' I'd say it was almost brilliant for a note left in a chimney." She chuckled.

Marie Claire smiled. Raven recognized that smile as the Marie-Claire-Public-Servant face, the same one she used for small children who wanted to share why they liked "The Cat in the Hat."

The second page held similarly dull, trite exchanges about "looking into your eyes," "holding you close," and "counting the minutes." The third page was a copy of a receipt from Wolf's marine store for $10.50 dated in the spring. The item was "WB," and the count was five.

"Oh, I think this is in here by mistake." Betty pointed it out to Marie Claire.

"No mistake. That was the back of one the notes written in the thin handwriting."

"Really?" Raven looked closer at the page.

"WB for water bottles?" Betty guessed at the abbreviation. "It'd make sense for a cost and lack of tax paid."

Besides wondering who wrote these, Raven wondered what Charles had thought of them.

"He was extremely disappointed. He had so hoped he had found something for the national archives." Marie Claire said, her back to Betty and Raven as she made photocopies of the photocopies. "Just in case you don't find the originals," she said, handing them to Raven.

"Do you know if he figured out who wrote them?" Betty leaned on the counter.

"I don't know if he did. But I did." Marie Claire said as nonchalantly as giving a weather report and winked.

"You know who wrote these?" Betty straightened up.

Raven waited quietly for Marie Claire to continue. She read Betty's facial expression as shock and disgust for taking this long to get to the point.

"Sure did. Well, I admit I'm assuming. I don't know for sure. I think the girl is Laurie Eldridge. She's been the cleaning gal over there for years, and she comes in here from time to time to take out a book."

"I know Laurie," said Raven. "We went to school together."

Marie Claire nodded and opened up a tin box crammed with index cards, most of them crinkled and yellowing. She thumbed through the lot, although Raven didn't see how Marie Claire could read any of the tightly packed cards without pulling them out first.

"Here," she said, yanking out a light-yellow card. On it was printed Laurie Eldridge's name and address. Her signature splayed across the bottom, spilling across all the horizontal lines above and below it.

Raven placed the index card next to the notes with the frilly handwriting. Marie Claire had a point, both in the handwriting sample on the card and her reasoning to still conduct some work by paper instead of electronically. Betty leaned over Raven's shoulder.

Raven waited for Betty to argue against Marie Claire's thought, just to be a contrarian, or devil's advocate, as Betty always called it when she contradicted Howard, but she didn't do that.

"I agree with Marie Claire. It looks exact," said Betty. "So, who's the guy then?"

Marie Claire pushed her wire glasses up her small, wrinkled, pink nose. "I forgot to mention that all of the guy's notes were on the back of marine store receipts. I just didn't bother to copy the backs of them all."

Raven scrunched up her own nose. "So we're looking for a fisherman, a lobsterman, or at the very least, a man who owns a boat. What were the purchases on the other receipts?"

"Nothing. No purchases. The receipts were blank. That's why I didn't photocopy them. Why waste paper?"

"Just blank receipts from Wolf Marine?" Betty knitted her eyebrows as she looked at Marie Claire.

"Yes. Thin and flimsy paper to boot." Marie Claire shifted her feet, growing tired of the conversation.

"All from Wolf Marine, or were any from other marine stores too?" Raven thought of all the marine stores in the area, too many to count on both hands.

"All Wolf Marine." Marie Claire confirmed.

"Who would have blank Wolf Marine receipts?" Betty stated what Raven found to be obvious.

Marie Claire thought of the same obvious answer. "Wolf Marine."

Raven added. "The only two who work the register at Wolf Marine are Karl Wolf himself and that girl who works for him."

"The one with the nose ring," said Betty, and then quickly added, "I guess the other handwriting could be hers too. We shouldn't assume that the lover was a man." She smiled, trying to display her open-mindedness.

"Agree. But this chicken scratch says man to me. Just because a woman likes other women doesn't mean she's going to write like a man." Marie Claire, without realizing it, just one-upped Betty. Impressive, especially for her generation.

Betty's face reddened. She opened her mouth, and Raven quickly spoke to silence any retort. "We can explore both. We should look at it from all angles."

"That's right," said Betty.

"Karl's wife is the one who ran off with Rusty Poole, right?" Marie Claire didn't lower her voice to say it, not that there were many in the library to hear it. Raven was surprised that Marie Claire was interested in the town gossip, or maybe she was offering that information from the research librarian's perspective.

Betty tsked at the mention of the scandal and scowled. She may have been hip about gays, but she remained old-fashioned about infidelity.

"I don't know how Evelyn gets up in the morning and faces the town, day in and day out, from that perch at the cash register," Betty added. "You know people are whispering behind her back."

"Like now," said Marie Claire.

Betty reddened again all the way to the roots of her dyed blonde hair.

"I need to look for a new bird book," she said, with a snort, pushing off the counter to wander the stacks.

Raven looked back at the photocopied receipt from the marine store. The handwritten date said "May 3." About two months before Sarah Wolf and Rusty Poole left town. Who started the cheating first—Karl or Sarah? Seemed like everyone in town was fooling around on their spouses. She thought back to "Shannie" on Marcel's phone, and a pit of pain developed in her gut. How had she been so stupid all this time?

Chapter Twenty-One

Raven found Betty leaning against a tall bookcase with her eyes closed and rustled a few books sticking out as she approached so as to not frighten her.

"Is the witch done lecturing?" Betty said without opening her eyes.

Raven whispered. "She's an icon in town and actually quite nice. Don't let her get to you."

Betty straightened and opened her eyes.

"You'd think at my age no one would get to me, but every once in a while, that little child inside of me hurts."

"Wanna tag along to see what we can learn at the marine store?" Raven hoped a change of subject would cheer Betty. After her mother died, Betty took Julia's place in Raven's life and partially in her heart. Despite her brain going a little mush here and there—Raven agreed with Howard that it could be dementia creeping in—Betty was a stalwart whom Raven could rely on.

"I would love to. Do you think we could swing by my house so I could put my meat and such in the fridge first?"

"Absolutely." Raven was glad she had made the cabin reservations as "no housekeeping service" for this long weekend. She didn't have to worry about her guests until they checked out, unless they texted her earlier.

Howard greeted Raven in the kitchen with the requisite kiss on top of her head.

"You two out causing trouble?"

"I hope so," said Betty. "Otherwise, why bother?"

All three jumped at the loud knock at the front door, an entry rarely used.

Howard left to answer it.

"Look what the cat dragged in," said Howard. Behind him lumbered Johnny.

"Saw your car, Raven, hard to miss it." Johnny held papers tightly clasped in his right hand and a paper coffee cup in his left. "I figured this was the gathering of the Sherlock Holmes Society, and I should crash it to share my information."

"Oh, you learned something about Charles' death," Betty turned to Johnny, her face back to its happy smile.

"Not his death, but his business."

That interested Betty less. She turned back to unloading her groceries.

"I talked to a buddy of mine down in Boston. He claimed that Charles had to have a bodyguard down there. Some dude was threatening to beat him up over his testimony. Stalked him. Allegedly smashed his windshield with a baseball bat."

"Remind me again what Charles did for a living?" Howard gestured to Johnny to take a chair in the adjacent sitting room. Johnny sat in the floral chair closest to the wood stove.

"Can I get you something to drink?" Howard waved towards the kitchen.

Johnny shook his head and raised his hand, showing his cup of coffee. Raven hoped, as she always did, that it was just coffee in that cup. He answered Howard's first question. "He was an expert witness for construction-type issues, usually testifying on behalf of the State of Massachusetts or another plaintiff."

"He was an engineer?" said Howard.

"Not exactly. More like a math nerd. Did something with the calculation of things."

Betty perked back into the conversation. "Ah, like what happened to UConn's new library back in the day. The builder never added in the weight of the books, and eventually, the bricks started flying off it and whacking students." Betty sat down on the edge of a loveseat, now interested. "Remember it was encased in bubble wrap when Barbara was there studying nursing?"

Barbara was Betty and Howard's middle daughter and the most normal in the lot, from what Raven had observed. She only had met her twice, however. Barbara didn't spend much time with her parents.

"That's a bit of an exaggeration, but yes, I think that's what Johnny means," said Howard.

"You wouldn't call it an exaggeration if you had a brick fall on your head." Betty protested.

"I don't think any students were clunked on the head, Betty," Howard said.

"I disagree," Betty said back, her face reddening.

"Did you find out who was trying to beat up Charles?" Raven stood against the door frame, hoping to refocus the conversation back to Charles. Not only did she not care one iota about a Connecticut college, she wanted to hear what Johnny learned.

"My buddy is getting the guy's whole name, his real name, the one who smashed the windshield, but he did say that he's known down there as Sammy the Shark. Probably hired by someone else."

"Sammy the Shark. That doesn't sound too good." Howard's dignified face soured.

"My money's on Sammy," said Betty, "Sammy for the kill."

"Betty, that's disgusting," said Howard. "This isn't anything to joke about."

Betty stiffened in her seat. Raven brought up the article she had read online about the North Shore construction company and its two billion dollar loss.

"Two billion?" Betty's eyebrows shot up. "Now that would be worth killing for." She eyed Howard, and Raven wondered just how much Howard was worth. Since moving up to Secretly, he and Betty had fully renovated their old colonial and spoke of potential boats and cabins to buy. Raven was used to such talk from people from away, but with Howard it felt like a reality he could pull off. In cash.

Johnny nodded. "Yeah, the North Shore guy. From Swampscott or Peabody. Yeah, my buddy mentioned him. They're looking into his connections to the vandalism, too, but I'm sure he's kept his nose clean. That's why you hire the Mob."

CHAPTER TWENTY-ONE

"The Mob," Betty swiveled to face Johnny. "There's no more Mob."

Howard shook his head and rolled his eyes.

Johnny laughed, not at Betty but at the notion that the Mob was a dead organization.

"Oh, there's the Mob, all right. Sure, the newfangled gangs and drug lords get more publicity now, and RICO took a lot of the punch out of the Mob. At least initially. But the Mob is alive and well, I assure you, and comes in many colors and languages. Don't you worry now."

Johnny said it lightly, like he was offering a menu of dessert items to Betty.

Howard had his laptop on a tray table next to him. "What's the name of the construction guy?"

"Sammy the Shark!" Betty said, jumping to her feet, her hands on her hips.

"No," said Howard, Raven, and Johnny in unison. Betty's face reddened again. She sat back down.

"Sammy's the potential mobster. The baseball bat-yielding guy." Howard explained to Betty, his fingers poised over his keyboard, as if typing in the name of the Boston Construction owner would magically morph into Charles' killer.

"Now I'm confused," said Betty.

"Obviously," said Howard. Tears formed at the rim of Betty's eyes as Howard looked toward Johnny for the name he was waiting for, ignoring his insult to Betty.

Johnny looked uncomfortable but responded. "It's easy to get all of these guys mixed up," he said to Betty. To Howard, he said, "The North Shore construction guy is Nick Billoni."

"Baloney? Like the meat?" Howard started typing.

"In sound, yes, but not in spelling." Johnny pulled a small, crinkled paper from his pants. "Billoni. B-I-L-L-O-N-I. Billoni. Nick. Nicholas."

Howard took the paper and, after studying it for a moment, tapped in 'Nicholas Billoni Massachusetts' on his laptop and read off the titles of many links to various news articles.

"'Billoni Construction Liable for Full Damages'"

"'Billoni Construction owes the city of Boston thirteen point five million dollars for faulty city building'"

"Wow," said Betty, moving closer to the edge of her seat and forgetting about her slight from Howard.

"I love this one," said Howard with a grin. "'Full of Billoni —Construction Owner Denies Any Wrong Doing'"

Johnny snorted. "Gotta love Boston reporters!"

Howard continued. "'Nick Billoni vows revenge.'"

"That one sounds good," said Betty. "What else does it say?"

"Let's see." Howard clicked it open to read out loud to the room.

"'Nicholas Billoni, owner of Billoni Construction of Peabody, Mass, vows to fight the charges against him, levied first by the City of Boston, and then by neighboring municipalities and private companies, totaling, by this reporter's estimate, based upon public filings, as over two billion dollars.'"

Johnny whistled, and Betty inhaled. Raven nodded. Here was the two billion dollar proof.

Howard read on. "'Billoni stands by the structural integrity of his buildings and claims that anyone who is saying otherwise needs to prove it or else. Billoni refused to elaborate on what "or else" meant.'"

"I think we can guess what 'or else' means. This guy sounds promising. I think he's our man," said Betty.

Howard pondered. "The question I have is why off Charles up in Maine when it would have been less noticeable in the Boston area."

"Good point," said Johnny, rubbing his hand over his graying five-o'clock-shadowed chin.

Raven had a hunch. "Try 'Billoni' and 'Maine' together in a search."

Howard typed. One link came up. For property taxes in Whale Harbor. Nicholas Billoni owned a mansion on the water in the neighboring town.

Chapter Twenty-Two

"Well, la-di-da! Pay dirt!" Johnny stood up and clapped his hands together.

Howard shut the cover of his laptop. "Imagine having a million-dollar home on the water where you come to escape your problems, and you keep running into the guy who you think caused them?"

"I know I'd be pissed seeing Charles Kearns' face up here if I was Billoni." Johnny leaned against the wall.

"So what's our next step?" Betty still sat at the edge of her seat.

Johnny straightened. "I'll share this information with Marcel and my Boston buddy. Let them run down the whereabouts of both Billoni and Sammy the Shark in and around Halloween. If that's when the coroner thinks the murder happened."

Raven agreed. "I think the Halloween bonfire is the last time anyone saw Charles."

Johnny continued. "I'm sure that Marcel's team or the state is checking an electronic trail of Charles. My bet is it ends on Halloween or the next day. I'll give my buddy a range of dates, say October 31-November 2. See ya!"

Johnny waved as he went out the kitchen door. He was gone as quickly as he arrived. Here one moment. Gone the next. Like always.

Howard's chest inflated. "I don't think I've ever helped with a murder investigation before."

Betty squished her eyebrows together. "Since you're such an expert now, I'll be sure to leave you clues to follow after I murder you!"

Both Raven and Howard cocked their heads at the puzzling message.

Another mixed-up thought floated out of Betty's brain. Raven hoped it was because of Howard's poke at her and not a medical reason.

To distract Betty again, Raven reminded her that they still had interviews to do.

"If you feel like it. If you have time."

Betty beamed. To be useful and needed again. She had all the time in the world.

"I'd love to! I love investigating."

Howard mouthed a 'thank you' to Raven as Betty pulled on her coat and fleece hat, her back to Howard.

"I'll drive," Raven suggested. "Let's go to the marine store first."

Karl Wolf was standing at the register when Raven and Betty walked in, wrapping up a sale with Clark Christianson. Raven held the folder with the photocopied messages against her chest. She suddenly felt shy confronting this burly man whose own wife had been missing for over three months.

She saw Betty's eyes widen. The marine store was a site to behold. First, it looked like it hadn't been swept or dusted since 1901, the year above the door, stating its inception. In fact, it looked like it was abandoned. Half of the items appeared too old to be functional. Shelves were littered with boxes of nuts and bolts and unpainted buoys. Ropes for lobster pots, chains for moorings, and orange life jackets hung around the store on the walls. A paint area sat to the right side of the counter but was not neat with cards of optional colors like in a normal hardware store. In addition to a plethora of bottom hull paint, this one had some used cans with dribbles down the side showing bright reds, blues, and yellows, and more neon spray paint than could be used in a decade.

Rufus, Karl's large Newfoundland, sauntered up to them, drooling as he came. Raven ruffled the fur on his head, and he sat on her feet.

Betty chuckled, "Better you than me."

Clark turned away from the counter to leave and stopped in his tracks when he saw Raven.

"Hey, you. Saw your hubby yesterday, ayep."

"You did? Where was that?" Raven was just making small talk. Marcel was always everywhere in the county at any given moment.

"In Whale Harbor," Clark said, dropping the r's and dragging the 'o' to sound like an 'a' like all good Mainers did unconsciously so 'Harbor' came out 'Habah.'

"Cold down there this time of year," said Betty, chiming in to be included. Whale Harbor was only five miles from Secretly, but that bit of a difference always changed the temperature for the good or the bad, depending on one's preference and the time of year.

Clark nodded politely towards Betty and focused back on Raven. "Good to see Tom, too. Hadn't seen him in ages, and I got to meet the new DA." He whistled like a construction worker watching a mini skirt pass by. "I feel so special." He chuckled and patted Raven on the arm as he passed by and left the store.

Raven felt the nerves in her arms and legs. Shannon was again with Marcel? Why were they spending so much time together? How often were they together? Why didn't Marcel tell her? That 'Shannie' text was to have her meet him last night. She found herself holding her breath as she replayed seeing it on his phone screen.

How frequently was this happening? She tried to think if there were any late nights that Marcel had been working, or anything else that was amiss that she had brushed off.

Lost in her thoughts and worries, she hadn't noticed the empty space between her and the counter, or Karl staring at her. Betty gave her a little nudge, bringing her back to the present. She tried to steady her breathing and slow her heart's pumping as she stepped forward. All she could think about was Shannon. And Marcel. And losing him to her.

Focus. Focus. Pushing Shannon and Marcel a bit aside, she cleared her throat and tried to remember why she and Betty were at the marine store.

Karl's winter beard was coming in, more gray this year than last. His dark hair was neatly trimmed with more graying around the edges. His skin seemed smoother and his eyes brighter since the last time she had seen him. Not the usual look for a man whose wife had run off with another man. Maybe Sarah's absence did him good. He smiled broadly, revealing a missing tooth on the left side of his mouth. He actually didn't look much different than his great-great-great-great grandfather, Johan Wolf, who had started the store and whose faded portrait hung behind the counter behind Karl.

"You getting a boat there, Raven?"

She shook her head. Focus. Focus. Breathe. She had no energy for anything coy.

"I hate to say it, but Betty and I are playing detective."

She introduced Betty as her neighbor, knowing that Betty also would have had no reason to have ever been in the marine supply store to meet Karl.

"Detective? Like in 'Magnum PI'?" Karl leaned forward on the old wooden counter. His smile widened. Also, not a normal reaction if he had anything to hide.

"Exactly! But without Hawaii as our backdrop!" Betty laughed. "Oh, I wish!"

Now that she stood in front of Karl, Raven didn't know where to begin. If she brought up Charles' death, it might sound like she was accusing him of murder, yet, why else was she in the store with the love notes? She'd have never guessed that Betty would come to her rescue.

"Actually, I'm a history buff," said Betty, "and we were chatting with Marie Claire about secret passages and such, and she mentioned the secret brick hiding place in the chimney at the Lane Mansion."

So, throw Marie Claire under the bus, Raven thought. Karl would probably chalk it up to old age or being a town gossip.

Karl's face reddened at the mention of the Lane fireplace. Raven let Betty continue. She still didn't know how to go forward with the conversation or even show what they found.

Betty took the folder out of Raven's hand and opened it up. "So Marie Claire had copies of notes from that chimney. Charles Kearns, from the Lane Mansion, had found them when the chimney was being repaired and brought them to her, not realizing they weren't old."

"And the intriguing part," she added, with a slight tone of manufactured naïveté, "is some of the notes were written on the back of receipts from this store." She showed him the photocopy.

Karl stared at the photocopy of the Wolf Marine Receipt. Seconds ticked by. He looked up at Raven and then Betty and finally nodded.

"Yep, that's my receipt."

Raven had barely been paying attention, her thoughts still floating in and out on Marcel and Shannon. Betty, however, was laser-focused. And patient. Now it was her turn to let seconds tick by, mimicking Raven at the library.

Karl shifted his weight.

"Anything else?" He shuffled papers on the counter. A sign for them to leave.

"Yes." Betty herself shifted on her feet. "Marie Claire had two backs she didn't copy. She said they were also your receipts."

Karl shrugged. "My receipts are all over town."

Betty wasn't giving up. "They were blank. Blank receipts."

Karl stood motionless.

Betty now went in for the kill.

"Who has access to your blank receipts?"

"Myself. And Anna." The part-time high school student.

"We believe this would be a man's handwriting." Betty flipped back through Marie Claire's photocopies and turned the paper around for Karl to study the handwritten note found on the back of the marine receipt. "Do you agree?"

She showed him the note with the poor rhyme.

"Tick. Tock. Tick. Tock. How slow the hands on the clock move." Betty read the verse out loud. Raven waited for her to criticize the poem, but Betty paused her tongue. She was a naturally charming interviewer.

Karl's face reddened. Maybe he heard the bad rhyme, too? Or was he preparing to confess to being the author?

He closed his eyes.

"Yes, all right. Yes, I wrote that."

"To Laurie Eldridge." Betty said it as a statement.

"Yes, but please leave her out of this. And you have to believe me, I would never have taken up with Laurie if Sarah hadn't already been sleeping around."

"With Rusty Poole." Again, Betty was to the point.

Karl looked at his hands. "Him. Others before him. I assumed she'd eventually stop. Get it out of her system. 'She's a young filly,' my pop said when I married her. 'Be prepared for her to break down the fence once in a while before she settles into your pasture,' he said. So, when I caught her before the wedding with Tom Pinkham," both women inhaled, "I cut her slack. I chalked it up to Tom fooling around with everyone's wife and sister."

Raven wasn't surprised to hear this about Tom. He had a ladies' man reputation, but she was disappointed to have it confirmed he had no respect for a wedding ring or a commitment. She was also surprised to hear Karl act nonchalant about his wife's cheating.

"But Rusty Poole?" Karl made a face. "Older. Pot Belly. That surprised me. Had to be for his money. But it also showed me that she would never settle down, never be faithful. And for the record, I'm not like that. I was sick to my stomach cheating on Sarah despite all she did to me."

"Are you still seeing Laurie?" Betty sounded like a journalist now with her impartial tone.

Karl nodded. "We'd move in together if I could find Sarah to serve her with divorce papers. Enough's enough. They've been gone for four months now. You'd think they'd have run out of money by now."

Rusty was known for being wicked cheap, "having his first communion money," as it was said. In general, many lobstermen kept hundreds of thousands in cash, not being very trusting of institutions and also preferring a cash-driven economy. Rusty might have enough money to be away for years.

Betty turned to Raven. "Anything I missed?"

Raven shook her head. "Thanks, Karl, for speaking to us," she said.

Karl nodded. A look of relief swept across his face. The truth does set you free.

The women turned to leave, and Betty twisted back.

"It would have sounded better to rhyme Tock with Clock, by the way." She walked out of the store while Karl scratched his head.

Raven shook her head and shrugged. Betty just had to get that in.

Chapter Twenty-Three

"I think that went well, don't you?" Betty adjusted her seatbelt as Raven backed out of a parking spot. "Now on to Laurie? This investigating stuff is fun!"

She hadn't felt this good in years. She hoped Raven didn't mind her taking charge, but Raven had paled in the store after that lobsterman's comment about the DA, Marcel's ex-girlfriend. Can you call it an ex-girlfriend if they dated in high school? Betty had never taken any high school relationship seriously, her own or those of her daughters. The fact that one of her daughters was now married to her "high school sweetheart" didn't change Betty's viewpoint.

Betty glanced over. Raven hadn't acknowledged her comment and was still looking sort of out of it, but she was driving away from the marine store and across to the other side of the peninsula, the upper part, still considered Secretly, about a twenty-minute drive. The lower part of the peninsula led to Whale Harbor. Betty decided to let her be.

Instead, she turned her thoughts to her next interview. Betty had never met Laurie Eldridge but had heard of her. She and Howard had just moved to Secretly when Laurie's husband died. Tragically. She couldn't remember the details, just that Laurie was young, and they hadn't been married long. Also, that Laurie moved back in with her mother after his death. Oh, and that it was all tragic. Over and over, the mumbles around town, always "what a tragedy" if Laurie's name was mentioned. Betty made a mental note to look up the article on what happened to Laurie's husband when she was looking for something to do.

Keeping things in a veil of secrecy reminded Betty of her family when she was growing up, like the whispering when Aunt Sue had cancer, or when cousin Herbert had to go off to a court-ordered "summer camp"…for five years. She thought of her own white lies to her daughters about miscarriages they didn't know about or her own struggle with depression. Betty was deep in thought about the dangers of secrets and what secrets did to children when she heard a stifled sniffle come from Raven.

Looking over, she saw tears running down Raven's face as she drove.

"Is it all getting to you?" Betty reached over and touched Raven's arm.

Raven nodded and swallowed a sob. She turned right to drive along the bit of the coast that touched the northern part of Whale Harbor, even though it was the long way. Good, thought Betty. The ocean breeze was a healer.

"To find anyone dead is traumatizing. I found my mother, but she was in her own bed. Died from natural causes. At age ninety-nine. Never made it to one hundred." Betty almost said, "What a tragedy," but held her tongue. That really wasn't a tragedy but a blessing. Her mother hadn't been able to walk on her own, or feed or change herself, for years.

"But to find a body where you don't expect it," Betty said, forcing herself to refocus back to Raven, "and a partial body at that, and to have it turn out to be a crime, and against someone you know. Well, that would overwhelm anyone. Truly." Betty leaned over again and rubbed Raven's arm.

Raven nodded again, this time with a louder sob escaping. She pulled the car into a scenic turnoff to catch her breath and wipe her face. Betty marveled at the waves crashing up on the rocks as Raven steadied herself.

Raven asked for a tissue from the glove compartment. "What kind of investigator arrives in tears," she said, trying to make light of her crying.

"A sensitive one, that's who." Betty leaned back against the passenger window to study Raven. "This isn't about Charles' death, is it?"

Raven shook her head and blew her nose.

"You're worried about Marcel and that woman." Again, Betty making a statement, not a question.

"Uh-huh." Raven looked up at Betty, the rims of her eyes red and an abundance of tears filling up and spilling over.

"Oh honey, don't worry. No one loves you more than Marcel. No one. He adores you." Betty attempted to give Raven an awkward hug. Awkward for many reasons—the smallness of the front seat and the fact that Betty too was worried about Marcel and that woman. All men had a wandering eye. Sometimes, they acted on what the eye saw.

Raven's expression of self-doubt didn't change. She shrugged and wiped her face with a new, dry tissue.

"The last thing you want to do is worry. Don't bring a problem into your marriage that isn't there. Trust me. I know."

Raven coughed and swallowed and blew her nose again. "You're right. Her showing up could be about actually needing to learn her new job."

"Yes, and to prove that you could call around and see if she's doing the same with the other law enforcement departments in the county." Betty heard how horrible that sounded, especially if it proved Raven's fears, and quickly recanted the advice. "Scratch that. Bad idea. Don't listen to me. It might only be with Marcel, and it would be perfectly normal to ask an old friend, even an old boyfriend, to show her the ropes. Now listen to me—and this is actually good advice—wipe your face one more time, and let's get back to our mystery. It's a good distraction, and we're helping Charles." Betty smiled and handed Raven a clean tissue.

After smoothing back her hair and taking a gulp of water from a water bottle always kept in the cup holder, Raven began to maneuver the Mini back onto the road. She slammed on her brakes to avoid a shiny black SUV with Massachusetts plates speeding by, at least fifty miles an hour over the speed limit on the winding, narrow coastal road.

"Yikes! Why do all the BMW drivers think they own the road?" Betty said as she gripped the dashboard in front of her.

Raven looked again over her shoulder and ventured out. Within two miles, they pulled into the gravel driveway of an old Cape-style home set up on a hill with a sliver of a view of the ocean. The red paint on the clapboards was peeling, and the white trim also needed a re-do, but a bright orange mum greeted them in a chipped planter on the front step. There were no cars in the driveway.

Before they were out of the car, the front door opened. A frail elderly woman in a thin, light blue house coat with silver snaps stood behind the glass storm door. Her white hair was short and wild. Too old to be Laurie's mother, Betty thought, hoping she wouldn't look like this woman when she was the same age. A high-pitched yip from a small dog drifted out.

Raven waved and shouted. "Hi, Mrs. Luft!"

Quietly, Betty said, "That's Laurie's mother?"

"Great-Great-Grandmother."

"Whew. I was wondering if I looked that bad, too."

Betty received a small smile from Raven and took that as a reminder to remember that she wasn't from around here.

Betty quickly said under her breath, "She looks awesome for a great-great-grandmother!"

"Raven Fossett, I haven't seen you in ages!" said Lorraine Luft, using Raven's mother's maiden name, as she held open the screen door. "What brings you over to this neck of the woods?" She smiled a toothless grin. Betty assumed, and hoped, Mrs. Luft just hadn't had time yet to put in her teeth.

As the door opened, the extremely small dog, maybe a chihuahua mix, ran out, yapping and running zigzag between their legs.

"Jackie. Get over here." Mrs. Luft called out. "Treat. Cookie. Chew. Snack."

The dog stopped on the word 'snack,' and Raven bent down and scooped it up. She then stepped up on the concrete landing and gave Mrs. Luft a peck on the cheek as she handed Jackie back to Mrs. Luft's outstretched arms.

"We were hoping to see Laurie. Is she home?" Raven smiled in a way that reminded Betty of her daughters selling Girl Scout cookies, friendly but direct. "Would that be two boxes of Tagalongs or three?"

Mrs. Luft shook her head. "That girl is off working. What a hard worker she is."

Raven nodded. "She definitely is. Cleaning houses still?"

"Yep." Mrs. Luft stroked Jackie, who squirmed. Probably waiting for his treat. Or was it a snack?

"Any idea whose house she's at?" Most likely, it belonged to a person from away, and only Laurie would be in the house this time of year. Betty was glad that Raven had the idea to track her down there.

"Nah. I never know where she is." Lorraine steadied herself. "Wait, she said something about going down to Whale Harbor and enjoying the view while she cleaned."

That made sense. That's where all the muckety-mucks lived, according to Howard, who didn't consider himself one despite their bank account.

Howard's voice echoed in Betty's head, chastising her as usual. "Betty, just because we have money doesn't mean we have to spend it or look like we have it. Especially up here." Was it a crime she loved her designer purses or chic tennis outfits? Did it make her a bad person that she missed some glitz of living in Connecticut? She hadn't appreciated the sophistication when she had it.

Raven turned to Betty, "We could drive along the point and look for her car at all the houses on the water."

"Sounds like a plan to me." Betty smiled at Lorraine. "Do you know what kind of car she drives?"

"A red car." Lorraine stroked Jackie's ears.

"That'll do," said Raven.

How helpful, thought Betty. A red car with Maine plates. Well, most likely not a red Porsche or Mercedes. Based on the condition of the house, they were probably looking for some rusty old thing without hubcaps in front of a waterfront mansion. That should actually be easy to find.

You're a snob and a boar, Betty said to herself. Why can't a hard-working cleaning woman have a nice car?

She looked back at Mrs. Luft's kind face. So what if the house wasn't painted. That took time and money, neither of which these people might have enough of. Betty wondered when she became so negative and judgmental. She lived in a beautiful place and was becoming ugly.

Raven and Betty drove in silence back down the coastal road. Whale Harbor had been one of the best-kept secrets of the Maine Coast until the past ten years or so. For well over a century, many had already flocked and saturated Boothbay, Camden, and Kennebunkport, among other seacoast Maine towns. Now Whale Harbor was getting slammed. Acre upon acre of trees had been cut down despite the state law of not clear-cutting along the coast. Those with the money coming in from southern New England, New York, New Jersey, and the Mid-Atlantic states came for one reason: to see the ocean. There was no way they were going to allow Maine legislators in Augusta to cause a pine tree to block part of their view on the estate they just spent millions on. Betty didn't understand the logic. If they wanted a coast that looked like the southern United States with its stripped shoreline, they should have moved to the Carolinas or Florida.

She once heard someone say at Lane's that they would do what they wanted with their land and just claim they didn't know if asked about it. Or blame it on the contractor, one had replied back. Even though Betty missed more of an urban bustle, she respected the environmental laws that protected Maine and kept it beautiful.

She was grateful Raven was driving. The roads in Whale Harbor were narrow, with no shoulder or painted line down the middle. They curved this way and that, often with a blind corner or hill. Raven had taken a left to drive down to the dead-end section where the Whale Harbor Lighthouse stood at the bottom. Famous for its depiction on stamps, postcards, and articles about Maine, it had stood as a beacon for centuries to warn cargo ships and fishermen about the dangerous rocks. Now Betty saw it almost as an evil demon who had accidentally signaled to too many to move to this great peninsula. Maybe evil was too strong a word as it hadn't done anything intentionally or against its nature.

There were many dirt roads shooting right and left off the road to the lighthouse. All marked private. Betty knew at the end, each one opened up to the cliffs and were littered with houses that you could only see by boat. Laurie's car could be anywhere among these homes.

Raven took the first right and drove down to the end, passing four or five driveways before hitting the shore and three additional driveways. No red cars in any of them.

She drove back up to the paved road and turned down the next dirt one.

Nothing. Then the next. Three times a charm, and on Indian Ledge Road, they hit pay dirt. The large mansion at the bottom took up three lots and had a shiny red Toyota SUV in the driveway with a Maine plate and two bumper stickers. One sticker said "Eat Lobster. Support Maine Lobstermen." The other said "A clean house is a clean heart."

Chapter Twenty-Four

"There she is!" Betty yelled, pointing to the SUV. Raven swung the Mini Cooper into the spot next to it. She wasn't as confident as Betty sounded, although this was probably Laurie's vehicle.

Before getting out of the car, Raven craned her head to take in the house. The seaside mansion stretched before them, more wide than high. Its wood-clad boards were painted light grey. Like Maine's coast needed another grey-painted house. Obviously owned by a person from away. No Mainer would ever paint their house this dull color. Instead, they'd let the natural shingles take their course, fading beautifully with age and the weather, fitting right into the area and needing minimum upkeep. It was bad enough to have to paint trim every couple of years.

To the left was a looming two-car garage, which was also something not common among Mainers, despite the winters. Even those with garages parked their vehicles outside because the inside was full of snowmobiles, tractors, kayaks, and other more important things than a car. At least this garage was a separate structure. She never understood the garages that were attached to houses. Getting in and out of your car, or garage, was an opportunity to wave to your neighbors.

A thick glass door appeared as the only entrance into the house from the back. Betty had already walked up to it to peer in, her hands cupped up to her eyes to block out the sunlight from interfering.

"Do you see anyone?" Raven said.

Betty shook her head and kept looking. She stepped back and tried the door. It opened.

Turning back with the door handle still in her hand, Betty looked at Raven and shrugged. "Shall we?" Motioning with her hand for them to enter the house.

"How about just calling into the house first?" Raven joined Betty on the stoop.

Betty nodded. Propping the door open with her elbow, she cupped her hands around her mouth to mimic a bullhorn. "Hello?" She yelled in and waited. Silence. She tried again, louder. "Helllloooooo?"

A faint "hello" came back, followed by "Coming."

Both Betty and Raven stepped back to allow whomever it was to have room to come out.

Laurie Eldridge, her face red from either coming quickly or scrubbing something, came to the door. Seeing Raven, she smiled, waved, and stepped out.

"Hey, Raven. How are you?" Then, her face clouded. "Is everything okay? Did something happen to Nana?"

All legitimate concerns with having an aging great-great grandmother at home and unlikely visitors who come to find you at work.

"Your nana is awesome," said Betty, a little too enthusiastically. Raven knew that Betty was gearing up to plunge into an interrogation and wanted to damp her down.

"Yes," said Raven, touching Betty's arm as a signal to cool it. "We're just..." now it felt odd to be there..." following up on some..."

Raven was struck by how odd it felt to be facing Laurie after years of distance. Not that anything specific occurred. Just life moving on.

"Leads," said Betty, ignoring Raven's touch.

"Leads? For what?"

Raven sighed. Betty had the patience of a bucking bronco. Now Laurie had her guard up. Raven tried to backpedal.

"Just "I" dotting and "T" crossing."

"We talked to Karl." Betty blurted out. Raven closed her eyes. This was not only going to go nowhere, they were creating a town enemy.

"Karl? So what?" Laurie snapped at them, her eyes flashing in anger and her lips tightening. "It's none of your goddamn business what Karl and I do."

Betty stepped back, shocked at Laurie's outburst. Raven, not surprised at the snarl, stayed put.

"Laurie, we're not here to judge. Just to confirm you were Charles Kearns' cleaning person," Raven said.

"What do you mean 'was'? I still am." She shoved her hands into her apron pockets. "Or did he send you here to fire me, the wimp?"

"Oh, you may not have heard yet," Betty started. Again, Raven cut her off.

"Sorry to share this news, Laurie, but Charles Kearns has passed away."

Laurie's anger turned to shock.

"What? When?"

Raven continued. "We're not sure yet on the details. When was the last time you were in his house?"

Laurie softened. "Mid-October, I think. He was coming up for the Halloween bonfire, and he asked if I could make the second floor a bit livable for him. You know the place is a disaster with the chimney construction. So much dust."

Raven nodded in agreement.

Laurie went on. "And he isn't much of a neat freak either. Always leaving food around, and wrappers. I try to warn him about mice." She paused and looked at her feet. "Tried. I tried to warn him."

Raven nodded again, thinking of the mess in his office-bedroom. It was obvious that Laurie hadn't been back since mid-October based on the amount of garbage that she and Johnny found.

Laurie gathered herself and continued. "He told me he'd let me know when he was coming back up for the holidays. I had told him it was wasteful for me to clean for him regularly with all the construction going on if he wasn't going to be there. He loved that plan, but I never heard from him before Thanksgiving. I assumed he stayed in Boston."

"When did you start working for him?" Raven smiled, hoping that Laurie was understanding that she and Betty were truly not the Secretly Finger Pointing Committee.

"I came recommended from the previous owners," Laurie said, becoming defensive again, narrowing her eyes at Raven.

"Oh, so you've had access to that hiding place in the chimney for a while then," said Betty.

Betty! Raven's jaw tightened. How could she have done such a great interview with Karl and now be totally blowing it with Laurie?

"What are you saying?" Laurie's voice raised, and she stood defiantly with her hands on her plump hips, her weight and anger aging her although she was close to Raven's age of thirty-five.

Raven wanted to give Betty the "cut it" sign by slicing her hand across her throat, but she didn't want to cause more drama. Instead, she rushed to again calm Laurie down.

"Laurie, we don't care about what you do with anyone. Honestly. That's not the point of our visit. Like I said, we're just dotting some "i's." Thanks for confirming you hadn't been in Charles' house since before the bonfire. Sorry to bother you, and sorry to bring bad news. Thank you for the help."

Raven turned and started walking back to her car, her feet crunching on the white stone driveway. Betty mumbled a thank you, finally realizing the need to keep it to a minimum.

"Wait," said Laurie, calling out to them. "Why is it important—the last time I was in the house?"

Betty stood outside the Mini, waiting for Raven to respond. Before she had a chance to, a black BMW SUV with Massachusetts plates screeched down the dirt road and entered the driveway at such a speed it kicked up white rocks. One pinged off of Raven's Mini side panel. It was the same idiot who almost ran into her by the scenic turn-off.

Raven stared as a middle-aged, balding man exiting his SUV wearing casual clothes that implied Boston or NYC in both their style and newness. He slammed the door shut with his large hands and lumbered toward the house, ignoring her and Betty standing outside her car.

"This damn place. Nothing's open." His round, red face showed pock marks from prior acne. His black hair was slicked close to his head. 'Closed for the weekend.' It's just Thanksgiving, for Christ's sake." He seemed oblivious to Raven and what damage he may have done to her car.

Laurie's demeanor completely changed upon seeing him. She gave him a huge smile and held the door for him to enter.

"Hi, Mr. Billoni. I'm almost finished." She glanced at Raven and glared as the reason she wasn't finished.

Billoni?

"Nick Billoni?" Betty called out. Raven held her breath.

Chapter Twenty-Five

Deputy Sheriff Tom Pinkham had just pulled into the local donut shop in Eelsboro when his cell phone rang. The caller ID said "State Crime Lab."

"Hello, gorgeous," he said as he swiped to accept the call.

"Now, how'd you know it was me," said a friendly female voice with a giggle.

"I'm all-knowing," he spoke as he exited the SUV. He knew it was a terrible stereotype for a cop to be getting a coffee and a donut, but he was hungry and tired, and this joint gave it to him for free.

"It could have been my boss," said Lucille Stanford, director of the Maine State Crime Labs. She giggled again.

"But it wasn't," said Tom. He also knew that Lucy's position was as high up as it went at the crime lab. He doubted the police commissioner, whom she reported to, would be calling from a crime lab phone should he ever need to reach Tom. Tom had never spoken personally to the Commissioner and didn't even remember what he looked like. In fact, he could be standing behind him right now in the coffee lane and not know it.

He peered slightly around the lobsterman who stood in front of him and looked up to the next customer, a family of five with designer clothes that screamed Boston. Nope, definitely not the police commissioner.

He normally liked to talk on a mobile phone on speaker, but he had shut that function off when he had entered the cafe to keep matters confidential. "So, what's up?" he said as he waited his turn.

"I got your gun info," said Lucy and then deepened her voice. "Maybe you should come get the info in person."

He grinned. Now that was a great idea. Except Augusta was about sixty minutes in one direction, and Marcel made it clear he wanted to know the information as soon as possible, mainly to keep the State Police from barging in.

"I wish I could, Lucy. Hold on a sec." He lowered the phone from his face and ordered a large hot coffee, light and sweet, and a jelly donut.

"Where are you?" Her voice was still husky.

"Getting a coffee." No need to get further into it.

"And a donut. I could hear you, you know. You better watch your figure, Deputy Pinkham, otherwise no one else will."

"Hey, that's my line."

"Where do you think I learned it?"

Tom stepped aside to wait for his order. "So, really now, what have you learned about…the thing." His uniform and vehicle were enough to scare people without saying 'gun' out loud.

"Are you sitting down?"

"Yeah." He lied.

"That gun you found on Whale Beach? I still need to run a couple of more tests to be one hundred percent, but I wanted to give you the heads up that it's most likely a match for the bullet markings in the bones found in the woods."

He grabbed the waxed bag with the donut and the paper cup of coffee and nodded thanks to the cashier. He needed to be in his vehicle to ask more questions. He didn't want to risk being overheard.

Once settled back in his SUV, he continued. "Let me make sure I get this straight. The gun we found at Whale Beach is the same one that shot Charles Kearns." Now, they were getting somewhere.

"We believe so."

That pointed to a local in his eyes. Not a hitman from Boston like Johnny had floated as an idea. Find out who owned the gun, if it was registered, and they'd find the killer. Case closed in two days. Tickety-boo, to quote his long passed Canadian grandfather.

"There's more," Lucy said and waited as Tom gulped coffee to help swallow the donut crumbs and then sneezed as the powdered sugar went up his nose.

"More?" He sniffled to push the sugar out. Ugh.

"Guess who the gun belonged to?" Lucy continued to keep her voice low and flirty.

"Santa Claus." He hated guessing.

"Nope." She giggled.

"Jesus."

"Nope. One more guess."

He sighed.

"Your mother."

With this guess, she roared with laughter. "Oh, that's a good one. Except the only person she might be interested in shooting is you for not marrying me."

"Oh, jeezem crow." Tom had met Lucy's mother once, and she practically took her own wedding ring off for Tom to give to Lucy after only one date. "Just tell me who owns the gun. Please."

"The gun belongs to Peter Poole. And it's registered in Secretly."

"Peter Poole? Hmmm. Wonder who that is? I know a bunch of Pooles, but I don't know of any Peter Pooles. Oh wait. Peter Poole! That's Rusty Poole!"

Rusty Poole. The lobsterman who had run off with Sarah Wolfe in July. No one had seen him in months. His wife Evelyn was a cashier at Lane's. She'd been looking forlorn ever since he left town. Poor thing.

So, Rusty came back in October or November and shot Charles Kearns? Why would he do that, and where was he now?

"You still there?" Lucy's voice came through the car Bluetooth as Tom drove away from the donut shop in Eelsboro and headed towards Secretly and Marcel. He had radioed him without response and decided to swing by the house.

"Yeah. Thanks, Lucy. Let me know what else you come up with."

"Okay." He heard the flat tone in her voice, disappointed either because their conversation was ending or because they had no plans for meeting up for a fun time. He was sure there weren't too many law enforcement officers who were willing to flirt with the head of the state crime lab.

Tom ran through the top reasons for killing someone, specifically in Maine. Most Maine murders were between two people who knew each other. Usually a domestic violence crime, sadly. There was too much of that in Maine. And domestic didn't mean romantic. It meant someone you knew, like a tenant strung out on heroin, killing landlords who were evicting him, a drug addict son murdering his parents to inherit, and those in the drug trade killing each other.

Other usual motives for killing besides domestic issues or money involved jealousy and lust. And hiding something, usually concealing another crime.

Secretly was small. Chances are Rusty Poole and Charles Kearns knew each other and had run into each other somewhere. Charles definitely would know Evelyn Poole both from shopping at Lane's—Charles lived next door to the store—or even seeing her get in and out of her truck in the store parking lot.

But what relationship could Rusty have had with Charles? Did Charles try to date Evelyn? Tom pictured Evelyn—a little dumpy with mousy brown hair and not the brightest light on the Christmas tree, as his Grandmother would have said. He usually used himself as a measuring stick on personal matters, and he would not sleep with her, so he figured Charles, too, wouldn't have bothered to get mixed up with a married woman who wasn't that desirable.

There was Rusty's supposed mistress, Sarah Wolf, who was also a cashier at Lane's. She was married to Karl Wolf, the marine store owner, but Karl didn't seem to care about Sarah fooling around. In fact, he didn't even seem to notice the couple of times before their wedding when Sarah was "at her mother's," and she was actually at Tom's. That was a couple of years ago, though. Tom had suspected Sarah was seriously "shopping" for a new guy, and he ended any tête-à-têtes with her quickly. No surprise she ran off with Rusty for his bankroll, but maybe she also was stringing Charles along, Boston money and all. Of course, everyone in town suspected Karl, too, had someone on the side, but while Karl might not care who Sarah bedded down with, Rusty might be crazy enough about Sarah to not want to share her with a third guy.

If Charles and Sarah were having an affair, did that mean he'd come across Sarah's body too one of these days? Did Rusty get rid of both of them? Maybe they were killed together, and a coyote relocated one of the bodies. This wasn't the last of the story; that's all Tom knew. It only opened up more questions.

Then he thought, what if the motive for murdering Charles wasn't lust but secrecy? Did Charles discover something Rusty wanted hidden?

He remembered the video of the Lane Mansion that Raven had taken with Johnny. Marcel mentioned wanting Tom to compare it to the one Tom took on Wednesday night. He was going to the Ouellettes anyway, since he hadn't heard back from Marcel yet. If Raven was home, they could watch both videos then.

Tom drove the back way into Secretly. It took him past Johnny's property, a small white Cape on a former goat farm. The barn still stood, as did many other outbuildings. Tom guessed that Johnny kept a riding mower in the barn and not much else.

He slowed and glanced through the trees. Johnny's truck stood in the driveway. He swung in to say hello.

Chapter Twenty-Six

The large, angry man froze in the doorframe, his open windbreaker with the polo rider emblem flapping in the breeze. He slowly turned back and narrowed his eyes at the two women by the Mini Cooper. "Yes, I am Nicholas Billoni." He spat the words out in staccato form. "What's it to you?"

Betty stepped forward with her hand extended.

"Betty Hart," she said, giving him her widest and most charming smile. "From Secretly, just up the road, formerly from Essex, Connecticut." She threw around her fancy Southern New England roots whenever needed.

Nick backed out of the doorway and stepped off the landing to shake her hand, still not smiling. Laurie stood on the step, still holding the door, her mouth agape. Which word roped him in? Connecticut? Or, specifically, Essex? There was a lot of money in Essex, Connecticut, and the surrounding Connecticut shoreline and river towns. Maybe Nick saw it as a business opportunity to be gracious to Betty. Raven was impressed.

"I'm glad to see you up here, getting some much-needed R&R." Betty continued smiling, her voice a bit singsong, like a sorority girl reeling in a frat boy. She motioned behind her without losing his gaze. "This is my neighbor, Raven Ouellette. She owns Pine Acres, that adorable camp on Duck Puddle Road. She elevates the word "glamping" to a new meaning." Her smile widened.

He finally smiled back at Betty and nodded toward Raven. Betty knew how to work a man, that's for sure. Raven could use some lessons from her if Shannon McGrath became more of a problem.

"Her husband is the local county sheriff, Marcel Ouellette, by the way. Should you need him." Betty continued to smile. "In case any reporters have followed you up here."

Now his eyes focused like lasers on Betty, and his smile vanished. Replacing it were tight lips that sneered over excessively white, straight teeth, like a wolf ready to pounce.

"Why would reporters be following me?" His voice was low, almost too low for Raven to hear.

Betty continued as if nothing had changed in his demeanor. "We get news up here, Mr. Billoni. We know how your name has been dragged through the mud over some silly math calculations. Someone trying to make a name for himself."

Nick relaxed again. "Exactly. That's exactly it." He slapped his right leg. "Where were you when I needed some good defense and an uplifting talk?" He chuckled and winked.

Betty mirrored his laugh and raised her hands to the sky. "I'm here now."

What a flirt she was! Raven dared to walk closer to Betty.

"You should have come up here sooner," said Betty. "When was the last time you treated yourself to your beautiful Maine home?"

Boy, she was sly. Sneaking it in to find out when Nick had been here. They could double-check this with the information Johnny received from his friend in Boston.

"I wasn't aware that the locals would be supporting me. All of Boston has gone soft. I forget Mainers are stalwarts."

Betty gave him a Cheshire Cat grin. "That we are."

Raven wasn't sure what he meant by calling her a stalwart. She was against big business, just like other people, if that was what he was implying.

"I've been hiding out at sea," he said, laughing. "My in-laws have a house on one of those South Carolina islands that don't seem much like an island to me if you can drive to it."

"I totally agree." Betty wasn't going to let him slip off her fishing line.

"And then I took my parents—the whole family actually, my wife and kids and my siblings and their kids too—on a month-long Mediterranean cruise for my parents' sixtieth wedding anniversary. We just got back on Monday in time for Thanksgiving turkey."

Betty clasped her hands together in enthusiasm and held them against her heart. "What a son! I'm sure you made your mother cry."

He leaned closer and whispered with a chuckle. "I'll be honest. The timing was perfect. Between the publicity and Halloween, there was no better timing to be out of dodge."

"You were in Europe for Halloween?"

"Yeah, sipping Negroni while Boston's running around in costumes, ringing doorbells, throwing tiny, wrapped chocolates into plastic pumpkins. I hate Halloween."

Betty nodded and whispered back, putting her right hand to her mouth in case a little one overheard her. "Me too."

Raven hadn't had a trick-or-treater in ten years, and she knew Betty hadn't either. The kids in Secretly all did Trunk or Treat now, or whatever they called it, in the firehouse parking lot. Besides, the houses were too far apart to walk to them, and most parents didn't want to drive the kids around.

"Well, I don't want to keep you from enjoying your time up here. And how nice you have Laurie making sure the place is spit spot."

"Who?" Billoni squinted.

"Laurie." She motioned with her chin to the young woman still standing on the step, still holding the door, still in shock with her mouth open. Betty lowered her voice as softly as it would go. "Your cleaning lady."

Nick threw his head back with a laugh. "Ah!" He whispered back. "Laurie. Thanks." He straightened. "Nice to meet you both."

"Same here." Betty gave a little wave even though he was only two feet away.

He started up the stone driveway and turned back

"And I hope I don't need your husband," he said to Raven.

She cleared her throat. "I hope so, too."

On the drive back to Secretly, Betty and Raven ran through the Nick conversation.

"You know, just because he was in Europe on a boat for four weeks doesn't mean he didn't get off at a port, fly into Portland, drive up here, shoot Charles, and fly back to the boat." Betty's excitement over the Nick conversation remained, and she barely sat still in her seat despite the buckle. "When Howard and I went on a Caribbean cruise, we got off the boat at least six times. In the Mediterranean, he could have disembarked in Nice or Naples or—"

"Or," said Raven, "he made himself an airtight alibi with that cruise and had Sammy the Shark do his dirty work while he was out of the country."

"Oh, I like that even better." Betty clapped. "Actually, his passport would scan in and out if he came back. Scrap my theory. Even if he landed in Montreal and walked into Vermont, Canada would still have to scan it."

Raven hadn't thought of bypassing US Customs by walking in through Canada, but she assumed it was quite possible in many places on the northern border.

Betty continued her theorizing. "Or Quebec City. That is closer to Maine. That would be the more likely airport to fly into. He could have a fake passport. Maybe even a Canadian one. He's rich enough and connected enough." Betty fantasized about Nick the Gun Man.

"Then he wouldn't need to walk across the US border in the woods. He could just drive through with his fake Canadian passport." Raven added.

"You're right. We should have asked to see his ID. I wonder what he would have done."

"Probably slugged us. Or called the police, which means Tom or Marcel would have come and found us there." The last thing that Raven needed was Marcel finding her in the middle of the investigation.

"But they would have asked him for ID, and then they could have seen his fake passport." Betty's index fingers were extended like an orchestra conductor, highlighting her point.

"Which we don't know if he has, and he would have coughed up his Massachusetts driver's license anyway."

"True. Darn." Betty sat back in the seat and watched the pine trees whip by and then perked up. "We could ask Laurie to look for the passport."

"Betty," said Raven, halting the speculation from going down the wrong road, "I don't think he used a fake passport to get into Canada and walk into Maine or anywhere to kill Charles. Let's table him for maybe hiring a hitman, but nothing more."

"You're right, you're right. I'm getting carried away…because if he had a fake Canadian passport, he'd just fly back into Boston anyway and drive up with his own car. We could check the electronic tolls."

"I'm sure Johnny's friend is checking that."

"When will Johnny have the information from his friend?"

"Maybe this afternoon."

"We could swing by now."

"We could." Raven had no appetite for going to Johnny's. She actually had never been to his house despite being invited many times over the past two years. She told herself that it was because she needed to keep her distance literally in order to keep her distance emotionally, but if she was honest with herself, she also didn't want to feel bad seeing his cold and lonely existence. Not that he didn't deserve that. He did. She just didn't want to visualize it.

"I actually liked him," said Betty. "Nick." She clarified when Raven shot her a puzzled look. "He doesn't seem like a scum ball contractor to me."

"What does a scum ball contractor seem like?" Raven hit the brakes to allow a line of turkeys to cross the road without needing to take flight. It was always awkward watching a wild turkey fly, even though they were quite good at it. So good, actually, they flew up to roost in the trees every night, but there was something about their rapid, awkward take off that always bothered Raven and made her squirm—that large round bottom coming off the ground. She always expected the wings to give out with the heavy lift, but so far in her life, she had only seen successful turkey flyers. Still, she didn't need to force the issue and always gave them a wide berth to simply cross the road by walking.

Betty chuckled. "I was about to say a scum ball contractor looks like an Italian mobster, so I guess Nick does fit that bill, more or less. I suspect it's his charm that helped him get ahead."

"Maybe for all of those city contracts." Raven mused over that option. Betty might be sucked in by him, but to Raven, he was just a bigwig, pushing his weight around. Wouldn't a city councilman feel the same? Raven guessed it depended on what was in it for the councilman.

"But from what Howard read to us this morning, it sounded like his charm ran out." Betty pointed into the woods as they sped up. "Fisher cat. Or is it just fisher?"

"Fisher." The lean black animal slinked across the road ahead.

"Fisher cat sounds better. Well, the name, not their sound." She chuckled again. "Do you think they were tracking the turkeys?"

"I don't think that's in their wheelhouse. Maybe just the poulets when they're around."

"The what?"

"Poulets. Baby turkeys. In the Spring. They're grown turkeys now and blend in with the rest."

"Oh, I learned a new word today!" Betty clapped her hands together like a two-year-old getting a new balloon.

This was the second time Betty clapped today. Was Howard right in his fear that she was regressing into a simpler state? Or was she just delighted to be out doing something? Regardless, Raven noticed a happier Betty.

"Nick doesn't seem the worse for wear for having to pay out thirteen billion dollars, or whatever it was," said Raven. She couldn't imagine how much money that really was.

"Maybe that's just a drop in the bucket for him. More of an insult to his reputation than a hole in his wallet?"

"That could mean he has a whole lot of money hidden somewhere." Raven steered the Mini toward Johnny's road.

"Hmmm, maybe that's what he'd like to protect more than his reputation— his bank account. Oh look, Marcel's here." Betty commented on seeing the country sheriff's SUV in Johnny's driveway as they drove up it.

"That's Tom's car," said Raven. For a brief moment, she hoped Johnny was okay. Of course, he was. She pushed any feelings of concern for Johnny away.

Betty's thoughts were still on Nick. "I'll bet his next cruise will be to the Cayman Islands or Bermuda," she said.

"Why's that?" Raven parked the Mini next to the SUV.

"Money laundering," Betty said with an obvious tone.

"I think you watch too many crime dramas."

But at least Nick's next cruise would have a business purpose, thought Raven. To go on a cruise as a vacation was the last thing Raven would ever want to do.

Chapter Twenty-Seven

Johnny moved into the 1840 Cape Cod-style house when he came back to Secretly after his retirement from the Boston police force. He initially had envisioned, even if unrealistically, reuniting with Julia and getting to finally know Raven. He knew that he had a lot of apologizing to do, a lot of years to make up for, and a lot of explaining, but he also knew, at the very least, he had been fiscally responsible to Julia and Raven with his monthly payments. Julia had never acknowledged or thanked him for a dime. Not that he deserved thanks—he definitely didn't—but it wasn't every deserting drunk of a husband and father who mailed away half of his paycheck every month.

By the time he retired, however, and moved back up to Maine, Julia had passed away. He wasn't totally surprised that Raven hadn't told him about Julia's death or hadn't invited him, years prior, to her wedding to Marcel, or updated him on her life in general. He wasn't totally surprised, but if he allowed himself to admit it, he was a little surprised. After all, he had done the best he could to help support her while working like a dog and getting himself sober. It signaled to him how hurt and angry Raven was for her entire upbringing. Again, he couldn't blame her or Julia. He owned it.

Since moving back, he took advantage of every crack in Raven's thick armor and every opportunity to be around her to show his sincerity. He never brought up the monthly payments, and neither did she. He heard Marcel whisper to her once, "He's a nice guy. Give him a chance," when they were in their kitchen. He had also heard her response: "Easy for you to say."

He knew the destructive nature of resentment, and if he was a religious man, he'd have prayed for Raven's soul. He simply hoped for the best for her, for him, and for their relationship, and kept trying.

In the two years he had lived in Secretly, he had never had a visitor to his home. He had invited Raven multiple times, most of the invites were met with silence. After the first year, he gave up asking her. Now, as he was putting the mayonnaise jar back in the fridge, he heard tire tracks on the dirt driveway.

Peering out the front window, he saw Tom Pinkham exiting his sheriff's county SUV. What brought him? His breathing quickened. He hoped Raven and Marcel were okay.

"Tommy!" He called out, opening his front door. He felt braver meeting whatever news it was head-on.

"Hey Johnny, I hope I'm not interrupting," said Tom, carrying his coffee cup in with him.

"Not at all. Just about to have a bologna sandwich. Would you like one?"

"Sure," he said, brushing errant powdered sugar and donut crumbs off of his blue sheriff shirt. "Always up for eating. I haven't had bologna in years."

"Excellent! And how about a refresher on that coffee, too? I have a pot already on."

Johnny always had a pot of coffee on. That's what kept him from drinking other stuff. Never the decaffeinated junk. High test all the way.

As he pulled out the luncheon meat, he still wondered what brought the deputy to his door. He hadn't lapsed on his car registration or his sobriety. It had to be about Raven or Marcel. He'd let Tommy do his job and tell him in his own way, although the suspense was making his heart pound. His doctor had warned him about getting worked up. Usually not an issue. His natural demeanor was calm and relaxed. That's what helped him be a good cop. Hard to rattle him. But this anxiety over potentially bad news about Raven or Marcel surprised him and also pleased him. Not that he doubted his feelings for them, but this proved how important they were to him. He wondered if they'd feel the same hearing bad news about him.

"I hope you don't mind me just barging in," said Tom.

"Not at all." Twice now apologizing, thought Johnny. It must be real bad.

He breathed deep to say, "Mayo or mustard?"

"Both, if you don't mind."

"Mind? Never." As Johnny reached for the condiments on the refrigerator door, the sound of more tires on the dirt driveway signaled a second vehicle. It must be Marcel to tell him about Raven. Jeezum crow, this was really bad.

He held his breath and rushed to the door. Raven's Mini Cooper had parked next to Tommy's SUV. She and Betty were already out and walking towards the door. They looked fine. Betty was smiling and laughing. Marcel must be okay, too, then. Deep breath back in. Shoulders down from the ears. Too much old work trauma, always assuming the worst. But what the heck finally got Raven to his house?

"Wow," Johnny said, flinging open the door. "Had I known I was having a party, I would have gotten a cake!"

Raven looked up at him and smiled slightly. Betty, however, gave a huge grin.

"Cake? Did you say cake? I love cake."

"I could make brownies." He chuckled, thinking of the box mix in his pantry.

"Got any vanilla ice cream?" Betty's eyes widened. "Brownie sundaes!"

Raven had already entered the house. He never thought he'd see the day when she'd walk down his hallway, but there she was, heading for his kitchen. She passed him with only a nod. Not even a hello. Oh, well.

"Great minds think alike," said Tom, rising when he saw Raven and Betty.

"Now if only someone would share these thoughts with me," said Johnny. "Bologna sandwich?"

Raven shook her head no.

"I'd love one," said Betty. "And that brownie, too."

"Coming right up!" Johnny pulled out two more pieces of bread. He grabbed two eggs from the fridge in preparation for the brownie creation.

"I'm only here because I'm waiting on Marcel. I was headed to your house," Tom motioned with his chin towards Raven, "but thought I'd stop in to say hello on my way because I think Marcel's on a call."

"Oh, I'm a time waster, I see." Johnny laughed and frankly, didn't care. It was delightful to have company. "Sit, please." He motioned to his kitchen table and chairs.

"Well, we're here with a real purpose," said Betty as she pulled out a wooden chair and sat next to Tom, folding her hands on top of the table.

Johnny realized that Raven still hadn't said a word yet. She was the driver, so it wasn't like Betty forced her to come here. He coached himself to relax and give Raven time and space. He had said this to himself almost every day for two years. Patience.

"What's your purpose?" Tom took a bite of his sandwich. "Delicious, Johnny. Thank you. Just like my mom used to make me as a kid."

"I'm delighted." Johnny beamed and handed Betty her sandwich. "Are you sure, Raven, I can't get you anything?"

She shook her head again. "No thanks." She remained stiff, still standing in the kitchen.

Betty accepted the sandwich on a plate. "Thanks." Turning to Tom, she touched his arm and said, "Our purpose is twofold."

Johnny hadn't seen Betty this excited about anything. Purpose did amazing things, he knew that. He pulled a brownie mix from a cupboard and read the back of the box, gathering the rest of the short list of ingredients. He eyed Raven out of the corner of his eye. She had moved next to the kitchen table but still stood, now looking out the picture window into his backyard. Was she taking in the view of the small pond in the back, watching a duck swim, or was she counting the minutes before she could run from his house and speed away in her car? Would he ever get her back here again? He could hope that the Universe was giving him a sign that his luck was changing. He needed to make this visit count just in case this was his only shot. He glanced at the photo hanging on the wall, a picture of him, Julia, and a three-year-old Raven. Had she seen it yet? Should he point it out?

Before he could decide, Betty squirmed in her chair and lightly pounded her fist. "We're nosy. Johnny, did you hear from your Boston contacts about Nick and Sammy the Shark?"

Tom wiped his mouth with a napkin and laughed. "Nothing like getting right to the point."

"Exactly," she smiled. Raven turned her attention back to the room for Johnny's answer.

"One sec!" Johnny called out as he stirred the brownie batter with a wooden spoon. "Forty-eight, forty-nine, fifty! My mother said to never stir muffins or brownies more than fifty times. You make them tough. There. Now you know my baking wizardry secrets!"

He laughed and looked right at Raven, hoping for a smile. Nothing.

He poured the batter into a metal pan and smoothed it out while he shared his news.

"So, yes, I do have information. I had planned on dispersing it today, so sorry for the delay in getting this out to you all." He popped the pan into the heated oven and started a timer.

"I'm on the edge of my seat," said Betty. She literally was.

"I have to admit I am too," said Tom, "but I think it's more for that warm brownie."

He, Betty, and Johnny laughed.

"I agree! With ice cream!" Betty clapped her hands like a three-year-old at a birthday party.

"Let's make this a real party! I'll get out the jimmies, too." Johnny pulled a jar of chocolate sprinkles out of a cabinet. "So, let's confirm the timeline first. Do we know for sure when Charles died?" He looked at Tom.

"Wait." Betty swiveled to also eye Tom. "Do we even know for sure if it was Charles?" She laid a hand on Tom's knee.

"I'm supposed to have all the answers? I've been too busy getting coffee." Tom lifted up his paper coffee cup with a large grin and shifted away from Betty, although her hand somehow still stayed. "Okay, okay, so yes, we do know that it is Charles, sorry to say." He looked over his shoulder at Raven, who grimaced and nodded.

"And the approximate date of death?" Johnny took out four bowls.

"Well, we all know he was at the town bonfire on October 31st. And the decomposition speaks to the end of October or early November. Since no one remembers seeing him after the bonfire, we're saying November 1st as the date for now until we get his cell carrier's complete information."

Johnny took a kitchen chair and flipped it around. He crossed his arms on the top of its back and rested his chin on his hands.

"Here's the scoop that I have. The Boston PD fished a body out of Boston Harbor on October 30. It was bloated, like it had been in the water for a couple of weeks. Bullet hole in the head. Execution style. Based upon the fingerprints, they IDed the poor sucker as one Raymond Samarci. Also known as Sammy the Shark."

Betty gasped and threw her hands up to her mouth.

Chapter Twenty-Eight

"Well, that crosses one suspect off the list," said Betty.

Tom nodded but didn't add anything. He checked his phone and then put it back on the table.

"That also puts Nick Billoni in the hot seat." Betty smiled a bit like the Cheshire Cat again, Raven thought, banking this newly discovered information about Betty; in case Betty ever personally gave her a look like that, then she'd know that Betty was holding something back.

Johnny shrugged. "My sources swear Nick was on a cruise from mid-October to mid-November. Sounds crazy to me to be on a cruise ship that long, but that's what I got."

"A cruise ship sounds like a set-up alibi to me," said Tom. "He could have disembarked at any port and flew to Maine."

"I thought the same thing," said Johnny. "And asked the same thing. There is no record of his passport being scanned back into the US until this past Monday."

Betty's eyes glowed. She glanced at Raven. "Can I say?"

"Of course," said Raven, nodding. Betty was the one who pried the information out of Nick, and it wasn't Raven's place to feel ownership for any of the details. The last thing she wanted was for this event to be a part of her life. Since Wednesday, too much sadness had crept in—Charles' body, Johnny's ever presence, Marcel and Shannon. She swallowed deeply. Concentrate on Betty.

"So, we have our own news, Raven and I." She pointed to Raven and back to herself and related how hunting for Laurie Eldridge led them to track her down at a house she was cleaning for…drumroll…Nick Billoni!

"Really? In Whale Harbor?" Johnny jumped up just as the brownies' timer went off.

"Yep. It's a gorgeous piece of property. Don't you think, Raven?" Before Raven could wager an opinion, Betty gulped in more air and continued. "And while we were there talking to Laurie, guess who drove up?"

"Santa Claus," said Tom, relying again on his favorite answer.

Betty giggled and grabbed Tom's knee again and squeezed. "Nope, silly, and frankly, I feel like Santa Claus myself giving you guys this gift! It was Nick Billoni!"

Tom's eyes widened. Johnny slammed his hands over his face, covering his expression, but the "oh, no" leaked out.

"What? Isn't that great?" Betty's face had hurt and confusion on it. "I thought you guys would be thrilled."

Raven knew the reasoning behind their reactions. Laypeople interrogating a murder suspect before the police did was a sure sign of a guilty person being able to cover his or her tracks. She hoped she and Betty hadn't tipped him off.

"Don't worry about it," said Tom, using his hand to brush away both Betty's hand and any concern. "Tell us what you learned."

"Well," said Betty, her red, puffed-out cheeks coming down a bit in size and color, "we were able to confirm what Johnny's source said. Nick told us he took his whole family, even his extended family, on a European cruise for a month. He only got back Thanksgiving week."

She sat triumphant, again pleased with their work, despite the earlier dismay of Tom and Johnny. She continued.

"And I'm thrilled to hear you've already checked out the possibility of him sneaking in. Any chance he got into Canada and walked across the border? We're debating that as a possibility."

"We're" not debating that, thought Raven. She didn't mean to make it obvious by sighing, rolling her eyes, and shaking her head, so that it showed that it was just Betty's idea, but it was too late. That was how it came across.

Betty glared at Raven. "What? We talked about it." Betty's defenses went up.

Her lip quivered a little, like it did when Howard criticized or challenged her. Maybe Howard was right about Betty's mind slipping. Didn't Raven read somewhere about people needing more psychiatric drugs in their seventies than in their thirties? Not that Betty was psychotic. Just ultra-sensitive lately.

"One scoop or two?" Johnny had four bowls on the counter, each with a dark square in the bottom. He stood poised with a metal ice cream scooper in one hand and a quart of local vanilla ice cream in the other. She realized he was good at diffusing situations, redirecting attention for everyone's benefit. She'd seen him do it even with her when she wasn't giving him an inch or if she ricocheted a grouchy comment off of Marcel. A style like this aided him in being a good cop, even if he wasn't a good dad.

She didn't know if she'd ever be able to forgive him for abandoning her and her mother, for upsetting their apple cart, and making her mother be afraid. The loss of him, his love, and his income. Did that sorrow cause her mother's cancer? Would she still be alive if he hadn't left?

Raven put those questions aside for the time being. "Just one scoop for me, thanks."

Johnny froze briefly, his eyes drilling right into hers. Did he read minds, too, and did he know what she was just thinking? Her face felt hot, but she resisted touching it. He came out of the trance.

"Great! And whipped cream? Jimmies? Unfortunately, I'm fresh out of maraschino cherries. I haven't bought them since I gave up drinking Manhattans." He laughed.

Was it funny? Maybe it was funny because Betty and Tom laughed. It wasn't funny to Raven.

Johnny handed out the bowls. The ice cream and whipped cream partially melted and swirled together over the warm brownie. He put the jimmies container on the table. Raven had to admit the smell was enticing. Her stomach growled, and she realized she hadn't eaten since yesterday.

Before Tom dug into his, he cleared his throat.

"Okay, now it's my turn to share." He smiled, looking like he was slightly embarrassed or uncomfortable, having held back his information while everyone else reported.

"Oh?" Betty's spoon hung in midair, a bit of ice cream dribbling off it. "I hadn't realized you were holding out on us."

His face turned a little pink. "Now, don't turn me into Marcel for telling you this bit of info," he said, eyeing Raven.

Was he blushing because of not telling this group earlier or because he was nervous over telling too much?

"Scout's honor." Johnny held up the three-finger Boy Scout salute. "What happens at Johnny's, stays at Johnny's." His grin widened, and a low chuckle came out.

"Never," said Betty. "Cross my heart and hope to die." She made an 'x' over her heart. "And just for good measure…" she made the sign of the cross, touching her forehead, heart, and both shoulders. "Is it sacrilegious for a Congregationalist to pretend to be Catholic once in a while?" She giggled.

Tom shrugged and then pointed at Raven. "It's this one who needs to commit." He grinned.

Raven finally smiled. "Mum's the word." She motioned her fingers across her lips, mimicking zipping them closed.

"Okay, just want to be sure." He adjusted himself on the kitchen chair. "So, this morning, the state crime lab called me."

"The crime lab? Oh, this is going to be good." Betty cuddled her bowl like it was a bag of popcorn at a suspense movie.

"It is, actually, if I do say so myself," Tom continued. "Anyway, Lucy called." He flushed when saying the woman's name. Raven was surprised Betty didn't pounce on that, but Betty was too focused already on hearing the details of the case, not Tom's love life.

Clearing his throat, he began again. "The crime lab called and said they had analyzed the gun we found in Whale Harbor and had some results."

"Ah! Whale Harbor. Another connection to Nick! I think we should figure out if he really did sneak back into the country." Betty said. Her "we" made the group sound like a Scooby-Doo mystery club. Raven amused herself, pegging Betty as Velma, the short, less attractive one with the glasses, although, Raven had to admit, Velma was the smartest and most level-headed of the bunch. She looked around the room. Johnny or Tom probably had to be Velma based on that definition.

Tom ignored Betty and finished his sentence. "And that the bullets remaining in the gun probably match the wound marks in the bones that were found in the preserve."

"Charles' injuries," Betty said, clarifying.

"Yes."

"We don't want to lose sight that those 'bones,'" she made air quotes, "were actually poor Charles Kearns."

"Totally agree," said Tom. Raven saw him shake off Betty's comment. Tom and Marcel, and the entire force saw too much of everything all the time, and for their own sanity and health, they needed to de-individualize a situation from time to time. Raven knew Tom as being a sensitive law enforcement officer and a caring person. He treated everyone with respect, regardless of age or ethnicity. In fact, some Wabanaki Indians requested Tom by name if they needed a sheriff. They knew he held no prejudice. Losing sight that the bones found in the woods were Charles's was one thing that Tom could never do.

"Was the gun registered?" Johnny ceased eating his sundae and was licking the stickiness off of his fingers.

"Yes, it was." Tom paused, leaving that news to hang in the air.

Betty dropped her spoon. "It was? To whom?"

Tom, appearing less interested in sharing now, perhaps his patience with Betty running thin. Raven had seen the same expression on Howard's face after Betty had corrected or scolded him.

"Are you going to make us beg," Johnny said, laughing. He read the situation Raven assumed. "Or make us sign an affidavit in our own blood?" He chuckled again.

Tom's shoulders relaxed, and he smiled. "The gun belonged to Peter Poole."

"Which Poole is that?" Betty looked from face to face.

Tom added. "Also known to all of us as Rusty Poole."

Johnny sat back in his chair and whistled. "Jeezum crow."

Betty looked again from Tom to Johnny to Raven. "Rusty Poole? The missing guy? The one who ran off with the wife of Wolf Marine? Sarah Wolf? The Lane Market cashier's husband? Evelyn's husband?"

"Yep. One and the same."

Johnny whistled low again.

"He and Sarah have been gone for ages." Betty counted on her fingers. "Something like three to four months. Didn't they run off around the 4th of July? I only remember it because the store was packed with customers, so many tourists in town for the holiday weekend, and Lane's was down to one cashier. Evelyn. She looked exhausted, ringing up all the orders. In fact, I spoke to Chris Lane about it, asking why he hadn't scheduled two cashiers, and he said he had, but Sarah hadn't shown."

Only in a small town could one not only inquire to the store owner about staff but have the owner answer in detail, Raven thought. She wondered if Betty realized what a perfect fit she was for the town, its gossipiness and all. Then Raven's thoughts swirled toward Rusty Poole. He shot Charles Kearns. But could the case be so easily closed? Why did he do it? What made him need to come back to Secretly in the first place? Was it just to kill Charles? Or did Charles see him in town? That seemed too drastic. Unless he was doing something he shouldn't be. There were rumors he stole from other lobstermen's traps. Did Charles accidentally witness that?

Or was it as simple as Charles saw him in town, and Rusty didn't want to be seen by anyone? It wasn't like Rusty was an escaped convict. Evelyn would have questions, of course, and Karl Wolf. Was Sarah Wolf with him? Did they kill Charles together? And where were they both now? On the lam, obviously. It all sounded too dramatic to believe, like a movie.

Johnny's voice pulled her back to the room. "So, what does Marcel think?"

Tom picked up his mobile phone again and looked at the screen. "That's just it. That's why I made you swear not to tell Marcel." He put the phone back on the table and stared at it. "I haven't been able to get ahold of him for over an hour. I've left several messages. So you guys actually know before he does."

Raven felt the nerves in her legs twitch. Marcel not communicating with Tom? Did something happen to Marcel? Was he okay? She made herself breathe. Then a horrible thought, a dark thought that rivaled the possibility of Marcel being hurt, pushed its way through. Her face paled, and the room spun. Maybe, just maybe, he was occupied in a different way.

Chapter Twenty-Nine

The news of Rusty Poole killing Charles was startling but not that startling to cause Raven to turn white and again look out the window, disengaged from the group, Johnny thought. Was it the concept of neighbor killing neighbor that made Raven ill or something else? If he had a close relationship with her, he'd have pulled her aside and asked what was bothering her, even risk injury to his own fragile ego and feelings in case the answer was him. But his fatherly instinct told him this wasn't about him or Charles Kearns but something much deeper and much more painful.

Another incident that impressed Johnny was the fact that she was in his house, and she actually ate something he made. She ate at his kitchen table. He was seated next to her. He could pretend this was how it always was and always had been. If there was a God, please, oh, please, he thought, let this be the first of many times; let this be how it will be from now until it isn't.

Betty sat up straight, beaming. An odd reaction to a murder investigation, but Johnny knew it was because an idea had flickered on in her brain.

"Maybe Nick's responsible after all? Maybe after Sammy the Shark got killed, Nick needed to find a local person to take Charles out?" Betty took out a small notebook from her purse and jotted down a thought. "With modern technology, websites, and all, do you think there is a place now where you can sign up to be a hitman? Kinda like 'Killer Dating' or something like that."

If it wasn't Betty, Johnny'd be worried about the enthusiasm and warped humor surrounding murder. But she did have a point. Could Nick have hired Rusty? He may have known him from the lobster pound in Whale

Harbor. Rusty sold right off his boat, cheap. Most gazillionaires are looking for a bargain. That was how they became gazillionaires.

"I'm not aware of any hitman websites per se, but I'm sure there's an electronic network," said Tom. "Another angle is Rusty had been fined for selling some undersized lobsters. There's also a couple of complaints about him taking catch out of others' traps. Marine Patrol has a thick file on him, so to speak."

"Stealing?" Betty wrote that down. "Maybe Rusty owed money for his drug problem, and that's why he became a hitman."

"Rusty had a drug problem?" Johnny stayed away from any rumors of drunks or addicts in town—helped keep himself clean—but he had never heard of Rusty snorting or anything. He had heard, however, about the lifting of lobsters from traps that weren't tied to his brown and green buoys.

"Just speculating," Betty said, still making notes. "Why else would he be stealing?"

"You know what happens when you assume, right?" Tom said, with more of his deputy sheriff voice than his "I'm everybody's friend" voice. Unlike Johnny, whose laid-back style was part of his DNA, Tom's calmness was more learned behavior.

"I thought this was brainstorming?" asked Betty. Her face clouded, deflated.

"Here's a barnstorming brainstorm idea," said Johnny, keeping it light. "I say, Tommy, we go to talk to Nick while he's in the area." Then he backpedaled. No need to look like he was undermining a sheriff. "Well, I mean you, Tommy. If you think it'd be necessary. Don't mean to tell you what to do."

Tom's face looked relieved at having an option to leave. Maybe the need wasn't to vacate Johnny's house but Betty's biting commentary and frisky hands. He jumped to his feet. Johnny admired Tommy and would love to go out on Tom's lobster boat one day. Despite Tommy's smaller statue, Johnny knew he was incredibly strong and agile.

"No worries at all, Johnny, and I'd love your company. Want to tag along?" Tommy's eyes were as wide as his smile, pushing Johnny out of the kitchenette.

"You don't have to ask me twice. Let me grab a sweatshirt." Johnny's frame wasn't as limber as Tom's, partially due to his almost six-foot stature and partially due to his nearly seventy years of wear and tear on his body. He abused it for many years between the drinking and the police work, and it occasionally paid him back with a tinge in his shoulders or hips. All and all, however, he knew he was fortunate to move as well as he did.

Betty and Raven also rose from the kitchen table.

Tom turned back to Raven. "Oh, I almost forgot. Marcel said you have a video or pics to show me, of when you and Johnny combed through the Lane Mansion. We want to compare yours to the one I took on Wednesday night, to see if anything had been changed."

Raven's face was as serious and blank as when she came in. She nodded. "Yes, I have that."

Johnny studied her clouded expression. She had seemed a bit lighter eating the brownie and ice cream. Did he misread that? Did he say something? He reviewed the last few minutes of conversation in his head. It was mostly Betty and Tommy bantering back and forth. He didn't remember anything he had said, not that it would be the first time he didn't remember saying something, but that usually happened when he drank, not eating ice cream and brownies.

Tom was still talking to Raven. "Is it okay if I come back to your house, after the Nick interview, to look at the videos?"

Betty made a slight huffing sound as if she owned the rights to speak to Nick Billoni. Or as if she needed to be invited to join him and Tommy too, to act as the Nick translator. Poor thing. She really was a nice lady. Johnny thought she just needed more to do. Not everyone adjusts to retirement easily or to moving to the rural parts of Maine.

Raven responded to Tom. "Sure. Come by anytime." She headed out the door first and turned back to Tom. "Have you heard from Marcel yet?"

Tom checked his phone again. "Nope."

She lowered her eyes to the ground and asked. "Any calls about an accident he might be responding to? Or a domestic?"

Tom shook his head.

"Are you worried something might have happened to him?" Betty said in a low voice, touching Raven's arm.

Raven shook her head as Tom responded to Raven's questions.

"No calls have come in this morning except for a couple of speeders," said Tom as he headed for the SUV.

Raven shrugged off Betty's arm and resumed walking towards her Mini. Johnny's eyes followed the back of her head, which was still lowered. She seemed to be studying her feet, stepping carefully, deliberately watching where she planted a foot. Was that what this was about? She was worried about Marcel being hurt, and it had nothing to do with him. Not everything was about him, Johnny reminded himself. People carried many burdens. Not just him, but everyone.

Chapter Thirty

Raven and Betty drove home in silence. Raven's energy for exploring the crime diminished with the news that Marcel wasn't responding to Tom's calls and texts.

If he wasn't on a call, there was only one explanation. Shannon McGrath.

The thought of that name elicited tears to form on the edges of her eyelids. Wet, burning tears that she willed to stay put. She didn't want Betty to see them. She wished she had sunglasses on or was alone in the car. Her chest heaved. She was afraid she was going to explode. The air inside the car was thick and dissipating, like she was buried alive and soon would run out of oxygen. She cracked open her driver's side window a few inches and inhaled the cool November breeze. She regained a bit of her composure.

Betty broke the silence in the car. "So, tell me about Rusty Poole," she said

It wasn't the question that Raven was expecting. Was Betty clueless to Raven's emotions or simply trying to distract her? She wanted to know about Rusty Poole. Who cared about Rusty Poole or Sarah Wolf? They could have each other. All stinking, rotten, cheating people could have each other. They deserved each other. Raven felt her sadness turn to anger. And Karl Wolf deserved too to have Sarah cheat on him since he cheated on her. The whole lot of them could burn in hell for all she cared. Or rot in jail, as in the case of Rusty. Who cared? Even bringing Charles' killer to justice fell off of Raven's list of priorities that she didn't know she had. Who. Cared. Not. Her.

But she didn't say any of those thoughts out loud, and Betty wasn't one to give up despite no response.

Betty prattled on. "I think he's the one I bought two lobsters from a couple of summers ago, right off his boat. The 'Marie Sue.'"

"'Forgotten Sue,' " said Raven, minimizing the sound of a sniffle from prior to tears.

"'Forgotten Sue?' What kind of name is that? A girlfriend who got away?"

"Named the boat after his mother, I believe. Or his grandmother. One of those women used to say that the lobsters always came first, and their men always forgot about them. So in tribute, or to taunt, when he got his own boat, he named it 'Forgotten Sue.'"

"Oh, I like that." Betty fell silent and then mumbled, "It's so easy to forget your mother. To take her for granted."

Raven wondered if Betty was referring to her treatment of her own mother or how her three daughters treated her. Despite knowing Howard and Betty for years, she had only met two of their three daughters. Betty talked about all three as if one hadn't been ignoring them, but Raven imagined deep inside it hurt.

Betty said, "Where do you think Rusty and Sarah are? Wouldn't their credit cards give them away?"

Raven shrugged. "I don't think anyone's tried to trace them. Probably now they will."

"Or ping their cell phones?"

"Yeah, that would work too."

"I think you have to have that feature turned on. I do. I want Howard to know where I am at all times in case my kayak tips over or a coyote drags me off into the woods." Betty laughed. "Did you hear about the mountain lion sighting? And the black bear? Both caught on those night cameras."

Raven nodded, although she found both hard to believe between the growing population in Secretly and the fact that even the state wildlife officials were poo-pooing the mountain lion claim.

"Cameras don't lie. I know the person who posted it, too. She's in my garden club. So, it's not like someone who grabbed a video from somewhere else."

Now that Raven heard it was a garden club member, she grew even more dubious of the information. Not that Garden Club members lied; they just weren't tech-savvy based upon Betty and others who Raven had met at Betty's house when she had accidentally stumbled across a meeting when bringing over freshly baked cookies.

"Here we are. Home again, home again, jiggetty-jig." Betty unbuckled as Raven stopped the car in front of the Hart home and pulled up on the emergency brake, a tip she learned from her grandfather, who had taught her how to drive, including the best way to handle a manual transmission vehicle. Part of her love of driving a stick shift was out of dedication and memory to him.

"Keep me posted on any new developments," Betty said, sticking her head back into the car before shutting the door.

Once home, Raven took Lily and Dukie out back for a quick walk and bathroom break. The two rented cabins both looked empty, but neither couple had indicated they were checking out. Both had them rented and paid for in advance until tomorrow. With their vehicles not in the large driveway, she assumed the visitors were shopping or hiking or whatever people from away did in late autumn.

To her, it was an in-between time. Not cold enough for snow and all that came with that—frozen ponds for ice fishing and skating, or fields with enough snow for cross-country skiing or snowmobiling. She hadn't been on a snowmobile in a couple of years. There hadn't been enough snow to use the trails in Secretly, and Marcel traveled with Tom and other guys up to Caribou or over to Rangley. Maybe she and Marcel could plan a weekend away to do that this winter. Betty could watch the poochies. Somehow, Raven had fallen off doing things with Marcel that he loved.

Dukie had found an old tennis ball in the bushes and brought it to her feet to throw. She picked up the faded yellow orb and underhanded it across the back yard. He raced after it like a greyhound on a track, tucking in to beat an imaginary adversary. Lily trotted behind and then turned away to follow a scent. Dukie got to the ball first. Of course, he was the only one racing. Lily, who loved going after balls, too, had learned long ago that she'd only win against Dukie if she was standing near where the ball landed. Her short, stubby runt-of-the-litter Lab legs were no match for his Portuguese Water Dog athletic style.

Raven looked over her shoulder to confirm that Lily was rooted in the same spot under the barren lilac bushes. She was smelling and pawing the ground to improve the whiff. Hopefully, she wasn't uncovering another mystery, thought Raven. They still hadn't solved the first one Lily had led them to.

Raven was still outside when the sound of tires on the gravel hit Raven's ears. While it could have been one of the guests returning, Raven hoped it was Marcel. She walked around the house to look. Tom and Johnny were alighting from Tom's SUV. Still no Marcel.

"No luck," said Johnny. "Nick skedaddled back to Boston already, the little weasel. Betty must have frightened him off." Johnny laughed, although they all knew it was partially true. The main reason people needed to leave investigations to law enforcement professionals, besides potentially putting themselves in harm's way, was they actually might be on to something and botch it for the cops. Like this.

Raven resisted asking Tom if he reached Marcel. The words hung in her throat, causing her breathing to suffer. She was glad she was far enough away from the two men for them not to notice her attempts at regulating her breath to slow it down.

Then another thought came to Raven.

"Tom, when you guys found that gun, Rusty Poole's gun, it was in Whale Harbor, right?"

"Yep," said Tom, strolling up towards Raven and the house. He leaned over to scratch Dukie on the back. Dukie pranced around, his fluffy black tail high in the air. Now he looked more like a circus dog, a poodle, which was in his bloodline many centuries ago, almost a bit too foo-foo, which is why Marcel initially wasn't keen on the gift of a PWD. "Not masculine enough for my reputation," he had teased. Now they were joined at the hip. Raven heard Marcel's voice in her head and tears sprung again to her eyes. Where was he?

"Who found the gun in Whale Harbor?" Johnny asked.

"A lobsterman named Clark Christianson. He's also a part-time beach-comber with his metal detector."

"I can understand that," said Johnny with a big grin. "Diversify your portfolio. I'm thinking of doing that myself."

He didn't say how, and no one asked either. Raven knew he received a pension from the city of Boston. He had lived like a king for years while she and her mother had to move in with her grandfather to survive. All the sheets washed, and floors scrubbed to keep Pine Acres going and a roof over their heads—her mother's hands red and raw from hanging out laundry on cold winter days to avoid running the dryer to save money. She had never thought of it before, but now she wondered how Johnny had done his laundry in Boston—did he bring it to a cleaners or did he schlep it down to a laundromat, or maybe he had a nice place to live with a washer and dryer, and he did it while he cooked a meal or unwound in front of the TV with a cold beer and the game on the boob tube. Her grandfather's voice. Boob Tube. Probably why Raven never watched much TV herself.

Tom and Johnny now stood in front of her, waiting for her to invite them inside. She turned to the front door and whistled to the dogs who came running to get their small biscuit for coming inside. The three took their shoes and boots off in the foyer and walked into the main house in their stocking feet. Raven continued the same line of questioning, driving toward her main thought.

"Who was with you when you and Clark went to get the gun?" She asked as she took off her shoes.

"Well, we didn't have to get the gun. Clark picked it up with a piece of driftwood to avoid touching it and put it in a bag. We were only at the beach so Clark could show us where he found it."

"You and Marcel?" Johnny asked Tom, then looked at Raven. "Mind if I have a cup of coffee?"

Raven waved towards the coffee pot as Tom responded to Johnny.

"Yes, Marcel and me. And Shannon."

"Shannon?" said Johnny, but Raven barely heard his question.

Shannon.

She already knew that.

Chapter Thirty-One

Tom noticed Raven swayed, first a bit to the right and then a bit to the left. He rushed over and reached out his arm to steady her.

"You feeling okay? Why don't you sit down?" He led her from the kitchen to a chair in the living room area of the main room.

Johnny also rushed over, abandoning his coffee hunt. "Have you eaten today? I mean, besides a brownie sundae? Maybe your blood sugar peaked and then plunged? Want me to make you something? Egg Sandwich? Hamburger? Pasta?"

Raven didn't answer Johnny, but Tom nodded in agreement that it could be food or water-related. He had seen that too many times, especially with cyclists, runners, and senior citizens. Blood sugar or dehydration. With either, it caused the person to plop on the ground out of nowhere, right where they were. Sometimes, that meant into oncoming traffic, and other times, it could be under a dinette table. He had scraped up folks from the sides of roads and kitchen floors too many times to count. He only exhaled once Raven was seated.

She looked pale but not clammy or shaky. Her eyes were closed, and her hands were knitted together on her lap. She sat on the edge of the seat. He wished she would lean back.

"Let me get you a glass of water," he said, kneeling next to her, and then rose to stride over to the cabinets for a glass.

Raven found her voice, although she didn't open her eyes. "I'm fine. Really." She shook off whatever had possessed her and started to rise. Johnny put his hand on her arm to hold her back.

"Why don't you sit here a moment," he said gently. Tom continued his journey for that glass of water.

Johnny must have been an awesome cop, thought Tom. Gentle, compassionate, funny, and yet, Tom suspected, serious, and even tough when he needed to be. He was grateful to be getting to know him. He sensed a lifelong friendship coming on. People made mistakes, especially when they were young. True growth came by learning from them—taking ownership and evaluating what you needed to do to move forward, to be in a better place, or to be a better person.

The dogs barked and rushed out of the room. They weren't warning barks but excited yips. Tom heard the front door open. Marcel was home.

"Hey, stranger," said Tom when he saw his boss walk into the kitchen. "I've been trying to reach you all day—did you shut your phone off?" Tom beamed at Marcel, knowing Marcel would never do that, but remembering the young rookie who did in order to go to his girlfriend's house for some afternoon delight. Tom couldn't remember the rookie's name because he hadn't lasted long under Marcel, but the joke remained within the department. The 1970s song about skyrockets played in Tom's head.

Raven rose and faced Marcel, hearing Tom's question. Tom noticed Marcel and Raven hadn't yet said hello to each other. In fact, Marcel hadn't looked at any of them since entering. He stayed crouched near the dogs who were demanding his attention, burying his face into their necks.

"Something like that." He mumbled and then stood and faced Tom. "Sorry. I should have told you to radio me. My phone was run over at my first stop of the day." He tossed the smashed cell phone on the counter.

The flattened cell had more than a cracked screen. It resembled a metal pancake.

"Ugh. How'd that happen?" Tom filled a glass with water from the tap, the beauty of having a well. Tom appreciated the lack of chlorine smell as the water poured into the glass.

Marcel, still rubbing the dogs' heads, said, "My own stupidity. I put the phone on top of the Jeep and backed up. I did remember it was on top before I got too far, but by then, I had run it over. In fact, I'd say it was the crunch sound that made me think to look."

Tom chuckled. "Where were you?"

Marcel blushed, the pink color going up his neck and clear to the roots of his greying crew cut. Tom wasn't used to Marcel blushing over anything, and he guessed Raven wasn't either. He noticed out of the corner of his eye that Raven had stiffened and paled again with Marcel's physical response.

What was going on? They were the most solid couple he knew. Could it be about Johnny? Tom knew that Marcel was growing tired of Raven's stubbornness in letting Johnny into her life. Both Tom and Marcel understood the pressures of law enforcement, and seeing Johnny come out the other side and begin again was all Tom needed to embrace him. He understood that Johnny wasn't his dad, and he didn't have that history with him, but didn't Raven say once she didn't know him as a father at all. Maybe her mom made up stuff. Wouldn't be the first mom who colored her kid's view of her father.

These thoughts quickly ran through Tom's mind as he walked over to Raven, not as speedily as last time, but still wanting to be nearby in case she swayed again. He handed the glass of water to her, and she took it without drinking it. Marcel still hadn't looked Raven's way, so he hadn't seen her need for potential medical attention.

"Oh, this is going to be good," said Johnny with a chuckle, also noticing Marcel's discomfort.

Marcel's blush continued. "I hate to admit it. I was at the Donut Hole Dozen. So stereotypical, right?"

Tom and Johnny laughed. Air returned to the room.

"Stereotypes come from somewhere," said Johnny, walking around to Raven, who seemed frozen in place.

"I was at Mashed Potatoes this morning myself." Tom eyed Raven who hadn't seemed to blink in way too long.

"Oh, how's that place?" Johnny had come around and also now stood in the kitchen area.

"Nothing like a donut with potatoes in it." Tom meant it.

Johnny laughed and shook his head. "Spoken like a true Mainer!"

"And so much for that healthy diet speech you give the rest of us," Tom said with a grin at Marcel but with his gaze on Raven. She still hadn't moved an inch or uttered a word. Finally, she took a sip of water and then another sip. Tom felt his shoulders relax.

Marcel, who had crouched back down to the insistent dogs, rose again from the tile floor, dusted off his pants, and leaned against the counter. The dogs still weren't done with him. Dukie sat on his right foot, and Lily leaned against his left leg, her heavy tail thumbing out a rhythm.

He focused on Tom, still not looking at Raven. "Why were you trying to reach me?" He asked.

"State lab called about the gun," Tom said. Why were Marcel and Raven acting like they were in different rooms?

"Luuuuuccccccyyyyy…." Marcel grinned and used his best Desi Arnez accent. Now, it was Tom's turn to blush.

"Cut it out." He joked back.

"At least she called you and didn't have her mother call. Like last time," Marcel said, his grin growing wider, referring to the time Lucy's mother called Tom directly on his county cell and asked for Tom's intentions with her daughter. Tom's intentions were to have fun, but he couldn't exactly confess that to a mother. In typical Tom fashion, when cornered about a woman, he stammered his way through part of the conversation and then faked a police call in order to hang up mid-sentence.

Tom heard a loud exhale from Raven during this banter. He glanced over and saw color was returning to her cheeks.

Marcel straightened and came over to Raven, standing in front of her. She looked up at him, and he kissed her on the forehead, drawing her in for a hug. She seemed to melt into his arms. Gosh, that sounded cliche, but that was what it looked like. Must be where the saying came from. Like stereotypes, cliches came from somewhere, too.

Maybe, Tom thought, he should give some thought to settling down. Maybe Lucy's mother was right about starting a family, even if it wasn't with Lucy. Not to complain about Lucy. She was darn pretty and spunky, but she came with that mother who would be tracking Tom out of the corner of her eye, or even in front of his face, on a daily basis. Better to wait and keep on his current path, he decided. Especially if his intentions were just to have fun, right?

Marcel, still holding Raven, said, "You two compare videos yet?" He talked over her head toward Tom.

"You're a mind reader," said Tom. "We were just going to do that." He decided not to mention Raven's almost fainting spell. She could share if she wanted. It appeared that they had a lot to talk about.

"Yep, we're going to do that. Right after my coffee," said Johnny, chuckling, heading back to the coffee pot for a second attempt.

"Yes, please grab a cup. Help yourself," said Marcel. As Johnny passed by, Marcel reached out a hand and patted Johnny on the shoulder. Johnny smiled. Tom read appreciation on his face.

Tom marveled at how easy it was between Marcel and Johnny. They shared much in common, from law enforcement to Raven. Marcel had fully embraced, it seemed, having Johnny as a father-in-law even if Raven hadn't yet accepted Johnny as her father.

Marcel pulled back and looked into Raven's face. "What's the easiest way to show Tom the video?"

She cleared her throat. "It's on my phone," she said. Her look was serious as she stared into Marcel's eyes. No glimmer of a smile.

"That's where mine is, too," said Tom, hoping to keep the atmosphere light.

"I say we get cozy around the kitchen table," said Johnny, sipping on his fresh, steaming black coffee. He walked over to the table and pulled out a chair. Tom joined him, leaving an empty space for Raven in between them.

"You three work on that. I'm going to take a shower." Marcel kissed Raven again on the forehead and then lightly on the mouth and released her. She picked up her phone from the counter and, with her glass of water, brought them both over to the table.

After scanning through their phones, both Tom and Raven found the videos of the Lane Mansion. Tom gave his phone to Raven to hold, and both men leaned in toward her. They first watched Tom's from Wednesday night. The flash was on throughout since it was dark. Even though the mansion had electricity, it didn't have lamps on the first floor. The hall looked like it did when Raven and Johnny were in it. Piles of bricks were stacked everywhere. Papers were scattered on the living room floor. The kitchen was messy but barren. Only a tripod stood in the corner. The stairs in the video creaked like they did for Johnny and Raven. Light flooded the far room that Charles used as an office and bedroom. Again, a mess, with clothes and garbage from food wrappers. The printer was off to one side.

"Looks the same to me," said Johnny, "but worth comparing."

The video continued through the other two rooms and the bathroom and then stopped.

Raven's eyebrows furrowed.

"Did I F-up?" Tom laughed. "I thought I did a pretty good job."

Raven shook her head.

"Then what are you thinking?" he asked. Tom could almost hear her brain clicking through its gears. Finally, she spoke.

"The tripod. Let's go back to the walk-through in the kitchen. The tripod in the corner of the kitchen."

"Yes, I saw that," said Johnny. "I think it was there when we went back too. What's the significance of the tripod, Raven?" He drank more coffee as he waited for her answer.

She sat back in the wooden chair. "Charles was a bird photographer. Semi-pro, according to Betty. He even used a tripod. That's how serious he was. Which, to me, says he had a regular camera. An SLR. Probably an expensive big lens or two."

"Makes sense." Tom nodded. "Go on."

"So where are his camera and camera bag?" Raven, still looking at Tom's video, played it again from the beginning.

Johnny whistled at the question just as Marcel came into the kitchen from the shower, dampness and an evergreen scent following after him. He sat at the end of the table and spoke.

"Maybe now we have a motive," Marcel said, folding his hands together in his lap.

"Robbery," said Tom.

"I'm thinking more along the lines of what did Charles Kearns see through that lens. Is that what you're saying, Raven?" said Marcel.

She looked at her husband and nodded. Tom noticed their normal rapport was still off, despite the hug. It unnerved him to have them not be their normal happy-couple selves.

Johnny leaned closer to Raven to watch the video again. "Hmmm. What did Charles Kearns photograph?"

Tom said, "Find that camera, and we'll know."

"If that really is the scenario, I suspect that camera is long gone. Probably tossed into the ocean when the gun was dropped." Marcel shifted forward and rested his elbows on the orange and brown tablecloth. Still Thanksgiving colors.

"All we need is the data card. That's all the killer would have needed too unless they didn't understand new cameras," said Johnny. "I don't have one myself, but I remember our forensic photographer changing cards when one became full."

"And then uploading the images to a computer," Tom finished Johnny's thought.

"Okay, so, maybe Charles uploaded his photos onto his laptop?" said Johnny.

"Which we have. Well, sort of. It's in Augusta," said Tom.

"Let's look at your video, Raven, before we get too far down this rabbit hole," said Marcel.

Raven put down Tom's phone and picked up her own. Tom pulled his phone toward him just as it rang.

"Pinkham," he said into the speaker.

"Tom. Call came in about a car in Blue Heron Pond," the voice from dispatch said. "I tried radioing you."

"Really? Some numb skull drove down the logging road and straight into the water? Must be a drunk." Then he swallowed, thinking of the former drunk on the other side of Raven. He needed to watch his big mouth.

"I tried radioing Marcel too," the voice said through the cell phone speaker. "I know his phone is busted."

"Yep, it still is," said Marcel, looking over at the flattened piece on the counter. "But I'm right here, Andre." He put his hand out for Tom's phone. "Were there people in the car at Blue Heron?"

"Unknown. Most of the car is still submerged."

Tom closed his eyes. It was going to be a long day.

"Andre, please send a tow truck there to meet us. Tom and I are on our way," said Marcel.

The three gentlemen rose. Raven remained seated and still. Tom couldn't ever remember seeing her this quiet. He hoped she was okay, that she and Marcel were okay.

Tom pocketed his cell. "Johnny, want us to drop you back home? It's on our way."

"Super! Thanks!" Johnny touched Raven on top of her head. She turned a bit toward him.

"Talk to you later," she said.

Marcel went over to her, and she stood. They kissed a quick goodbye.

Before Tom left the kitchen, he turned back.

"Raven, do you mind sending me your video?"

"No problem," she said, still standing by the table.

And the men left.

Chapter Thirty-Two

Raven watched Marcel walk in to their home and then walk out of it. Barely staying other than to shower. Okay, so he was called away for work. He still wasn't at home. With her. Despite Tom's teasing and questioning about Marcel's whereabouts, she realized he never actually told them where he had been headed after the donut shop stop and his phone fiasco. In fact, he had had his coffee already before he left and had been limiting himself to water during the day, saving one cup of coffee for early morning hours or when work required a late shift. It had been years, however, since he was on anything but first shift. There weren't a heck of a lot of emergencies in the Midcoast, thank goodness. Except for lately.

He also never alerted Tom that he'd have to be reached via radio. He told dispatch, but not Tom? Odd with Tom being his right hand. No, Marcel didn't want to be found. Why? Where had he gone?

Could he have been picking up a coffee and a donut for whomever he was meeting? Who would that be? Raven only had one idea and she was about five foot eight and had flowing blond hair that she relished flipping. Maybe Marcel picked up a cruller, too, for Miss Shannon. Ms. Shannon, excuse me, remembering her campaign slogan, "Ms Shannon doesn't Ms Much." Trying to be clever. Flirtatious. Buying votes. Suddenly, Raven hated all pastries. Crullers were stupid. So were bowties and eclairs. She thought of Marcel bringing her a surprise treat at times at the end of the day, like from Dulce Vita, the Italian bakery in Thomaston, or from Sarah's in Wiscasset. His style. Well, now he was surprising someone else.

Raven had been happy with whatever he brought her—just as thrilled with something plain or with cinnamon and sugar. She wasn't fancy or fussy. Ms. Shannon would never stand for plain and never, ever for powdered sugar. Noooo. Too messy. She wouldn't want to soil her clothes with little white dust, although she had no trouble making a mess of other people's marriages.

Raven sat down at her laptop and put her head in her hands. She had to get a grip. She was shaking over doughnuts. She had acted this dramatically when Johnny first appeared in her life. Marcel told her to relax, see how it all evolved, to give him a chance, but no, she had to keep her walls up. Were those same walls so high she had now blocked out Marcel?

She glanced at her watch. She should have been sending Tom the video he had asked for, the one she had taken with Johnny, but instead, she opened her laptop and pulled up a search engine.

She typed two words: Shannon McGrath.

Unfortunately, there was currently some award-winning New York actress with the same name who exceeded the popularity of the measly county district attorney. Raven narrowed the search by adding the word 'Maine.'

Still too many hits on the popular name. Too many Irish Americans, Raven thought, although she had never thought about it before. She wondered if this would be a permanent new prejudice of hers, or just a strong dislike for one Irish American in particular. Despite the pages and pages of possible 'Shannon McGraths' in Maine, the County DA's campaign finally appeared in the mix.

Raven added the word 'attorney' to tighten the circle and have the Shannon McGrath of her wrath rise to the top. Articles of cases won when Ms. McGrath was in private practice popped up. Hmmm. Raven didn't realize that Shannon had been a defense attorney. That's kinda like switching teams to now be a prosecutor.

Reading the highlights further down the screen, the case of the murderer Cleary Holmes showed up multiple times. He had killed at least five young girls, one of them from Barrett County. And she had defended him, the scumbag, although Raven didn't know who was worse, Holmes or Shannon. Okay, too dramatic again. Raven remembered that case clearly because

Marcel and his team had worked diligently with the State Police and the other county sheriffs, with even some help from the FBI, to put Holmes away for life. I's dotted. T's crossed. As Marcel had put it. But somehow, Holmes was given a lighter sentence. Marcel was angry. Had he reached out to Shannon then to complain? Was that when the reconnection started? Was this part of Shannon's reason to get divorced?

Raven didn't remember Marcel saying that he knew the defense attorney in the Holmes case, but that was about the time Raven's mother developed her cancer, and Raven had her hands full running Pine Acres alone and tending to her mother, not realizing her mother would slip away so quickly.

Raven swallowed back the tears. Thinking of her beloved mother, her rock, going from a robust, healthy, laughing woman to a stick figure curled up in the bed was too much to bear at the moment. What a hard life her mother had, always wondering if they had enough money, having only Raven to rely upon once her grandfather had died.

Raven turned back to her laptop as a distraction. Memories stung. They poured over her heart like rubber cement, protecting the cracks, but also sealing it up. She didn't know how she'd ever soften enough to allow Johnny in. She didn't trust him, and she didn't forgive him for what he did to her mother. Her anger wasn't really about abandoning her. She was too young to remember him. It was about the pain he put her mother through.

Raven shook her head. Enough about her own past. It was safer, easier to look into someone else's. Digging back into the search engine, she wasn't sure what she was looking for on Shannon. She couldn't imagine there would be any indiscretions online at this stage, none that the news outlets wouldn't have already picked up on during the campaign. Not that Raven had paid any attention to any of the elections. She had only voted once in her whole life at the age eighteen, and the disappointment of her candidate of choice losing was all she needed as a turnoff for the whole process. Years of hearing arguments that it was her civic duty didn't sway her.

She scrolled past the dull campaign interviews and stopped at a scanned news article. It had been uploaded only a few months ago, but it was from Shannon's school days. Her high school days. Raven clicked it open.

The scan was black and white and grainy, but the words at the top, "Head Cheerleader Shannon McGrath wins Prom Queen," stood out. The article went on to say that senior Shannon was "escorted out onto the field as the Prom Queen by her date, the Captain of the Football Team and Prom King."

So trite.

Raven added cheerleaders to her growing list of people she didn't think she liked and continued scanning the article, moving down to the screen.

There, in all of his glory, was the captain of the football team, grinning with his arm around Shannon. Both were wearing crowns. It was her Marcel.

Raven slammed the laptop shut and jumped up.

She was mad at herself. She knew they dated in high school, but now she had a visual.

But he didn't marry Shannon, did he?

And they were kids. Does it even count as dating?

Raven tried to think of a boy she had a crush on while in high school. No one really came to mind. Well, if she had, she certainly wouldn't be attracted to him now, as an adult. Or would she? There were many happy couples in town who had grown up together since nursery school.

She put her head in her hands. She was bitter. She never used to be bitter. Could she blame Johnny? Her mother would have said no. "You create your own reality," her mother would have said, along with "Happiness is a choice. So is Misery."

So why was she choosing to be miserable?

Chapter Thirty-Three

Tom swung the SUV up Johnny's long dirt driveway.

"You can let me out down here," said Johnny. "I know you gotta get to that call."

"I sense it isn't a life and death situation anymore," said Marcel, his face serious. "One of the rookies has been dispatched to stand guard in case a crowd gathers."

Tom kept driving up the driveway, and Johnny hopped out when Tom stopped in front of his stoop.

"Thanks so much guys. Great to see you both. Good luck at the pond, and if I can be of any assistance with anything, please let me know."

"Much appreciated, Johnny. Truly." Marcel put up a hand as a wave.

Tom again marveled at Marcel's respect for his newly acquired father-in-law. Johnny's appreciation for it, too, was on his face as he waved goodbye.

Blue Heron Pond was a favorite place of Tom's in his youth. It was close enough to town to walk to if his dad had taken his car keys and secluded enough to be a great make-out spot, one of the reasons his dad would have banned the use of a family car. Now, with the addition of the logging road running along the side of the pond, it both opened up access to the trees for thinning out the forest, and also made it easier to get to the back of the pond at all hours. He hadn't taken a girl to Blue Heron in over ten years. As he and Marcel bounced down the rocky road to the preserve parking area, he considered revisiting this option as a rotation in his social life.

Trainee Roger Stanton stood on the shore of the pond, his hands on his hips. Next to him was a man older than him, holding a fishing pole. Fishing season had ended at the end of September, but Tom knew none of the officers were even going to mention it. This fisherman, knowing he was in violation of the game laws, had taken the good Samaritan approach and called in what he found. Tom chalked that up to their policing, making the citizens feel safe, and more or less law-abiding, without an iron fist. Tom remembered his basic training with the force. The head of police in Augusta reminded the new recruits to pick and choose their battles carefully. An expired fishing license wasn't on the docket today.

Tom and Marcel exited the parked SUV and walked toward the two men. As they got closer, Tom recognized the fisherman as Emil Bryant, the town's chimney repair guru. Wasn't he the one working on the chimney in the Lane Mansion, which was now Charles Kearns' house? Tom hoped this was just a small-town coincidence. He liked Emil and didn't want him to be caught up in a murder.

"Thank you, Officer Stanton," Marcel said formally, and the rookie nodded and stepped aside. "Emil, great to see you," Marcel stuck his hand out, and Emil returned his for a friendly shake. Tom and Emil did the same.

"What'd you catch today?" said Marcel. Normally, that would just be small talk, but at the end of November, it could be taken as an official, probing question.

Emil blushed and then realized Marcel just meant the sunken car. He pointed toward the middle of the pond.

"I threw in my metal weight over there," he said, pointing towards another part of the pond's edge, "and heard a clunk. So I came around the bend to this side and noticed the top of the car."

There wasn't much to see, but in squinting, Tom made out a light blue patch of metal, most likely the roof of the car. On a sunny day, that would easily be mistaken for a reflection of the sky.

A rumble was heard down the dirt drive, and all four men turned to look. The tow truck had arrived.

Raising his voice over the diesel engine, Marcel asked Emil, "About what time was that? Or," he turned to Roger, "did you already capture the details?"

"Yes, sir," said deputy trainee Stanton, also raising his voice over the tow truck sound as he opened up his notebook. "Would you like me to read you what I learned?"

"Please," said Marcel and waited.

Perfect case to learn on, thought Tom. No emergency. They could take their time. What a great opportunity for the rookie to have personal time with Marcel, too. Tom forgot how fortunate he was to be with Marcel as much as he was. He was a great mentor and friend.

The trainee cleared his throat. Emil smiled in amusement and tried to wipe the look off his face. He winked at Marcel and Tom.

"At 15:00, a call came in about a car found in Blue Heron Pond. I was approximately fifteen minutes away, so I radioed that I would respond. I asked Dispatch to tell the caller to wait for me," he looked up from his notebook and gestured towards Emil as the caller.

"Which I did." Emil offered with a slight smile still on his lips.

"When I arrived, at 15:15, Mr. Bryant indicated where the top of the car was peeking out of the pond. I received a call at that time from Dispatch to wait with Mr. Bryant as you and Deputy Pinkham were en route." Roger took a breath. "I interviewed Mr. Bryant who said he had arrived at Blue Heron Pond approximately thirty minutes prior to calling about the car. He called Dispatch the moment he realized what he had found, making that realization at approximately 14:55. Is that right, sir?" He turned to Emil.

"You got it. Good job," said Emil, recognizing that Roger was a new hire.

The tow truck had turned around and was now beeping as it backed up toward the men and the pond. The driver stuck his head out. "I hear there's a car to pull up?" A cigarette dangled from his lips.

The four men parted two by two to make way for the tow that was inching toward them. Tom went over to the driver's side door. "Give us one sec."

The driver nodded but then shook his head in annoyance. He stopped backing up but didn't turn off his diesel engine, the roar echoing across the pond and the smell of diesel filling the air.

It was Tom's turn now to shake his head in annoyance. Some people. Think they own the world.

Marcel motioned for the other three to walk to the side and huddle.

"Emil, you can go now."

"I'm happy to stay and help." Emil made no move to leave. Tom knew it was out of curiosity, not benevolence.

"Actually, I need to ask you to leave," said Marcel with a smile. "We'll be in touch if we need any more information." He put a hand out to touch Emil's arm in thanks.

Tom leaned in and whispered to Emil. "Time to put the pole in the back of the closet until ice fishing. And no more metal sinkers. Bad for the loons."

Emil nodded and began his walk down the logging road to the other part of the preserve where Tom assumed his truck was. The fishing pole and fish bag bobbed up and down with his every step.

The three officers turned their attention back to the pond. Tom put on the waders he kept in the SUV and sloshed into the pond. He could see the car's roof a little clearer the closer he went. A small compact. He couldn't think of any on the stolen list. First off, it was rare to have a car stolen in Secretly or Whale Harbor. And second, it was usually a teenage joy ride or a dare, and the vehicle was quickly recovered.

Based on the amount of growth on the roof, the car had been in the water for a while.

The tow truck operator, also in waders, walked out towards Tom with a large metal hook in his hands. His face, squished up as if in pain, showed what Tom's feet were feeling—the mushy, slippery, disgusting bottom of the pond. The silt had kicked up, making it impossible to see to the bottom of the water. The only good thing was there were no poisonous snakes in Maine. No water moccasins like he knew existed in Southern New England.

"Damn, this water is cold," said the tow truck driver. His cigarette fell out of his mouth and into the pond. "Damn. Damn. Damn. This day sucks."

Tom ignored the comment. He knew the driver would be well compensated by the county for this work. Probably triple his normal tow rate.

"Gross!" The driver said, plunging his hands into the water to look for the bumper of the car. "Ah, thank god." He must have found the bumper and secured the hook.

Tom slowly waded out of the pond behind the driver. He realized he could have made the rookie go in. They all had waders issued to them. Glancing over towards Marcel and Roger, he saw them chatting. Again, Tom was glad for Roger to have this one-on-one time with Marcel. Now, Roger would be even more comfortable reaching out to Marcel if needed.

The driver had returned to his cab and was slowly cranking up the metal chain, his head outside the window. The metal creaked as it reeled in the car from the pond. After a couple of minutes, the bumper, dripping with dead lily pad vines, finally popped out of the water with a suction noise as the car came closer to shore.

The driver pulled the tow truck a little forward to level out the car with the shore. Its wheels drove over the decaying skunk cabbage and onto the low grass. There was no sand or anything resembling a beach at this pond. Who would want to go into that murky water anyway, thought Tom. It really seemed more like a swamp. The preserve association should consider a name change to "Blue Heron Swamp." Tom decided to put that in their office's suggestion box.

The car was an older Toyota. Once blue. Now, a mix of brown from the mud, green from swamp grass, and an overall tan. Still, blue peeked through on the roof, parts of the hood, and a little on the doors.

Its tires seemed intact, and he didn't notice any body damage. If it was actually in decent shape, then his initial thought of it being junked wouldn't pan out. Besides, with so many non-profit organizations wanting junk cars as donations, the amount of cars abandoned had greatly decreased. A win-win for everyone.

The car windows, all closed, were caked with mud on the outside. At first, Tom thought the car was empty. He circled it.

Marcel and Roger joined him by the driver's side front door. Tom used his sleeve to wipe off the driver's side window and immediately jumped back in surprise. A grayish body sat strapped to the seat.

Chapter Thirty-Four

Raven forced herself to stop festering on Shannon McGrath and to concentrate on sending the video of the Lane Mansion to Tom. Instead, she allowed herself to get distracted again, this time by the Maine bird book that Johnny had brought from Charles' bedroom. He had brought it over when they came from his house to compare videos and had left it on the counter.

She flipped through it. Charles had bent down pages throughout the book, and as Raven went to those pages, she saw he had made notations by various the birds' photos. He added the date when he first spotted one in Maine, the time, and where it was.

She grabbed a small notebook from the counter and wrote down the list of birds with notations. The ones he saw in or near Secretly were extensive, with the most concentrated area being the Blue Heron Pond Preserve, including the snowy owl, the one he photographed with the full moon. In fact, July of that year was when he wrote he had seen it for the first time.

Did someone kill him for his bird photographs? Were they worth that much money? She researched the snowy owl he had photographed and learned it was common in Maine and elsewhere in the US and Canada. Anyone could find it and capture a photo of it. His photograph just happened to be stunning with the July full moon glinting off the white wings and the reflection in the pond of both the owl and the moon. Maybe there were other equally as beautiful shots of other birds that someone wanted to get their hands on, yet it seems like a stretch to kill him for that.

She finally turned back to her original task—sending Tom her video of the Lane Mansion. She tried sending it to his cell. First, it took forever for the blue line to get to the end, and then after three "not delivered" returns, Raven realized it was never going to go through. Maybe it was because he was at Blue Heron Pond and didn't have good cell coverage, but she suspected it was the size of the video file.

Then she tried to email it to him from her cell and was met with a similar error message: "file too large."

She opened her laptop again. The photo showing Shannon as Prom Queen and Marcel as Prom King was still up on the screen. She quickly clicked out of it and logged into her cloud account. Yes, her video was there in the clouds.

She again tried to email it to Tom. Again, it failed for being too big a file for his email to receive.

Maybe the county had a website to send files to—they had to for court documents and such. She did a brief search on the county sheriff's website, as well as the state police and the state court system. Nothing that was apparent, at least not to the general public. She'd ask Tom to find out when he and Marcel came back from the pond.

Raven looked again at the bird book next to the laptop, picking it up and flipping through it. She always liked birds—how could she not, having a nickname after one of them—but she never really got into recording sightings or studying the details, other than tracking the return of the hermit thrush in spring. She loved the melody rising above all others as she walked the poochies in the woods. She had countless audio recordings of that species, sometimes the dogs are wandering and sniffing in front of her, their jingling collars also heard. Sometimes, it's just sunlight streaming in amongst the trees.

She picked up her phone to find one of the videos, to hear the soothing sounds of the hermit thrush. When was the last time she recorded it? Scanning back to June, she found a video that had a thumbnail showing just trees. She clicked on it and saw the icon for when a video was downloading from the cloud.

The cloud. Maybe that's where all of Charles' photographs were. In the cloud. Most likely he shot large data files, maybe even raw files, not that she fully understood what that meant, but she knew their size could be huge. He would have realized quickly that no amount of laptop or phone space could possibly hold all of his files. He would have to store them somewhere else, like on a thumb drive or in a cloud account.

Find either of those and find his photographs, she thought. And find his photographs and find out what he saw that got him killed.

Chapter Thirty-Five

"Holy..." Tom couldn't even get the rest of his words out. He felt his stomach lurch and moved away from the car.

Marcel looked in, then stepped back and squinted. Seeing a dead body never got easy. This was a woman. A brunette, although most of her hair was missing.

When Marcel stepped back, the new cadet also peered in and gasped. He ran to the edge of the pond. The sound of his wrenching was muffled by the diesel engine. Poor kid. It might be his first dead body, and this one was a doozy.

Tom straightened and looked back at the car. It couldn't be her, could it?

Marcel tapped on the cab window on the passenger side. The window rolled down.

"Can you cut your engine, please?"

The tow truck shut off. Tom saw the tow truck driver shaking his head and muttering, his hands gesturing his frustration.

"Do your job," Tom mumbled to himself and had actually mumbled it about himself, not the truck driver. Doing his job would keep him focused.

He pulled out his cell and requested a forensics team. Two dead bodies in Secretly in less than a week. Unheard of. Charles Kearns' body had sat in the woods for a while, a few weeks. The body in that car had definitely been there longer than that.

The body. Could it be her?

The rookie came back, wiping his mouth with the back of his hand. He looked pale and sweaty. Clammy was probably more like it.

"Sorry, sir," he said, addressing Marcel although he kept his gaze down at his own shoes. He heaved a bit, and Marcel unconsciously stepped back.

"It happens, son," said Marcel. "Is this your first dead body? At least on the job?"

"Yes, sir. Anywhere." He still kept his gaze down. Then, realizing he might be considered rude, he looked up and into Marcel's eyes.

"You'll be happy to know it never gets easy, but you do learn to deal with it. I'd like you to still stay here with us, but you don't have to get close to the car or the body," said Marcel.

Distracting himself from the body until the forensics team and the ME arrived, Tom thought of his own first years on the job. Did this rookie realize how lucky he was to have a boss like this? Tom had learned so much from Marcel, entering in under Marcel when he was second in command under the prior sheriff. Tom had fallen in love with his job. It was a natural fit with his personality. His cadet class teased him that he was a combination of Florence Nightingale with his desire to help, the Dalai Lama with his calmness, and Bozo the Clown with his humor. Tom had to agree.

When the last sheriff retired, Marcel was encouraged to run for the role, as it was an elected official, the only elected law enforcement type role throughout Maine. When Marcel moved up, so did Tom, assuming the role as second in command, having been already promoted to detective along the way. Now, only doing speed traps as a summer back-up, and instead, investigating larger crimes like theft as his main job, he had fallen in love with his position all over again.

He had worked on his share of murders in his years on the force, not that Barrett County had many, thankfully. In fact, the whole state of Maine hovered between twenty to thirty murders a year. Too many in Tom's book, especially since most of them were domestic, involving spouses and partners, children, and a landlord thrown in here and there, but it still was better than Massachusetts.

Why did Mainers always compare themselves to Massachusetts? Not neighboring New Hampshire, not even New York. That tie, the former ownership of Maine by Massachusetts, still had a residual effect. If it wasn't about crime, it was about salaries, or traffic, neither of which were high in Maine. It was the crowds of people that Tom couldn't stand with their "keep up with the Jones" cars and houses and all that stress that went with that appearance. If Tom never went to Massachusetts again, he wouldn't care.

He wandered back to Marcel and Roger.

"Estimated time for the forensics team is thirty minutes."

Marcel nodded. Roger still looked like he was about to pass out.

"Anyone need a water?" said Tom, heading for his SUV. He did. Oh, please don't let it be her.

"I...I...I could use one," said Roger, "if you don't mind."

"I'll take one too," said Marcel. "Thanks,"

"Yes, thanks." Roger's voice was now also shrinking. He'd be okay going forward if he got through today, thought Tom.

Tom grabbed three waters and a box of granola bars. He handed out the water and opened the box. Marcel took one. Roger hesitated. Tom knew it was because Roger was afraid of throwing it up.

"Better to have something in your stomach," said Tom with a gentle, knowing smile. "At least that's what I've experienced personally."

Roger met Tom's gaze and smiled back. "You're right," and he took one.

Tom tapped on the tow truck's driver's side window, and the window lowered. A scowl was large on the driver's face. He did nothing to hide his contempt for being kept waiting.

"Granola bar," said Tom with a large grin, ignoring the Negative Nancy behind the wheel.

The driver was about to say no, but paused, studying the box.

"Sure." He reached his hand out. "Thanks."

"Take two. Or three," said Tom. He had more in the SUV, keeping them handy, not just for himself but a stranded driver, a frightened child, or whomever needed a pick-me-up. It was amazing how far a free granola bar could help.

Tom provided the driver with an update. "We have a body in the car. That's our hold up."

"Oh," said the driver, his face relaxing. He appeared embarrassed by his earlier impatience. "I didn't realize."

Tom nodded. No judgment. "Neither did we until we looked inside. In case it's foul play, we need to make sure we handle it the right way, so a forensics team is on its way." He glanced at his watch. "Probably here in twenty minutes. You're welcome to get out and stretch or walk the other preserve trails. Sorry to hold you up."

"Oh, that's okay. I understand. Let me just call my wife." He pulled out his cell. "How far a walk do you think it is between here and Lane's?"

"A couple of miles. Maybe less."

"If I had on different shoes," said the driver, getting out of the cab. He looked down at his work boots. "I'd have blisters by the time I got there." He finally smiled.

"I hear you. Thank you for your patience, and our apologies again."

"No, no, no need. I'll just be over here if you need me." He meandered towards a wooden bench placed by the preserve organization to encourage leisure and meditation at the pond. Now, all it did was allow the person seated to view a mud-covered car that contained a dead body. And not just any dead body.

Chapter Thirty-Six

The Cloud. If Charles had taken a large volume of bird photos, he must have had a cloud account. Of course, he could also have put all his records on a zip drive, a thumb drive, that the killer had already found, although Raven didn't think that someone would go back to the Lane Mansion recently if they had everything they needed. Nope, Charles' photographs were still untapped. When Tom came back with Marcel, Raven would ask him to call the offices in Augusta to look for a saved account on his laptop.

Maybe she should call Tom at the pond to get the search started. Her watch showed a little after 3 p.m. Some state offices closed at 3:30 in the afternoon, and others at 4:30 p.m. The chance of her reaching Tom at the pond and him reaching a live person in Augusta and then the person doing the work before the close of the workday was probably nil. Not probably. Definitely nil. Especially on the Friday after Thanksgiving.

All she really needed to know was Charles' cloud provider, if he had one, his account name, and his password. She could look it up on the cloud provider's website using her own laptop.

She shook her head at the words in her head. "All she needed." She had made it sound so simple, but it still involved both needing to know what service to use and how Charles got into it.

But Charles was older. He might be one of those who wrote down website names along with account names and passwords, like in a notebook or on a scrap of paper, despite all the cybersecurity warnings not to do so. The answers she needed might well be in the mess in his bedroom-office on the second floor of the Lane Mansion.

She sighed and looked out the window.

She made up her mind. Worth a try.

She packed up her laptop into a canvas bag. She could use her phone's hotspot for wifi if she was so lucky to find an answer.

"You guys wait here," Raven said to Lily and Dukie. They witnessed her donning her coat and assumed, despite her words, that it was time for their afternoon walk. Lily refused to take no for an answer and pushed her way past Raven when the door opened. Dukie, not to be outdone or end up last, wiggled his large fluffiness between Raven's legs and also ran outside before Raven could shut the door.

They stood facing the way to the woods, tails-a-wagging.

"Not right now," said Raven, "but you can come with me in the car, and maybe, a big maybe, we can go to a preserve afterwards on our way home." She hoped she'd actually be back home quickly, answer or no answer. She opened the backdoor of her Mini Cooper, and Dukie and Lily hopped into the small backseat.

Lane's Market had only a handful of cars in the parking lot. She didn't know how it stayed in business without the tourists, especially with that large chain grocery store opening up in Eelsboro last year. She passed the store and hung a right into the driveway of the Lane Mansion.

Looking up at it from her driver's seat, she felt a sadness about the house. The windows without curtains made the entire structure seem hollow, forlorn. Did it long to return to the Lane family? Did it know its current owner had died?

While she sat in the car, she saw Chris Lane exit the front of the store and step back to survey the area. He either didn't notice her parked in the driveway, or he chose to ignore her if he had seen her. Her car was too recognizable to not know it was her.

She waited for him to return to the store before exiting the car, although she didn't know why she didn't want him to see her go in. Maybe to not be delayed on her mission? Maybe to not be seen at all? If she was honest with herself, something nagged her about Chris. She remembered the way he had sneered at Charles around the campfire that October night and his constant drive to reunite the mansion with the Lane family. Marcel thought now would be the best chance to do so, with the house in such a dismantled state. Something a local would forgive in order to get it, and the price now might finally be right.

Chris walked up the two concrete steps and disappeared into the store. Raven opened her car door and stepped out. She reached in for her canvas bag containing her laptop and phone and left the windows half rolled down and her sunroof open for air for the poochies, even though it was forty-five degrees out. She hoped she'd be back in ten minutes or less. It was peace of mind, however, to know the dogs were getting airflow and were safe.

The mansion's front door was closed the way that she and Johnny had left it. She clicked on the latch, and it swung open only an inch, looking like it did when Johnny and she found it opened. Using the toe of her Bean boot, she pushed it open further.

Mounds of bricks still littered the hall, although Emil's crew did seem to have made a bit of progress. She was surprised Marcel had allowed the work to be done so quickly after finding Charles's body and not knowing where he was actually killed, but he had said all the forensics had been done at the house, and it made no sense to cost the workers a day's pay.

Her heart twinged at the reminder of his sensitivity toward others and then stilled at the image of him laughing with Shannon McGrath at their prom. Was Raven being overly sensitive? Was Marcel just showing kindness to an old friend? Or politically being friendly for when his position came up for re-election? Or were they, in fact, rekindling something they once had?

She shook her head to stay focused—enough of this Marcel and Shannon soap opera, she told herself—and headed for the stairs. Before advancing up, she poked her head into the disheveled kitchen. The tripod still stood in the corner, waiting to be reunited with its camera and its operator. It would have an eternity to wait.

The wooden staircase creaked in the same spots it did when she and Johnny climbed up it, causing the same goosebump reaction for Raven. The murder, the empty, torn-apart house, and the unanswered questions about it all enveloped her as she briskly walked down the upstairs hall, feeling like the house was swallowing her up like a mist in a bog.

"Darn it all," she said, realizing she had failed to bring a real flashlight. The light on this side of the house left first, and already the room was dim without the sunlight. At least Charles's bedroom had an overhead light that worked.

She switched it on, and the room illuminated. Papers and food wrappers were strewn everywhere in the same spots that she and Johnny had left them. Streaks across the wooden floor showed where Johnny had scooted under the bed to grab the bird book, with the dust clinging to his clothes.

Why had Johnny ferreted that bird book away so quickly?

Well, she hardly thought Johnny was Charles's killer, so those questions were more out of curiosity than purpose. She really didn't know him. She again focused on the task: find a thumb drive or find a cloud account and a cloud password.

Raven started at the most obvious place—the area used as a desk. There were no obvious external drives on the table that Charles was using as his desk. She then went into cloud account mode. Inspecting each piece of paper individually, she sifted through mostly blank, unused printer paper. At the bottom of one pile was a small black moleskin notebook that she and Johnny had missed.

On the first page was the word PASSWORDS. Just as she suspected for his age.

He even had the email addresses and account names associated with each account. Listed were Email, Math Association, Banking, Health Insurance, Car/Home Insurance, Electricity, Propane Delivery, Amazon, and the last one. Cloud. The same company she used.

Bingo.

Chapter Thirty-Seven

"Tommy Boy," Clint from Forensics called out as he and his partner, Hailey, alighted from their state car, a dusty Ford Fusion with official Maine magnetic labeling on both front doors, the large lettering reading 'Crime Lab.' Never a good car to see in one's own driveway, Tom thought. He was sure Clint's neighbors stayed away from him.

Clint continued. "What are you guys doing out here in Secretly? Growing dead bodies?"

Tom shook his head and grinned. Clint was more of a joker than he was.

"Although," Clint went on, "the fact that both bodies aren't recent tells me you're not that good at finding them." He laughed.

Tom guessed that if he had to work with all of the bones and soft tissue decay that Clint did, day in and day out, he, too, would be even more sarcastic.

Tom waved to Hailey, who stood next to Clint, also grinning. She was pretty with short brown hair—a pixie haircut, his mother would have called it—with a wide, friendly smile. She was also tall, almost six feet, which was a good half-foot taller than Tom and probably the only reason he hadn't dated her. One of the few of the state workers whom he hadn't.

Hailey checked her watch. Her wrists were long and slender. There was no ring on her left hand. Not that rings meant anything to Tom, in many circumstances, but they often meant something to the woman who was wearing them, and he respected that. The one thing he never understood was why a married woman, or even one in a committed relationship, would ever think he'd be interested in her long term, knowing she was a cheater. Once a cheater, always a cheater, was his motto.

His mind flashed back to the woman in the car. If it was who he thought it was, he had helped her cheat on her significant other. Was he any better than her? So, she said the guy was boring, and they might not make it long term. That was a couple of years ago, and, no surprise, they hadn't.

"We'll have to wait for the medical examiner," said Hailey. "He should be here in about fifteen minutes."

"Why's that?" Tom needed confirmation now. He needed the car door opened and the face fully visible. On Wednesday, Clint went with him and Marcel straight to Charles Kearns' body in the woods before the ME's arrival. Why the hesitation now?

"The body hasn't been exposed to oxygen. Once we open the door, decomp will start in rapid fire. We want to make sure we're all on the same page, see the same thing, the ME and us." Hailey was matter-of-fact. A good straight man, so to speak, to Clint's clown.

Marcel and Roger had joined the small group.

"Long time, no see, Sheriff," said Clint, saluting.

"Let's not make a habit of this," said Marcel.

"I hear you." Clint stuck his hand out towards Roger. "Welcome to the team."

"Thank you, sir." Roger had slightly recovered from his previous loss of lunch. He had been standing there, probably debating if he had made a poor career choice, but the more he stood with Marcel, and now meeting the crime lab folks, the more he also probably felt he was actually home. Tom's grandfather always praised him for steering clear of the troublemakers and gravitating toward what his grandfather called "good people." The men and woman in front of him were good people, including Roger.

Clint smiled at the cadet's use of "sir," but didn't call it out as a joke, and embarrass him. He turned to Marcel.

"Funny seeing you twice in one day,"

Marcel nodded. "I know." He didn't elaborate, and Tom realized that Marcel actually never did say where he was the whole time his cell was smashed, and Tom had been trying to reach him.

"Where…" Tom's question to Marcel trailed off with the sound of more gravel. The Medical Examiner had arrived. All eyes turned toward the opening in the brush, where the logging road came into the clearing by the pond. A white van, the same one that had been at Marcel's home on Wednesday, parked next to the state crime lab car. The Medical Examiner, in the blue scrubs used by clinical professionals in hospitals and offices, walked toward them carrying a medical bag, obviously with tools to use on a human who had already passed on. Tom wondered what it was like to be a doctor for the dead. He probably had the same motivation that Tom had—to find justice for the murdered soul.

He was surprised the word 'soul' entered his vocabulary. Raised Catholic, including being carted off to a Catholic high school forty-five minutes away, didn't get the religion to stick, although maybe with the recent murders in his hometown, he was getting soft in his old age of thirty-seven.

The medical examiner approached, shaking his head. "You two," he said, looking from Marcel to Tom, "you really know how to ruin a holiday weekend."

"We try." Tom grinned, shaking off the dark thoughts of souls and Sister Mary Margaret in chemistry class.

The ME, Dr. Stuart Shaw, was in his mid-sixties and a real Mainer, drawl and all. Tom hoped to be retired and just puttering on his lobster boat by the time he was Dr. Shaw's age, but he knew many doctors felt like they had a calling, although he'd hoped the doc would give himself a break from death and end his career with saving lives.

Dr. Shaw stood by the muddy Toyota. "So, what's the lay of the land?"

Marcel nodded toward the newbie. "Officer Stanton, why don't you start?"

Roger, still a bit pale and trying to keep people between him and the car, edged slightly forward and swallowed. He relayed again the tale of the call, and speaking with Emil Bryant. He gestured toward the tow truck driver, who was now sprawled out on the bench with his feet in front of him and his arms crossed. Tom suspected he was napping. Or eavesdropping.

Dr. Shaw thanked Roger for the information as he put on his rubber gloves. He walked around to the driver's side, peered in, and then motioned to Clint to come over and take a photo.

"I don't think she'll be getting any online dates with that picture," said Clint. Tom winced. Clint had already documented the entire car and scene, as well as the deceased, through the window but took another photo of the victim per the doctor's request.

Clint said to the group, "Remember, when she comes out, there won't be a lot of hair on her head. It dies, too, when the person dies, and then it falls out. All the stupid movies showing a dead woman with long hair flowing around. Nope."

Dr. Shaw straightened up and surveyed the group. "Everyone ready?"

Roger's face said, "Ready for what?" even though he remained silent. He took a few steps back.

Dr. Shaw reached for the handle and pulled the driver's side door open. Thankfully, no water or snakes rushed out. A putrid smell filled the air. Tom was grateful it was November and not July.

Doc Shaw leaned in and then quickly pulled his head out.

"No one told me there were two bodies."

"Two?" Marcel walked quickly toward the open car door, as did Tom and the two from the forensics team.

"Two bodies?" Clint said. He had looked closely at the one on the driver's side. He even had looked a bit on the passenger side and in the back. No other bodies seemed visible to him.

Dr. Shaw stepped aside as they peered in one by one, holding their noses and their breath to block out the intense smell of rot.

The woman was strapped into the driver's seat, which helped keep her body in place. Seeing her up close now, without the smear of mud on the windows, Tom's fears were confirmed. In his mind, he saw her with pink flesh and wavy brown hair. He heard her giggle freely and blow him an air kiss.

The second body, a man, hadn't been wearing his seat belt. His bloated, grayish-green corpse had expanded and floated away from the seat and had pressed itself up to the windshield. With the slime and mud and his own discoloring, no one had noticed him. He blended in.

His face, although very distorted, was also recognizable to Tom. Tom knew him well.

He straightened up and turned to Marcel.

"I'm going to go out on a limb," said Tom, "and say that Rusty Poole didn't pull any trigger in October."

Chapter Thirty-Eight

Johnny had ants in his pants.

After Tommy had dropped him off, he entered his house and went straight to the kitchen, instantly seeing the mess of dishes he had made making the brownies and serving the sundaes. Ice cream and chocolate sauce remnants had hardened to the bowls. Jimmies were strewn across the kitchen table, along with a few stray ice cream drips. He filled a dishpan with hot, soapy water to soak the bowls, spoons, and brownie pan. A good chore to have.

The action triggered a memory. He was back in Rockland, doing dishes, when he and Julia were still together. The water was similarly hot and soapy as it was now in the dishpan. He was half in the bag. Maybe fully in the bag. Must have been a day off from the force or after a shift. Raven clung to his pant leg, balancing herself. She had just learned to walk, probably around two years old, maybe younger. He was bad with remembering things like how old she was when she took her first step or ate her first solid food or when she said "Da-da" instead of "Ma-ma" as her first words, much to Julia's disappointment. Unless Julia wrote it all down in a baby book, that information was lost forever with Julia's passing.

That particular day, he and Julia must have had a steak for dinner because he was wiping the blade of a sharp knife with a sponge when he swayed at the sink and lost his balance. The knife dropped from his hand. It aimed straight down to the floor. Only thing was, between his hand and the floor was Raven. The knife was heading toward the top of her head. It would have plunged straight into her skull.

The only thing he could do was shove Raven aside with his left foot. He pushed on her as fast as he could, and in doing so, she went flying across the linoleum in her stocking feet and landed hard on her butt just as the knife dug into the floor and stuck upright. It had landed directly where Raven had been standing.

Raven, startled, sat for a second, eyes wide and shocked, and then burst into tears and screamed. Julia came running and found Raven sobbing, red-faced with a face full of tears and a large chef's knife still standing erect on the floor next to Johnny while he clung to the counter's edge, trying to stay upright, loosing his sea legs from both the booze and the gravity of what might had happened.

"Get out! Get out! Right now! You're a monster! I hate you!" Julia had screamed at him as she lifted Raven up from the floor, checking her over for cuts and scrapes. Raven continued to wail at the top of her lungs.

Then Raven did something that angered Julia more. She reached her arms out for Johnny. She wanted Johnny to comfort her, not Julia. Johnny was the patient parent. The one who rocked her when she had the croup, the one who sang lullabies into her ear when she struggled to fall asleep, the one who bandaged her knees when she scraped them. She was Daddy's Little Girl.

He took a step forward to take her into his arms, to take her out of Julia's, but Julia turned her back, so Raven was out of reach. Raven squirmed and twisted in Julia's arms and flung herself over Julia's shoulder, arms still extended out to Johnny.

"Da-da!" Raven screamed.

Julia called over her shoulder. "Get out. I mean it."

So he did as Raven called for him until she was hoarse.

He walked out that day, leaving the knife stuck in the floor, returning later on his knees to apologize and beg forgiveness. It bought him a few more years with Raven and Julia, but when he finally realized he couldn't straighten out, he left for good, resigning from the Rockland Police and heading to Boston. He had called ahead to a cousin who offered him a couch. He eventually sat for the Boston Police Exam, passing it easily, and that was how life rolled up to this point, him continuing to send Julia money for Raven, begging her in the letters to let him come up and see her and Raven, begging to take him back after he had stopped drinking.

And he had stopped drinking, but not immediately. It had taken at least a decade, first not believing he had a problem, then going dry and then drunk, over and over again, until one morning, he woke up feeling worse than he ever had. It wasn't the hangover—the nausea and headache—he was used to that. It was the heartache of all he had lost, of the direction that his life had taken.

That was fifteen years ago.

He hadn't wanted to continue to pressure Julia to let him come home. She had never answered one of his letters, never sent a school picture of Raven as she grew, never once said she appreciated the money he had sent. Once a month. Half of his pay.

He had thought cash was an easier thing for Julia to receive, no check to cash, no town gossip from a bank teller, associating the check with Julia's failed marriage, but as a cop, he was afraid of the mail being stolen and the cash lost forever. It was a risk he took.

Julia also had never asked for a divorce. Had never even filed for one. Had never reported him for that day in the kitchen. Or tossing the Christmas tree, lights, and ornaments, onto the street. Or face planting too many times on the lawn. She had just told him to leave. For good.

Johnny stared down at the suds and stuck his hands into the water, now cooling down to a reasonable warmth. He picked up a sponge and began to clean the stuck-on, sugary remains of what had been the best day he had had with Raven since he moved back. It wasn't great, but it was something, and it took a murder in town to have it materialize. She hadn't come alone or even with an open heart, but she had come and come in.

"Please give me the wisdom to know the difference," he whispered towards the suds, speaking only the last line of the prayer he knew so well. He had fully accepted everything he could not change and continuously made an effort to change what he could. He still needed the wisdom—the guidance—to know which camp his relationship with Raven fell into.

Johnny was jolted back to reality with the sound of the sirens. Multiple sirens. They came from Eelsboro and headed further south into town past his property. Did something happen at the pond where Marcel and Tommy were heading, or was this for something else?

He shook the water off his hands, dried them on a dish towel, and grabbed his coat as he headed out the door to find out.

Chapter Thirty-Nine

Charles' cloud account was organized, unlike his bedroom. He had categories for construction work, court appearances, and birdwatching.

On her laptop, Raven clicked briefly on the construction thumbnail and then the folder marked "Billoni," but there wasn't much in there other than photographs of cracks in cement, which had meaning to Charles and the safety commissioners but not to her.

The birdwatching also had folders, and she focused on the Maine folder. Within that folder, he broke it down by date, not by bird. There were ten subfolders in July. What was the date of his famous owl one?

"The date of the full moon!" Using her cell's search engine, she narrowed it down to two folders. Within those, one was obvious with the large white snowy owl in about thirty frames. Click after click, the owl was in flight until it was directly over Blue Heron Pond. The beautiful white bird reflected in the pond with the shine of the moon and flew under the real moon and over the moon's reflection. No one could have staged it this well.

Raven zoomed in on the owl to appreciate the amazing clarity Charles had achieved. Then something caught her eye. Something in the pond. Backing up frame by frame, it was something sinking. A log? No, too wide. An old trunk? No, too small. Maybe a car? She shivered. Could it be the same car that Marcel was dredging up right now?

She scanned all of the frames in this section, and a vertical line was also moving a bit on the shore. Not a line. A person. She zoomed in on the person. The characteristics were grainy and blurry from being in the shadow, not the moonlight like the owl. She squinted and leaned forward toward the screen.

"Ah, now we can see what Charles saw," Raven said out loud.

A creak made her sit up. An outline stood in the doorway.

Evelyn Poole.

Chapter Forty

When Betty got home from Johnny's, she went right to her weekly chores—washing the floors, cleaning the bathrooms, and vacuuming. She was only a week behind on them and saw Howard's sideward glances at the dust balls. Taking off her rubber gloves, she now had the remainder of the day in front of her. Her earlier adventures with Raven were a dream—being a part of something meaningful hadn't happened in a long time—but now she was back to her same dull life. She hated to say that the town needed more murders, but Charles' death had definitely brightened up her world.

Howard sat in his leather chair and read. She admired the way he was always able to entertain himself. If she was honest, he didn't need her, and she didn't need him. So, how did two people stay together once their children were grown? Maybe they shouldn't.

She needed to get out of the house.

"I'm going over to Raven's," she said as she walked out the back door and to her car. She could have walked over to the Ouellettes, but she hoped that Raven would have a new plan for their next adventure, and this time, she'd be the driver.

Betty drove up Pine Acres's driveway as a fancy black SUV with a Massachusetts plate passed her in the opposite direction. The driveway wasn't wide enough for both cars, and Betty drove into a small ditch. When she tried to pull forward or back up, her tires spun. She was stuck.

"Darn it all!" She smashed her fist against the steering wheel. The last thing she wanted to do was ask Howard for help. He'd lecture her and point out new flaws that he had missed in the forty years of their marriage. Damn, those Massachusetts cabin renters!

Then Betty froze. Was it a BMW? A Black BMW SUV with Massachusetts plates? Could it have been Nick Billoni's? She had assumed the SUV was just speeding off in typical Massachusetts fashion, but maybe it was on purpose because it was Nick, and he had done something to Raven.

Betty gasped at the thought. Thankfully, she easily got out of her vehicle and walked as fast as her out-of-shape legs would carry her to the Ouellette house. Raven's Mini wasn't there, but Marcel's Jeep was in the driveway. She relaxed. Nothing bad could have happened because Raven wasn't there, and Marcel was everyone's protector.

Before she could walk up the steps to the house, she heard more tires growling up the driveway. Was that SUV coming back? Betty hid behind a birch tree in case it was Nick.

Chapter Forty-One

Evelyn and Raven stared at each other.

"I didn't hear you come up the stairs," said Raven, stammering as she caught up on her breathing, trying to slow her pounding heart. "I must have been deep in thought."

She was grateful her computer screen faced away from the door.

"Yes, you were. I heard you mumbling something about photos. Owls. Pond. Car. You have photos that Charles took." Evelyn said it as a statement, not a question, without moving from the spot. Her hair was wild, like she had been running her hands through it. She still had on her Lane's Market smock.

Raven had no plans to share what she was looking at. "Photos? No, I don't have Charles's photos."

"Then why were you talking about them?" Evelyn's voice was low. "Why are you sitting in his house on a computer?"

Raven's brain finally kicked in. She moved her finger gingerly on the tracker pad and eyed the "X" in the upper right-hand corner. Without looking at the screen, she ballparked where to guide the cursor and eventually hit it to close out of the cloud account. "No, I…I don't have any of Charles' photos." She paused and then steadied herself. "I hear he was a wonderful bird photographer, though."

"That's why he was in the woods that night."

"Pardon?" Raven pretended not to understand. She pretended she didn't think of Evelyn when she zoomed in on that blurry face by the pond in one of the owl photos.

"I heard you talking about his photos, Raven." Then she mumbled to herself. "This has all gotten bigger than it was supposed to be."

"I'm still not following." Raven felt a chill. "Well, Evelyn, nice seeing you. I have to get back home. Marcel will be wondering where I am." She shut her laptop cover and stood up.

Evelyn shook her head and reached behind her. Her right hand held a large metal pipe from the dismantled kitchen. She raised it in front of her.

"I need that notebook and your computer." She gestured with the pipe towards Raven.

Raven looked at the small notebook in her left hand, nestled on top of her cell phone. Her fingers clutched both. She knew she was holding something valuable for Marcel, evidence that led to Charles' killer. Maybe Evelyn and Rusty were in it together.

"Why do you need this notebook, Evelyn?" Raven was surprised by her bravery but also proud of herself for finding her voice, anything to distract Evelyn.

"You said it will show you what Charles saw. I need to stop you from seeing what he saw although I think you already did see it."

Raven felt every nerve in her legs and hoped they would keep her upright. She didn't want to collapse. Dig deep, she said to herself and, out loud, asked, "What do you think he saw?"

"You already know, but I'm happy to elaborate since you won't be telling anyone else." She hit the pipe in her hand like she was the lead bad guy in a 1930s noir film.

Raven looked at the pipe and then up at Evelyn. Evelyn was shorter and a bit older than her, but was in what her mother would have called "fighting shape." What was it with natural-ability athletes? She was positive Evelyn would swing that pipe as if Raven's head was a softball, and she was aiming for the bleachers to win the state championship again. Could Raven duck or block the swing in time? Probably not.

Mrs. Poole in the Bedroom with a Lead Pipe.

There was a reason the game of Clue had a lead pipe as a murder weapon. Because it could kill. Remember that, Raven, she told herself, remember that.

Buying herself time was Raven's only hope. Maybe there would be a noise to distract Evelyn, and Raven could make a grab for it. Or she could wait for Evelyn to let her guard down. Without taking her eyes fully off Evelyn, Raven took in the room, at least what she could see in front of her and peripherally. Was anything there to use as a weapon or for defense? Nothing that she saw. Maybe the wooden desk chair. She relaxed a little with her plan.

Steadying her voice, she said, "Okay, then why don't you tell me what Charles saw."

"Here's the thing," Evelyn said, bouncing the pipe into her left palm again, playing a mobster in an old movie. "I don't even know if he saw anything or understood what he saw." She stopped moving the pipe and shrugged. Did Raven even see a little regret in her eyes? Evelyn continued. "But he could have been there. Well, I'm sure he was there. I just don't know if he saw anything, but I couldn't take the chance."

Raven's head swam in the jungle of Evelyn's words. Was it her nerves, or did Evelyn talk in circles? No harm in asking questions.

"Where was Charles? And you? When you thought he saw something." Raven forced herself to exhale.

"At the Blue Heron Pond Preserve."

Evelyn said it like she was going there for a picnic. That was where Marcel and Tom were called. Her mother always said, "There is no such thing as a coincidence." Did Evelyn know about the police call? Is that why she was here? Raven needed to continue to play dumb.

"I'm still not understanding." Buy time. Buy time.

"This is about Rusty and Sarah," said Evelyn.

Now, Raven was thoroughly confused. Maybe Rusty did kill Charles. She had never known Evelyn to be a drunk or on drugs, but she wasn't making sense. Maybe she had a stroke. Maybe that's why she held Raven hostage with a lead pipe.

"I thought this was about Charles's…" She stopped short of saying Charles' murder. She didn't need to bring that word into the conversation, to plant that seed in regard to her own potential future.

"Not really, no.   It was never about Charles or his award-winning photograph." Evelyn smirked… "Just about what he might have seen. This has always been about Rusty. It wasn't even about that bitch, Sarah."

Marcel and Tom were called to Blue Heron Pond because a car had been found in the water.

"Does this have something to do with a car in the pond?"

Evelyn's eyes flashed, and she took a step towards Raven, the lead pipe raised. "How do you know about that? Were you there with Charles that night?"

Raven took a step towards the wooden chair and wished she hadn't mentioned the car.

"I…I…I don't know anything about a car." A feeble answer. A lie. Although Raven didn't know more than what she had just said.

"Tell me!" Evelyn demanded. She banged the pipe against the floor. Raven jumped at the loud sound.

Raven didn't have to explain. Sirens wailed toward them. Raven felt her heart leap with hope of help coming her way. Evelyn looked up to the ceiling and around her as if a helicopter was about to land in the tiny bedroom.

The sirens came close.

Closer.

Closer still.

Then passed the house.

Further.

Further away.

Until there was silence.

And Raven was again alone with Evelyn.

And her lead pipe.

Chapter Forty-Two

Johnny pulled his beat-up truck behind a second medical examiner's van, the first being closer to the crowd of official workers—uniforms of all kinds—county sheriff, lab technicians, medical examiners, and the State Police. Marcel must be pissed. Who called the Staties?

He walked closer to a muddy car attached to a tow truck.

"Sorry, sir, this is a crime scene," said a boy playing sheriff deputy. He put up his hand to imply that Johnny should not take one step further. Was this kid even old enough to shave?

"Johnny, come on over," said Tommy, waving him into the secret society. "It's okay, Roger. He's a consultant with the sheriff's office."

A consultant? A state trooper in the group raised his eyebrows.

"A free one; don't get your undies all tied in a knot," said Tommy to an officer more than double his size, both in height and girth. "Retired Boston cop and Marcel's father-in-law."

The information didn't make the state trooper relax. What part of what Tommy shared kept the tension in his face—Boston, retired, or related to Marcel? Whatever, Johnny strode forward and stuck out his hand to the cop.

"Ethan Johnson, but you can call me Johnny. Nice to meet you."

The trooper nodded but didn't extend his hand or his name Johnny's way. Johnny winked at Tommy, who grinned.

Tommy steered Johnny away from Debbie Downer and over to the side, out of earshot of the rest.

"Not sure if you're up on town gossip," Tommy said.

"I try my best," Johnny said with a grin.

"Well, last summer, Rusty Poole and Sarah Wolf ran off together."

"Yep, heard about it. Evelyn seems to have recovered, back to herself at the store."

"Yeah, well, they didn't get very far." With his chin, he motioned toward the muddy car.

"Inside? They're inside the car?" Johnny's eyes showed amazement and interest.

"Yep, the medical examiners are right now removing the bodies."

"But this pond isn't deep. If the car went in, why didn't they just get out of the vehicle? Heck, the water is probably only up to your waist."

"Try just over your knee except in the far corner. But that's with the drought. Even so, with the heavy rain we got in the spring, I don't think it would have been much more than the height of the car. Actually, it was a little over the height of the car. That's why no one saw it until now."

"Maybe they were drunk when the car went in?" As a recovering alcoholic, Johnny always had booze on the brain, sometimes as an innocent answer like this one, and other times as the demon who possessed and taunted him.

"We'll know when they run a tox report, but no, I think the real reason they didn't get out of the car is because they went into the pond already dead."

"Come again?" Johnny pivoted to look over his shoulder at the ME and lab team who were busily working the car over, wearing additional protective covering on their hands, head, and body. All four were also wearing goggles.

Tommy had followed Johnny's gaze and then added, "There appears to be evidence of bullet wounds to the skulls."

Johnny nodded his head in understanding. He had faced too many of these situations down in Boston. "Like a murder-suicide?" Sadly, true to Maine murders, the victim and the killer know each other well.

"Probably not. More like a murder-murder."

Johnny pulled back, surprised. In Secretly? Again? "Really!" The state cop turned back towards Johnny and Tommy. Johnny lowered his voice. "Really?"

Tommy nodded.

"Wow. Must be a local, though. Right? Who would have wanted them both dead? Karl Wolf?" Johnny thought of the nice man at the marine store. He didn't seem like the violent type, but that was usually the case. Hard to know what made someone snap.

"That would be my guess. We have a deputy over at his house now."

"Has the ME estimated time of death?"

"You mean month of death?"

Johnny shook his head in amazement again.

"Yep," said Tommy. "Probably right around the time they left town."

"So before Charles was killed."

"Yep"

"Is there a way they could have come back to town last month, killed Charles, and then got themselves killed?"

Tommy shook his head. "October weather was almost as unseasonably cold as November. The decomp would have been halted. These two," he motioned with his head towards the car with the flurry of activity, "have been in the pond a long time."

Johnny couldn't imagine the stench and the condition of the bodies. Four months locked in a car. Throughout the summer. Underwater. He was grateful that the body lying on a stretcher closest to him and Tommy was bundled in a sheet.

"So you guys are thinking that Karl took Rusty's gun and killed Charles?"

Tommy shrugged. "It's one theory, but it seems like a pretty solid one to me."

Johnny saw the sadness in Tommy's eyes, thinking about someone he knew and liked going off to jail forever. Tom continued.

"The part that doesn't fit for me, though, is the timing of this with the Charles Kearns murder. Are they even connected? I mean, if Charles saw Karl kill Rusty and Sarah in July, wouldn't Karl have killed Charles back in the summer? Why wait until October or November?"

"Unless Charles was blackmailing Karl. Maybe Karl didn't even know someone saw him until the first blackmail message arrived, and maybe he didn't figure out it was Charles until last month," said Johnny.

Tommy nodded. "That's a solid thought. We can look to see if Karl's been moving money around, even from the store bank accounts."

"Wonder if there's anything in those videos we took. Now that we might know what to focus on. Oh, and didn't Betty say that she and Raven had spoken to Karl and his new girlfriend? That's how we got the Nick lead that he was in town."

Tommy shook his head. "Another 'jump-the-gun' interview. Hard to believe that Betty and Raven had Karl on their radar before we did, though."

"Because of those love notes in Charles' chimney."

"I guess that could be part of the key to this all." Tommy checked his phone, both text and email. "Raven hasn't sent me her video yet. Maybe having trouble loading it up through the state system."

Johnny thought back to little Raven, two-year-old Raven, sobbing on the kitchen floor. All the years he missed, all the milestones, all the memories. He turned back to the crime scene so Tommy wouldn't see the tears forming.

Marcel motioned to them but only called Tommy back over to the muddy Toyota. Before Tommy walked out of earshot, Johnny called out to him.

"I'll catch you later." He had a strong need to see his little girl.

Chapter Forty-Three

"Stupid drought." Evelyn shook her head in disgust.

"Excuse me?" Raven continued to believe that buying time and keeping Evelyn talking was her best, her only, option.

"Nothin.'" Evelyn's eyebrows were so tightly knitted together that they looked like one brow. Unibrow. The word would have made Raven chuckle if she wasn't watching the Unibrow standing in the doorway, standing between her and freedom, and possibly life.

This is what the soldiers in war are taught, thought Raven. Dehumanize the enemy. If Raven thought of Evelyn as something other than someone she knew her whole life, someone she chatted with at Lane's Market at least once a week, she would be able to harm her, even kill her, to save herself.

If Raven called Evelyn 'Unibrow,' what was Evelyn calling Raven? She could guess after hearing what Evelyn had called Sarah.

Raven twirled the small notebook and her cell phone around each other in her hand, wishing she remembered how to call for emergency help without being obvious—maybe she could call one of these sirens back—but all she knew how to do without opening her phone was turn on her flashlight and camera.

"What are you doing?" Evelyn asked, raising the pipe and eyeing Raven's hand, her eyes wild.

Raven froze, keeping her eyes glued to Evelyn's face. "Listening. Listening to you."

Evelyn considered Raven's answer and lowered the pipe. She nodded, like a teacher who believed a lying pupil.

Buy time. Buy time. "Why don't you start from the beginning?"

"Now that's funny." Evelyn actually snorted out a laugh. Raven was a snorter, too, if something was really funny. Marcel said it was endearing to hear her snort. It didn't sound endearing to hear Evelyn.

Evelyn snorted again. "Which beginning? Meeting Rusty? The beginning of the end? How about marrying him against my father's wishes? Gosh, why didn't I listen to my dad?" She stared off into the distance. "He knew Rusty wasn't good for me and told me so." Evelyn refocused, back on Raven. "Sarah wasn't his first affair, you know. I think he's slept with everyone in town except Marie Claire and you."

Raven tried to steer clear of all town gossip, mainly because she feared what people said about her—being raised by a single mom and her grandfather, then marrying a sheriff, running an inherited business, and having a long-lost father return who ran around town, at times, like he owned the place. Okay, so she did hear gossip now and then, both about herself and others, but she couldn't recall much about Rusty and his conquests, or about Evelyn.

Evelyn's eyes pleaded for understanding, her face softening. "This time felt different. He was so happy it made me sick. Whistling around the house. Keeping his crap clean, especially his truck. Shaving. Getting haircuts. Even, ironically, coming home early, and eating supper with me, before going back out on his lobster boat." She used air quotes for the words 'lobster boat,' implying that he really wasn't going there. "And here I was working next to Sarah, who was also happy, always humming and cleaning her register, wearing perfume and make-up and her best clothes, acting smug, assuming I didn't know she was screwing my husband, which I didn't at first. When I figured it out, I couldn't take it anymore."

Oddly, Raven understood. It was bad enough to have a cheating husband, but to have his mistress flaunt it in your face day after day, Raven thought she'd crack too if in the same situation. Not resort to murder, she hoped, but lose it in some other way.

"I actually wish they had just run off together." Evelyn leaned against the doorframe, the lead pipe still in her hand but dangling low. "But I knew that would never happen. Rusty was greedy for his lobster money, and Karl

Wolf probably would never divorce Sarah, thinking of her as a prize trophy. Rusty used to say that. I guess until he, too, thought of her as a trophy, so I was stuck watching Rusty come into the store and give me a kiss on the cheek while winking at Sarah. Openly. Like they were buddies. She'd blush and giggle. I hated being made out as the fool, especially in public. I wanted them to know I knew."

Raven caught the line that Evelyn had said, wishing that Rusty and Sarah had run off. Didn't they? If they didn't, where had they been all this time?

Evelyn continued. "I'd lie in bed promising myself that the next time Rusty came into the store, customers or not, I was going to blast him, expose them both. But I'm not like that. I couldn't do it. Not there. Not at home. Not anywhere."

"So my hate just grew. Every day I fed it, and it grew, until I realized having them know wasn't enough anymore. I pictured them laughing at me when I confronted them. Saying 'so what' to me and making it out like I was the problem. That I wasn't pretty enough or young enough or thin enough or fun enough. I made up all sorts of scenarios in my mind."

Evelyn straightened up and looked Raven in the eye. "Until I got an idea."

Chapter Forty-Four

Johnny turned up the long gravel drive to the Ouellette's home and Pine Acres Cabins. Betty's vehicle was slightly off-kilter to the right of the driveway.

"Wonder what made her drive off the edge?" Johnny said out loud. He slowed to look inside, but the front seat was vacant. Further up the driveway, he saw Betty trying to hide behind a thin birch tree. He stopped the truck in front of it and lowered his window.

"I can seeee youuuuuu," He said lightly in a singsong voice, not sure of what type of reaction he'd get. Betty stepped away from the tree and laughed.

"Oh, I probably look foolish," she said. "I was afraid you were Nick Billoni coming back."

"Nick? Coming back? Is that who ran you off the road?" Johnny got out of the truck, keeping his engine running.

"Yes, well, I think so," Betty knitted her fingers together. "It was a large black SUV with Mass plates."

"Hmmm, could be one of a hundred SUVs running 'round Secretly and Whale Harbor on a holiday weekend." Johnny opened up the passenger door. "How about I drive you back home?"

"Oh, I wanted to talk to Marcel about it." Betty pointed to his Jeep.

"He's not home. He's with Tom at…" He stopped. Not his news to share.

"Where are they? Something to do with the case? Did they find Charles's killer?" Her eyes lit up.

"No, no. Something new," said Johnny. "I was just coming here to see Raven, but I see her car's gone."

"Yes, I was coming to see her, too. Maybe we can look for her together." She climbed into the cab of his truck.

"You don't want me to take you home?" Johnny glanced at her as he turned his truck around.

Betty grimaced. "I'd rather you didn't."

Johnny smiled and nodded. Most wives dreaded calling their husbands about a car accident. He was sure all her vehicle needed was a good push, but he'd leave it alone for now.

"Okey-doke. Mission 'Find Raven' it is," he said as he turned on the road toward the Lane Mansion. It was as good a place to start as any.

Chapter Forty-Five

Evelyn's eyes glistened as she shared her story with Raven.

"So, one day, I decided to carry out my plan. I hid in the backseat of Sarah's Toyota at the end of my shift. I knew she had to close. I crouched in the back behind the front passenger seat and prayed my legs could handle being crammed in that position for an hour or more. Good thing I'm short. I tossed the empty Mickey D soda cups to the other side of the floor, so I didn't have to smell the stale sugar smell. Who drinks that much soda? No wonder she was becoming a blimp."

Raven thought of Sarah Wolf at the register at Lane's. Her memory didn't reveal a fat person.

"Sarah was in such a hurry to get into Rusty's pants, she didn't pay any attention that my truck was still in the parking lot. I didn't even have to hide it. Plus, with it being summer, the parking lot was busy with tourists and seasonal folks who parked there to walk around town. The sun was going down. Perfect timing. I couldn't have planned it any better."

Evelyn stared off as she recalled the moment with pride, a smile on her face. She moved further into the room, leaving the doorway unguarded. Raven kept still, wondering if, during this reminiscence, there would be an opening for her to run past Evelyn and down the stairs before the pipe crashed down on her head.

"Thank God Sarah kept her windows down while she worked. Otherwise, I wouldn't have been able to stand it in that car with the July heat and humidity. I'd have ended up like one of the kids on the news where the dad claims to have forgotten to go to daycare, leaving the child all day in the car seat."

Raven refused to take in that news story or any like it. Her heart always broke for the parents. No parent does that on purpose. The media should leave them alone. She might do it herself by accident with the dogs if they weren't always jumping around and ready to get out of the car.

"I had planned on just offing her. Do you know what it's like to work next to the slut who is screwing your husband?" Her voice cracked.

Would Raven become Evelyn if Marcel took up with Shannon? Her heart pounded at the thought of losing Marcel, of him preferring someone else and not loving her anymore.

Evelyn continued. "Day after day of lies from her. 'I'm going home to do laundry...so booooorrrrring,'" Evelyn imitated Sarah. "Often, the slut's shift ended before mine. Going to do laundry, my ass. Just making more laundry for me by soiling my own sheets!"

Evelyn threw her back against the wall and let out a wail. It stunned Raven. Evelyn sobbed, still holding onto the pipe, head lowered. She wasn't far enough from the door for Raven to run, but if she moved a little further along the way, maybe, with the chair as a barrier, maybe Raven could get out.

Evelyn continued to cry. Real tears. Not crocodile tears. Months and months of pain. Probably years-worth. An avalanche of ache fell to Charles's bedroom floor in the form of those tears. The wetness darkened the wood grain in front of Evelyn.

Raven felt tears well up and roll over the brims. "I'm so sorry, Evelyn."

Evelyn's sobs quieted, and she wiped her tears with the sleeve of her empty hand. For a moment, Raven believed that Evelyn had come back to reality and was going to let her walk peacefully out of the house. Evelyn cleared her throat.

"I need to finish the story." She lowered her voice. "I need someone to know the whole story."

"I'm listening," said Raven. "Go on." *Please let me listen and live, Evelyn. What good does it do to tell me and then kill me, too?*

"I don't remember how I figured it out, that they were banging each other. Maybe Rusty smelled like her one day at home, or she slipped and knew something about me that she shouldn't. I don't really remember."

Evelyn paused to consider that memory, to see if she could find it to confirm when the painful truth set in, but it didn't come.

"Whatever. Anyway, when I was finally on to them, I'd wait fifteen minutes after she left Lane's, and then I'd call Rusty. No pick up. Then I'd call Sarah, prepared to ask her a question about the store or tell her she left something personal at her register. No pick up. Over and over again. Time after time. I'd repeat this, customer permitting, for about an hour. Just to annoy them. You don't know what it's like to be obsessed with showing someone that you know they are lying to you! How downright aggravating it is to know you are being lied to! You want to slap the person. To shake them. To cuss them out. It became my whole life. It was ruining me."

She gritted her teeth and made a sound like a growl. Raven held her breath. Instead of thinking of her own worries, she thought of her mother. Was Evelyn's torment over lies, the same torment her own mother felt when Johnny kept drinking? When he promised to stop, but kept doing it? When he left, did she think he'd come back? Did she wait for him to walk through the door? Did her mother privately sob? Raven never saw it, and she never asked her mother how long she waited for him to return. She didn't remember living in Rockland with just her mother before moving to Secretly to live with her grandfather. She didn't remember anything about her Rockland childhood. But she should. She was five years old.

Evelyn was speaking quietly, looking off, talking more to herself than to Raven.

"I'm sorry," said Raven. "I can't hear you."

"Oh, I was just talking to myself. Remembering that, I thought of telling Karl about what I suspected, but everyone knew he was screwing Laurie, so what would he care? He was as bad as Rusty. Maybe he'd be relieved. Happy about it. That would be no help to me. Misery loves company, and I definitely wanted someone to be as miserable as I was. Who better to make miserable than Rusty by taking away Sarah."

"And that's what got me thinking that getting rid of Sarah was a public service. Karl would be free to be with Laurie. And I'd have Rusty back." She paused and looked directly at Raven. "I like Laurie. Do you?"

Raven was thrown by the matter-of-fact random question but nodded. "I do."

Evelyn went on.

"I feel bad for Laurie, being widowed so young. And the way Hugh died. Anyway, with Sarah gone, I'd have Rusty back, even if the son-of-a-bitch would cheat again. At least it wouldn't be with my coworker. I'd have peace and quiet at my job and wouldn't have to look at that slut's face anymore. Karl could be with Laurie out in the open. Laurie'd have Karl and wouldn't be alone anymore. You can see where I'm going with this."

Raven really couldn't. Having an affair shouldn't be a death sentence. She needed to remind herself of that. Just in case.

"And my insurance was I'd use Rusty's gun to do the deed. That way, if he didn't settle back down, or if he did this again with someone else, I could call a tip line, and he'd be picked up and gone." She laughed. "Sent up the river, as they say."

Raven found her voice. "Seems like you thought of all the angles."

Evelyn took the compliment and beamed like a child praised for a good grade. Her energy level tripled. "I did. I really did. And I didn't even flinch with the wrinkle to my original plan when the slut picked up Rusty at the dock."

Evelyn boasted. Perhaps this was the best accomplishment of her life.

Chapter Forty-Six

Blue Heron Pond was two feet deep by the beach and sixty feet deep in the back corner that ran against the logging road. The deep section was a tiny area, made millions, maybe billions, of years ago, after Maine's volcanoes had erupted, after the glaciers slowly rolled through, and after North America separated from Africa. Whatever came through there made a large hole in just one small spot, and now that spot was opened up, possibly made dangerous, by the Preserve Association leadership authorizing logging in the back fifty acres.

Tom understood the reasoning. Thin the old-growth trees to allow newer ones to flourish. Many old trees kept coming down in the storms. Newer growth, including leaving the stumps of the cut ones to rot, gave way to changes in the wildlife that all areas benefited from. The money from the lumber also didn't hurt.

Tom pondered if the Toyota had, instead of taking the logging road around and crossing over to the beach, had gone off one of the edges by the deep drop, it would have been gone for good, or at least for a million or so years until this part of the earth dried up into nothing as the climate change scientists warned. The Toyota, along with Rusty and Sarah, would have sat for eons, barring some deep sea diver who mistakenly took a right into the pond preserve driveway instead of a left down the state route towards the ocean. He'd seen that happen before, too, with the person from away complaining that Maine didn't have enough signage. He usually liked to comment that Maine preferred to use its trees in other ways. He chuckled at the memory of many confused faces.

But this car didn't go in at the deep end. It went in at the beach, one of the shallowest areas, almost like it drove right in expecting to float or come out on the other side, drive up the embankment, and proceed on to the logging road. But it didn't do that. It sank, and probably pretty rapidly. With the excessive amount of late spring rain, it was easily covered by the pond's voluminous water supply. As that water evaporated in the heat of the summer, and with no additional rain by autumn, the top of the car probably was fairly visible, except it was a blue that almost mirrored the reflection of the sky. With the mud and slime, it blended in until even more water from the pond was lost, and the top of the car caught the eye of Emil who was illegally fishing.

Just dumb luck to have found the car at all.

Now, the medical examiners and Clint and Hailey were wrapping up their work. Two additional lab techs, who Tom didn't know, had also arrived and were sweeping through the reeds for any missed items. He wasn't exactly sure what would be apparent if the timing he estimated was right. Four months dead. Four months submerged. But who was he to question their job? He sure as heck didn't want them questioning his.

Roger was monitoring the radios for updates from the deputies that Marcel sent to Karl's marine store.

"Sir," Roger said to Marcel. He still stood away from the Toyota, and Marcel went to him. Tom also walked over.

"Sir," said Roger again, and lowered his voice. Tom had to give the kid credit for summing up Marcel's relationship with the state police quickly. Or maybe the same ice-cold trooper had glared at him like he glared at Johnny, or maybe Roger still couldn't stomach getting too close to the crime scene. Whatever the reason, Tom knew that Marcel would also be giving this young deputy brownie points for pulling him aside.

Roger continued. "Peters and Cheney would like you to join them at the marine store."

Marcel nodded. "Are they having trouble with the proprietor?"

"I think so." Then Roger, seeing Marcel's face at the wishy-washy answers, swallowed, and changed the answer to something more definite. "Yes, sir, they are. I heard the arguments through the radio, and I texted to tell them we three were nearby. Deputy Peters said things were in control but wouldn't mind another set of ears and arms. That's a direct quote. Sir."

Marcel nodded. "Thank you for monitoring that situation. Tom and I will go. Can you stay here until it's all finished up?"

Roger turned pale and then green but nodded. Marcel tapped him on his shoulder, passing him to walk over to Tom's SUV. Both he and Tom waved to the remaining crew, including Officer Debbie Downer. Hailey, in particular, gave a big wave. Did Tom imagine that? Maybe he shouldn't let height be a deterrent.

As they turned around, the tow truck driver got off the bench and came towards them.

"How much longer do you think?" He was polite, considering he thought he'd be here and gone hours ago.

Marcel glanced over at the lab team and then back to the tow truck driver, who looked like he needed food, coffee, and another nap, as well as a shave, a fresh set of clothes, and probably other things that weren't apparent, most of which couldn't be blamed on the delay or the Toyota.

"If I had to guess, I'd say thirty more minutes."

"Oh, okay, I can live with that." Like he had a choice. At least he chose the right attitude.

Tom maneuvered the SUV past the two ME vans, up the logging road, and out onto the state route. The marine store was on a side road off of the town green near Lane's Market, and Tom gunned it up the road and along the town green where the Lane Mansion stood next to the market.

Raven's Mini Cooper sat in the Lane Mansion driveway.

"What's she doing there?" Tom said out loud, slowing in front of the mansion.

Marcel chuckled and shook his head; he had given up years ago trying to figure out her or any other woman.

"Want me to stop?" Tom said, catching Marcel's smile.

"No, no, no. Our guys need us. We can circle back here if she's still here when we're through."

So, Tom and Marcel drove on past the Lane Mansion.

Chapter Forty-Seven

Evelyn was older than Raven by about eight years, giving Raven no school comparison information that often was helpful when dealing with a fellow local. All she really knew about Evelyn was that she was married to a lobsterman and worked as a cashier. Raven never judged people by their occupations because she didn't want to be judged by hers. She also didn't care if someone was formally educated because her mother and grandfather were two of the smartest people she had ever met, and her grandfather hadn't even gone past eighth grade. She also had definitely come across some college-degreed idiots, especially amongst her paying guests.

Yet, believing that being unflappable in a murder plot was a lifetime feather in one's cap didn't exactly reek of intelligence either. Imagine if Evelyn had channeled this creativity and planning into something else.

It also had never occurred to Raven that Rusty and Sarah had been dead this whole time. Since they hadn't been around Secretly since July, everyone assumed they had run off together. Even Evelyn's own embarrassment at the store seemed to imply that she had been left, abandoned, and definitely not that she was the cause of their disappearance. Raven also realized she had a prejudice against this type of crime, seeing it more as a jealous husband who'd commit it than a jealous wife. Another blind spot.

Evelyn kept talking. "I was almost ready to pop up and knock off Sarah when I heard Rusty's voice through the car window. He said 'hey there' or "whatcha doing here?' Or something like that. I knew the phrase well. I froze in my spot, shaking. I thought he was talking to me, that he had seen me on the floor of the backseat. But no, the pig was talking to the slut. He hadn't even noticed me. He even tossed his windbreaker over his shoulder when he got into the car. It landed on me, all smelly and dirty from lobstering. I flicked it off to the other side of the back seat. And get this! They didn't even notice that either, being all lovey-dovey and kissy in the front seat. In broad daylight. Disgusting! And rude!"

Evelyn's teeth gritted. Her face flushed to such a shade of red that Raven thought she might be having a stroke. Her whole body shook with rage, remembering the indecency she suffered, the betrayal she witnessed. Her voice was low and raspy.

"Sarah rolled the windows up and put the a/c on. Then I heard that slut gasp, and again I thought I was discovered. Wrong again!" She waved a fist into the air. "He was fingering her right there in the dock parking lot. I could see it through the bucket seats. I almost threw up. I wished the sun would go down quicker, save me from seeing this. I almost popped up then and there and blew their heads off, but I held back. I was patient. I talked myself out of it. 'Keep a lid, old girl.' I said to myself. I realized I had the opportunity of a lifetime. A two-for-one. I wouldn't back down now. I couldn't. How would I explain myself in the back of her car with his gun?"

Evelyn strolled around the small, messy bedroom and stood by a window, leaving the doorway fully open, unguarded. She absentmindedly ran her finger along the sill, dangling the pipe over her arm like a shotgun.

"They didn't drive far, turning into the Blue Heron Preserve. Naive me, for a nano-second, I thought that maybe I had misunderstood. Maybe they were just hiking buddies." She laughed, seemingly at herself. "It's funny what your own mind can do to you, to protect you. Hiking buddies. Yeah, right. Hiking buddies who finger each other." She laughed again and then started to cry.

Raven couldn't help but think of Marcel and Shannon. Work buddies. But worse. Former lovers. They'd know what each other tasted like to kiss and other things that Raven wouldn't allow herself to think about. Concentrate, she told herself, taking a page from Evelyn's own plot.

Evelyn remained by the window but kept an eye on Raven. Raven decided to not grab the desk chair if Evelyn turned her back to look out the window. The chair was closer now to Evelyn than her, but she could try to make a run for it and risk the pipe cracking her skull open. Risk the swing of a champion softball player. Maybe Evelyn hadn't swung at anything in thirty years. Maybe she would miss.

Chapter Forty-Eight

On their way back down the Ouellette's driveway, they ran into Howard by the mailboxes.

"Thank you for finally taking her off my hands," Howard said with a wink to Johnny.

Johnny grinned and laughed. Betty humphed.

"But seriously," said Howard, "where are you two off to so close to my dinner time?"

"There are plenty of leftovers from Thanksgiving," said Betty, leaning towards Johnny's open window.

"We didn't host Thanksgiving." Howard raised his eyebrows and gave Johnny a look that said "See what I mean? She's losing it!"

"Howard, I am well aware that we didn't host Thanksgiving. I'm not daff. There's no one at the Ouellettes." She pointed up the driveway. "Not even a barking dog. Go up there and make yourself a turkey and stuffing sandwich. Johnny and I are busy!" Betty sat back in the seat with a force that brought up dust from the cushion.

Howard shook his head while Johnny suppressed a laugh and a cough.

Howard crossed his arms and pointed toward Betty. "And you're not the only detective. I'm well aware that Raven's not home. I just saw her car when I drove home from Lane's Market. We're no longer out of Moxie, by the way."

"Oh good," said Johnny. "I'm glad to hear she's shopping."

"Oh, she wasn't at the store," said Howard. "I saw her Mini at the Lane Mansion. Dukie's head was sticking out of a window. I'm guessing Raven must be inside the house."

Johnny rubbed his chin, wondering what would have made her go back there.

"Thanks for the information, Howard. Enjoy your turkey sandwich," said Johnny, laughing as he let off the brake.

"And bring my car home!" Betty yelled the command to Howard just as the window closed.

Chapter Forty-Nine

Evelyn sniffled. In a faraway, soft, reflective voice, she said, "They didn't even have the decency to go very far. They didn't seem to care if they got caught. They didn't care if they were flaunting their affair right under my nose. Can you imagine? I'll bet Sarah could even walk to the preserve on her lunch break from the store. Meet him for a quickie."

Evelyn's face became more gray, more sad as she pondered the lack of concern Rusty had for her feelings, let alone their vows. She had never cheated on him. Her pause caused her to remember she was talking to Raven.

"Have you ever been to that preserve?"

Raven cleared her throat to form words, not knowing if she'd have a voice left, and grateful to talk about something that might help Evelyn get a grasp of reality.

"Yes, many times. It's beautiful."

Evelyn nodded in agreement. "Have you been there lately?"

Raven shook her head. "No."

"Why not?"

Now Evelyn was a nature reporter? Or a therapist? There was no real reason why she hadn't been there, but keeping Evelyn engaged gave Raven time to…to what?

Raven came up with an answer. "Because of the birds, they don't allow dogs off-leash."

"Ah. I see. Yeah, I saw your two in your car."

Raven's heart stopped. Had Evelyn hurt Dukie and Lily on her way into the house? All the energy she had drained down to her feet, and she felt lightheaded.

Evelyn continued. "Well, since you haven't been there in a while, you may not know they now have a small road that leads down to the pond and then around it to the backwoods. It's not that small, actually. It's wide enough for one of those huge logging trucks."

She stopped, waiting for Raven's response.

"No, I didn't know." Raven's mind was still on her dogs in the Mini, hoping they were safe. She actually did know about the road since a car had been found at the pond, but she didn't realize it was a new road.

"Yeah, they opened it up last year for some logging on the back side of the preserve. Doesn't make sense, does it? No dogs allowed because of the birds, but it's okay for logging trucks to come in and cut down the trees that the birds live in. I remember when that logging started. A customer had come in and asked what happened to all the baby birds living in their nests. He was crying."

She had a good point. Too bad Evelyn was a killer. She and Raven might have been friends.

"Anyway," Evelyn said, excited again to relay her triumph. "As they drove into the main preserve parking lot, before the slut shut off the car, I appeared over the front seats. Pistol waving. I felt like I was in a movie. Yee-haw! Ha! Ha!"

She grinned and waved the pipe in the air like it was a gun, and she was a cowboy, reenacting the moment. She twirled around and stopped in front of Raven, almost close enough for Raven to reach out and grab the pipe, or for the pipe to clock her.

"I think Rusty literally shit his pants because it suddenly stank in the car. Oo, boy, did it stink."

Raven understood, worried about her own bodily control as the pipe had bounced back and forth in the air. She expected Evelyn to forget she was in the house and pretend to shoot off the pipe like Annie Oakley at a county fair. Instead of bullets, they'd both hear the bangs of the metal as it hit the furniture, but Evelyn kept it in check. For now.

"Rusty twisted towards me to grab the gun, and I shoved it in his face and told him to sit back and keep his hands to himself. I reminded him I knew how to use it. He taught me. I kept the gun real close to me after that, so Rusty couldn't make a move for it. I made them drive down the logging road. Sarah's hands were shaking, and she was crying, bawling, barely able to steer. Kept saying she was sorry over and over. I bet she was sorry. For herself! She almost drove us off the road. I don't think on purpose or to save herself. I think she was just an awful driver. Heck, she was a lousy cashier, you know. Her drawer was always short."

Evelyn paused to recall Sarah's bad work habits as if the inability to count out change was worse than infidelity, or even murder.

Raven took the opening. "Hmmm, do you think she was stealing from the till?"

Evelyn shrugged, thought about it for a bit more, and then continued.

"Anyway, Rusty kept saying to me, 'Babe, it's not what it looks like.' Yeah, right. I knew exactly what it looked like! What else could it look like?"

Evelyn stopped imitating herself lording over the imaginary front seat and straightened up.

"And do you know what I said back to him for real?"

Raven shook her head, all of her words gone.

"I said, 'And this ain't a gun either.'" She snorted at her own joke.

Raven's head ached. She wanted Evelyn to stop talking. She didn't want to know any more and didn't want to visualize Rusty and Sarah's last moments. Her heart skipped in her body and sped up its pumping. She tasted bile in her mouth. Hearing how two people died was a preview of her own death.

Evelyn did stop talking. She placed the end of the pipe on the floor and leaned on the other end of it as if it were a cane. The tableau made a great portrait, one Charles could have captured if he had been there, alive. Raven worried that this odd image of a distraught, resting woman would be the last visual of her life.

Evelyn resumed her tale, quieter.

"Once we drove to the end of the logging road, I forced Sarah to drive over the brush and onto the sandy shore of the pond. She was blubbering and sobbing, still saying 'I'm sorry over and over.' I kept screaming at her to shut up, but that only made her cry louder. Even the power of a gun pressed to the back of her head didn't quiet her. Rusty, though, he was silent. I could see him watching me carefully, waiting for his chance."

Evelyn stared at Raven. "Like you are now."

Chapter Fifty

aven's hopes sank. Evelyn was fully of sound mind, as sound of mind as a person could be, having murdered three people and about to kill a fourth. Raven was simply Evelyn's confessor. She had no intention of letting Raven live.

"You should just relax and enjoy my story." Evelyn's suggestion came as she picked up the pipe in her hands again and held it like she would have held a softball bat. Champion stance.

One swing. That was all Evelyn needed. Raven didn't react until Evelyn motioned with her chin for Raven's attention. Like Lily did when she wanted a snack from the counter. Raven nodded.

"Good. Because it's an awesome story." Evelyn's shoulders relaxed, and she lowered the pipe again and held it near her leg. With a grin, she continued, proudly, eager to have someone know, happy to be in control. Raven's stomach lurched.

"With the gun against the back of Sarah's head, I then said, 'Keep the engine running.' Sarah whimpered that she couldn't swim."

Evelyn burst out laughing again; the volume and suddenness of the outburst caused Raven to jump.

"Imagine that. She was afraid of drowning. I reassured her. I told her not to worry. And then plugged a bullet into the back of Rusty's head."

Raven jumped again. The matter-of-factness surprised Raven, despite listening to Evelyn's tale and knowing where it was going. The outcome was two dead bodies, shot in the head and left in a sunken car. Marcel was there now, learning what she was learning at the same time. She fingered her cell phone. There had to be a way to get a message out. Marcel was close by.

Evelyn prattled on as if she was reciting the alphabet.

"Blood and pieces of his brain splattered everywhere, especially all over me. He slumped forward, kinda crumpled towards the floor. He hadn't been wearing a seatbelt. Sarah screamed, and I leaned toward her and shot her in the head, too. Her foot must have fallen off the brake because the car instantly started rolling into the pond on its own. I jumped out and slammed the door."

Raven wished she wasn't a visual person. She wished she didn't know Rusty or Sarah, wished she didn't know what they looked like alive, wished she didn't imagine what they looked like dead, bloody, and slumped forward in a beat-up, old Toyota compact.

"I couldn't have planned it better." Evelyn beamed. "The car eased itself into the pond on its own. Like in seconds, it was gone. They were gone. I was free."

A huge sigh emitted from Evelyn. She threw her head back and cried out.

"God damn you, Rusty Poole!"

Her head hung down, and she sobbed.

"I thought it was over. I thought I was free."

She sniffled and wiped her nose on her sleeve. She looked up and laser-focused on Raven.

"You don't know what it's like to have a lying, cheating husband. To smell another woman on his clothes, on his lips. As he kisses you hello, you taste her." The growl was low with a hiss.

All the little hairs on the back of Raven's neck stood up. She didn't realize she could feel more scared, more anxious, more sure today was her last day on earth.

Then Evelyn flashed back to her story. The need to tell her tale was greater than the need to wound another woman. At least at the moment.

"I don't know how long I stood there watching the pond, hoping the car wouldn't bounce back up. I flunked physics, you know, back in high school, so what did I know about cars sinking? And I was sweaty and shaking and covered in blood and brain parts. I couldn't wait to wash Rusty and Sarah off of me. And my hand throbbed. I hadn't shot a gun in years." She looked down at her right hand.

Raven remembered Evelyn having a bandage on her hand last summer. From a burn she had said when a customer in front of Raven asked about it.

"I stood there watching the pond. The reflection of the full moon on the now still water. An owl hooted. Mother Nature was absorbing Sarah and Rusty, and the woods were going back to normal, back to its evening rituals. It strangely felt peaceful."

"And then I heard a snap. A coyote, I thought. A large bird, probably that owl, flew off. I listened for more sounds. Nothing. Must have been that, I thought. I turned back to the logging road to walk out of the preserve and back the mile or so to Lane's parking lot for my pickup truck. When I drove out of the parking lot toward home, I passed someone else walking on the road, too, coming from the direction of the preserve, carrying a long, large object and a bag. Under a streetlight by the dock, I saw it was that nerdy guy who bought the Lane Mansion."

"Charles." The words escaped Raven's lips without a conscious thought. The connection was coming into focus.

"Yep. That one. Carrying a tripod and a camera bag. I hadn't thought he could have been in the same woods as me. I kept driving. I couldn't wait to get home to shower off the last of Rusty Poole."

Chapter Fifty-One

"Now that's a funny sight," said Tom, pointing out Johnny's truck at a stop sign with Betty on the passenger side. He and Marcel just left Wolf Marine. Karl had decided to calm down and cooperate, especially after hearing about Sarah.

"Wonder if they're going to the Lane Mansion to help Raven with whatever she's up to," said Marcel.

"We should all go and make it a party!" Tom glanced at Marcel. "Or not. I see you're anxious to get back to the swamp."

"Not really. I just never like delivering the news of a death to a loved one, especially knowing Karl." Marcel looked out the window. "Never get used to it.

"Do you think Karl's blasé reaction is telling?" Tom waved to Johnny as he drove through the intersection.

"No. I believe him when he says he didn't do it. We'll see how it all shakes out."

Johnny flagged down Tom's SUV by honking and flashing his lights. Tom pulled over, and everyone alighted from their vehicles.

"Hi, Tom," said Betty, almost with a wink. "Are you following us?"

"Yep." He winked at her. "Even though we weren't behind you. Trying to throw you off."

Betty giggled. Of all the women Tom flirted with in town, Betty was one of his favorites, although lately, he suspected if he was actually a bit more serious with her, she'd be the same with him. He had to be careful.

"What's the good word?" said Johnny.

"No good word at the moment," said Marcel. Tom knew there was nothing to share, especially in front of Betty.

Johnny's eyebrows came together close. "Am I to read between the lines? 'No Good.'"

Marcel smiled faintly and shook his head.

"What's your good word," Tom asked Johnny. Betty answered for him.

"We're headed to the Lane Mansion. Howard said Raven is there, and we're nosy."

"I'm nosy, too. C'mon, boss. Just a brief stop." Tom elbowed Marcel.

"Okay, okay, don't accuse me of being a party pooper," Marcel said as he got back into the SUV.

Chapter Fifty-Two

Evelyn and Raven stood in silence. Almost at the end of the story for Evelyn and the end of the line for Raven.

"Then the county photo contest winners were announced. And who do you think won for his July Full Moon Owl photo taken at Blue Heron Pond?"

Raven knew the answer. Poor Charles. And he had been so happy to have won. He may have even thought of being a bird photographer as a retirement gig. He definitely didn't see winning as a death sentence. Who would?

"I didn't know about the photograph until the bonfire when your ditz of a neighbor Betty brought it up. I should send her flowers as a thank you."

"Was he blackmailing you?" Raven still had delaying Evelyn on her mind, plus she was also wondering about this herself.

"Nope, but I figured it was only a matter of time. Or worse, he'd turn me in. He seemed like that sort, don't you think?"

Raven had to agree that Charles would be a law-abiding kind of fellow. She searched her mind for someone who actually would be okay with Evelyn eliminating her husband and his mistress and came up empty.

Evelyn moved from side to side. "I had gotten lucky with the car sinking. No one had really tried to look for Rusty or Sarah, not even Karl, but I knew eventually the car with them in it would be found, and that night might come back into focus for Charles, and he'd remember something." She snorted. "In focus. Get it?"

Raven barely nodded. She was exhausted from standing for however long it had been—she wasn't even sure—and from the stress of it all, and from being thirsty, and from a racing mind that hadn't yet provided a plan to save her. She again fingered her phone. There had to be a way without Evelyn noticing.

Evelyn continued, off in her own world. "After Betty brought it up, he bragged about his win, remember?" Raven did. "I took that as a hint towards me, like a signal that he knew what I did. 'I know what you did last summer.'" She laughed at her reference to the old horror movie. "Guess I've seen too many movies because I now actually don't think he knew anything about what I did. I was just being paranoid, but wouldn't you be if you were in my shoes?"

Again, Evelyn stared at Raven, waiting for a response.

Raven wanted to say a sarcastic "Absolutely" like it was normal to be worrying about being discovered as a murderer. Instead, she just nodded for the millionth time, agreeing with Evelyn on everything.

"And at least I think I taught him to not brag," Evelyn said. "My grandmother would have whacked him on the back of the head with a wooden spoon for bragging. She said it was against God's will to toot your own horn."

Considering how many times Evelyn had boasted about her own brilliant murder plan, her grandmother must be rolling over in her grave, wooden spoon poised for action.

Raven's mind flashed back to the bonfire. Someone, maybe Betty, maybe Chris Lane, had made a comment about his win. Charles hadn't even brought it up himself. Whoever said it was actually being mean and had also asked a contemptuous question about what Charles planned to photograph next, but Charles had answered it in earnest, going into detail about his plan to volunteer on the island with the puffins the following spring. Raven thought of the beautiful photographs that would never be, and how ironic it was that the person baiting Charles unwittingly cost him his life.

Raven, both to stall Evelyn and to also know, said, "How did you get him into the woods?"

"You'd be surprised what a pistol in your back will do."

Raven didn't want to experience that to know. Evelyn was eager to share.

"The day after the bonfire, Charles was outside this house, raking, and I simply walked up to him. We knew each other, of course, from Lane's. He stopped raking and rested on the handle to chat with me. I asked if he could help me with something, and he, of course, said yes, as I knew he would. Always the gentleman. He got into my truck on his own, and we drove to that preserve over by you."

"You didn't go into his house?" Raven thought of that drop of blood in the living room.

"Nope."

That blood could even have been from a repairman, Raven thought. She continued with her questions. "Did he question why you were bringing him to the woods?"

"Not at first. We got out of the truck and onto the path, and when he did ask me what we were doing, I pulled out the pistol and told him to keep walking. I made him get off the trail, and then I shot him. Bang. Bang. Maybe Bang-bang-bang." She shrugged. "That's the beauty of killing someone during hunting season. No one is paying attention to the shots."

Yeah, great, thought Raven. And what about killing with a lead pipe? Was there a season for that?

Mrs. Poole. In the bedroom. With a pipe.

Evelyn shrugged again. "So that's that. End of story. Well, sort of. Now, on to your story."

A chill raced through Raven. She braced herself to throw her arms up to try and grab the pipe.

"Time to go," said Evelyn.

Raven was confused. Go where?

"I'm sure people saw your car out front. Someone may even have seen me walk over. We need to go somewhere private."

Raven wanted to suggest Blue Heron Pond, knowing Marcel and other law enforcement officers were there, but held her tongue. She had lost her voice again anyway.

Chapter Fifty-Three

Best laid plans of mice and men.

Raven lived and now would die by that Steinbeck quote.

She didn't have the courage to make a grab for the lead pipe and meekly walked down the stairs and through the Lane Mansion, a chill up her spine. Evelyn prodded her along in the back, similar to the way she described using the pistol on Sarah, Rusty, and Charles.

The sun was going down. How long had she been in there with Evelyn? She still clutched her phone and the little book of passwords, her laptop left on the small table, forgotten by Evelyn and not needed by Raven.

She saw her Mini in the driveway with Lily and Dukie looking longingly at her, waiting for their promised walk or, at this stage, their dinner. Thank goodness they were okay.

At the very edge of the market parking lot, Raven saw Evelyn's pickup truck, as close to the mansion as one could park.

"Get in my truck, or I'll smash your dogs. I have a rifle in the truck, too, and you can tell I won't be afraid to use it. On you or those mutts." Evelyn kept the pipe on Raven's back as she said it.

Raven didn't know if Evelyn actually had a rifle too or was even a good shot—she may have gotten lucky at close range in the car and in the woods—but as long as she could pull a trigger or swing a pipe, she was dangerous to her and Lily and Dukie.

They walked across the lawn, away from her Mini and the dogs, and toward Evelyn's pickup truck. Evelyn told Raven to open the truck's passenger door. Raven glanced at her car as she pulled on the handle. Dukie, seeing Raven going somewhere without him, barked and, acting like the acrobat that he was, squeezed out the open car window. Lily, too chunky, whined but couldn't follow.

The sound and movement from Dukie caused Evelyn to turn her attention from Raven and focus on the Mini. Raven took her chance. She twisted and elbowed Evelyn in the face and then raised her right hand in a fist. Her knuckles banged against Evelyn's forehead, stunning her.

Evelyn fell against the truck, still clutching the pipe. Dukie lunged towards Evelyn. She swung to hit him.

Raven threw herself in the path of the pipe and Evelyn's arm, knocking both Evelyn, the pipe, and herself to the ground.

Dukie jumped on both of them. Raven didn't know if he intended to help, or if he thought it was a game. Raven and Evelyn rolled, pulling each other's hair and tossing Dukie to the side. Evelyn tried to bite Raven in the arm.

"Oh no, you don't," said Raven, head-butting Evelyn.

Dukie paced back and forth. He had never bitten anyone in his life, not even the UPS man whom he fiercely growled at from inside the house but slobbered on if he was outside for an encounter. But the UPS man didn't try to hurt his mama. Raven hoped he'd risk getting in trouble.

The pipe was left behind, and Evelyn felt the ground for another weapon. Midcoast Maine was loaded with rocks, metamorphic bedrock and igneous granite and everything in between, but the previous owner of the Lane Mansion preferred asphalt to gravel and had paved the driveway years ago. Her hand came up empty.

Dukie, who loved to bring gifts, scanned for something to present to the two women who scraped along the driveway and the lawn. A stick!

Raven felt something in her hair that wasn't Evelyn's hands and heard Evelyn scream. Evelyn released her grip, and Raven jumped up. Dukie had brought over a large branch with dead leaves on it. Shaking it over Evelyn, a nest of ticks fell on Evelyn's head. Easily, forty black dots crawled over her face.

"Help me!" Evelyn's pleas intensified.

Tom's SUV screeched into the driveway, followed by Johnny's pickup truck. Marcel jumped out of the passenger side before the SUV rolled to a stop. Tom was right behind, yanking Evelyn to her feet and then shaking one of his arms as the ticks fell on him too.

Marcel grabbed Raven in his arms, and Dukie circled them in a happy dance. And then darted off to find another gift.

Chapter Fifty-Four

Raven took a long hot shower, so long that Marcel checked on her three times, although Raven wasn't sure that he had ever left the bathroom. Her muscles ached, her legs and elbows were scraped, and she had a purplish lump on her forehead from the head butt, but with some ice, ibuprofen, hot food, and maybe a glass, or two, or three, of wine, she'd be brand new. She hoped.

Howard was actually at the Ouellettes when Marcel brought her home in the Mini with Johnny's pickup truck following closely behind, with Betty. Howard hadn't actually gone to their house for turkey leftovers—just Betty's car—but Betty had called him en route and told him to grab a lasagna out of their freezer. It was already baking in the Ouellette's oven, and the smell wafted into the bathroom and mixed with the lavender soap Raven used.

Tom said he'd come back as soon as he booked Evelyn and left her to rot in the county prison. He was already bucking for no bail.

Johnny had picked up Raven's cell and Charles' notebook with the passwords from the yard and found her laptop upstairs at the mansion. Even though she now knew the answers to both mysteries, she longed to see Charles' other photos, the ones he didn't submit for an award. Hard to believe that a photograph of an owl caused his death. No. No, it didn't. Evelyn was responsible, and her alone.

Dukie and Lily lay on the bathmat as Raven dried off. She looked down at their soulful eyes and wagging tails. Their faithfulness was beyond measure.

Of course, Evelyn would be given a fair trial. Could Raven stomach Marcel working with Shannon McGrath on it? What choice did she have?

Marcel poked his head in again. "Ready for dinner?"

Dukie and Lily jumped up and ran out of the bathroom. Marcel laughed. "Not them. They already ate."

"Oh, what's a bit more, especially for Dukie, the hero of the day?" Raven said, rubbing her dripping hair with the towel.

Marcel entered the bathroom and shut the door. Gathering her up in his arms, he kissed her very slowly.

Leaning her head against Marcel's chest, Raven sighed. "We don't have to rush. Lasagna always needs to rest."

Acknowledgements

This novel would not be in print without my editors, Verena Rose and Shawn Reilly Simmons at Level Best Books, believing in me, and without the support and patience from Deb Well. I am forever grateful to you all.

My earned confidence in my writing exists from both my MFA at Lesley University, with my advisors, Pat Lowery Collins, David Elliot, and Anita Riggio, and the feedback I've received over the years from my two writers' groups. The first group came out of Lesley with my colleagues Jana Van der Veer, Cheryl Lawton Malone, and Marjorie Moon. The second formed from a chance meeting at a Sisters in Crime Connecticut reading, giving me the outstanding writers Cori Arnold and Rhonda Lane to work with in our West End Writers meetings. I miss those nights.

Upon moving to Maine, I realized why many outstanding mystery writers live here. It's hard not to be enchanted by Maine's magic with its fog, woods, loon calls, laughing gulls, fish ladders, and the locals' thoughts on people from away. I'm grateful Cheryl encouraged me to start the Midcoast Maine Mystery series as a break from editing prior novels that I hadn't sold (yet). I also thank Cheryl, Jana, and my beta reader and cousin, Mary Rose Keeton Baier, for their feedback on *Blaze Orange*. Thank you to my great niece, Olivia Rivera, for her forensics expertise for this book and other stories. I'm grateful to my partner and muse, Tom Aylesbury, for making our move to Maine possible. He's a daily inspiration of drive and courage, and most importantly, has always wanted the best for me, a concept I wasn't familiar with prior to knowing him. Ironically, he is not a reader of fiction, and will never read this book and see the many sentences and teachings that have come directly from him, but that fits his humble nature to take no credit and seek no praise.

My final gratitude is to Steve Berry, thriller author extraordinaire, who gave an amazing lecture in Hartford, CT, in 2011. That day, he shared that his first eight novels were still in a drawer. His honesty gave me permission and courage to keep writing. *Blaze Orange* is my seventh novel. Thank you, Steve.

About the Author

Allison Keeton lives in Maine with her muse, Tom, and their two dogs.

AUTHOR WEBSITE:
  https://www.akeetonbooks.com/

SOCIAL MEDIA HANDLES:
  Facebook: Allison Keeton, Author
  Instagram: Allison_Keeton_Author
  Threads: @allison_keeton_author
  X: @akeetonbooks